TWO LISTS

A MALCOM WINTERS MYSTERY

THOMAS J. THORSON

The characters and events portrayed in this book are fictitious. Any similarity to real persons, living or dead, is coincidental and not intended by the author.

Thorshammer Books
ISBN: 978-1-7358366-6-9
For ordering information, visit: www.thorsonbooks.com

Cover and interior design by Stephanie Rocha
Front cover photo by Isai Ramos/Unsplash,
Freepik.com

Printed in the United States of America.

DEDICATION

Once more to my daughters Tierney,
Lourdra, and Gilleece, with the hope that my
small contributions to the literary world will
find a place on your bookshelf.

ACKNOWLEDGEMENTS

When I published my first novel in the Malcom Winters series in 2020, I was fortunate to have enlisted the invaluable assistance and expertise of people whose talents far exceeded my own and who worked to make my initial foray into fiction look and read more professional than perhaps it deserved. Remarkably, they've persisted through all five books now and my admiration and appreciation for their skills has only grown. My editor Kristen Weber, whose ability to make her critiques sound encouraging even as they require gutting entire chapters, has unerringly found ways to make even my best writing better. My faithful designer Stephanie Rocha, who's able to take my rough jumble of words and create brilliant art that captures the story's essence while navigating the maze of trim size and other things I don't understand to make the inside pages as beautiful as her covers. Steve Kirshenbaum of Looking Glass Books, whose enthusiasm for my characters is as infectious as it is inspirational. And of course the readers who've become invested in Mal's and Vinn's world, without whom my sweat and tears through all five novels would be meaningless. If this is in fact the last chronicling of their journey through the streets of Chicago and beyond, I owe you all a hot cup of tea.

AUTHOR'S NOTE

The two lists that play a pivotal role in this story and the order in which they're presented are real. They were noted in Kenneth Dutton's *The Wisdom of Psychopaths: What Saints, Spies, and Serial Killers Can Teach Us About Success* (Scientific American/Farrar, Straus and Giroux 2012) and reprinted in "The Professions with the Most and Fewest Psychopaths" by Eric Barker in the November 5, 2012 online edition of *Insider*.

ONE

"The salmon, really?" I ask Vinn as she places her order with the tuxedoed server standing impatiently between us. "Aren't you concerned that you'll offend one of its cousins?"

We're squished elbow-to-elbow with six other guests at a table more suitable for four only an arm's length from the rotund Caribbean Reef pool at the Shedd Aquarium, in which sharks, turtles, rays, and other assorted marine life swim among the coral branches in a constant swirl of activity that's hard to ignore. I swear an angelfish overheard Vinn's choice of entrees and is currently judging us as it stares out at the table from among its weedy hiding place.

Vinn smiles. "Mal, I seem to remember seeing both shrimp and mini crab cakes on your plate earlier," she reminds me. "C'mon, I've been sitting too long tonight. Let's take a walk."

We excuse ourselves from the company sharing our table, who like Vinn teach science at the University of Illinois at Chicago, along with their spouses. Unlike Vinn, they haven't won multiple awards and international acclaim for their contributions to their respective fields, nor are they intuitive geniuses recognized as such by their peers. The man across from us with the neatly trimmed goatee and comb-over did recently publish an article on immunology in a second-tier scientific journal which Vinn at the time said would set science back fifty years if it weren't rebutted. Which she took upon herself to do in a lengthy, scathing letter to the editor that was printed in the following issue. Call me cynical, but I have a feeling that that letter might have more to do with our pre-entrée walk than a sore tush.

Vinn rarely dresses up and the majority of her makeup probably has an expiration date from the last millennia. When she does put in the effort though, the result is stunning. Beautiful even in jeans and a hoodie, the tight-fitting burgundy dress with a teasing slit up the left leg lifts her appearance into a totally different dimension. As we circle the tank in the center of the room all eyes in the vicinity, both male and female, leave the colorful swimmers and follow us. My guess is that if a sketch artist suddenly appeared at one of the tables five minutes from now, not a single guest would be able to describe Vinn's date for the evening, which is fine with me. As the plus one, I know virtually no one here and would rather be at home with a hot cup of tea and Netflix. This being the wedding of the only daughter of her department head, Vinn not only needs to be here but has to behave while keeping her uncouth, rough-around-the edges lover from saying something that'll affect her standing at the university. I'm sure a bad movie and an early bedtime would be her preference about now as well.

"It was a lovely ceremony," she says as we stop to admire a school of parrotfish. "I especially liked when the dolphins leaped out of the water and splashed the wedding party just as the groom said 'I do.'"

"I don't know," I reply as we link elbows and continue our stroll, "it's hard to beat when the ring-bearer climbed over the rail with the intent of taking a swim. I was frankly disappointed that the best man has such good reflexes."

We continue our circular walk in a content silence, with Vinn occasionally nodding in acknowledgment to someone she recognizes. As we pass the tables for the bride and groom and their court, I can't help but notice that they're positioned exactly opposite of our own table, so that it's impossible to see us through the mini ocean. I wonder if that's a nod to the rumors that swirl around campus about Vinn's and my extracurricular activities, which usually place us in the middle of gruesome murder cases solved through elaborate, improbable, and often violent final confrontations of our own making. Improbable sounding but also true, and as vividly bloody as the images are that the rumor mill creates, they're actually tepid compared to what really happened.

Eventually we come back within view of our table where we see Emmett Sanders, the father of the bride, fulfilling his role of circulating among all the guests, talking and laughing with our tablemates. The black armband barely visible against his tuxedo explains his weary eyes and false smile but little else. Whatever tragic event it represents has been effectively buried in deference to this joyous occasion.

"I'll bet you ten bucks they're talking about us," Vinn murmurs under her breath.

"You're being paranoid," I tell her. "He just saw his daughter getting married. I'm sure they're recapping the dolphin splash, bouquet toss, or something like that."

In truth, while we've studiously avoided spreading word about our exploits to the rest of the faculty, we also haven't been shy about using students to help us out in our investigations when the need arose. It would be naïve to expect that word wouldn't eventually make its way to the ears of our colleagues, but given the social divide between teachers and the administration, we didn't think the rumors would go any higher than a handful of professors and teaching assistants. Given the odd expression on Sanders' face as he glances in our direction, that may have been wishful thinking.

"God only knows what magnified malarky those jabbering gossipmongers are regaling him with," Vinn grouses. "They're probably salivating to make me look bad in my boss's eyes. Probably best not to know."

Vinn's bitterness toward our colleagues probably has less to do with her attitude toward them personally and more to do with the fact that we've been drawn into the last couple of investigations against our wishes, or at least against our better judgment, as if we're a pair of moths that are unwillingly but inevitably drawn to the candle's flame. We've been singed more than once and have resolved to avoid any more activities that might result in being fatally burned.

Which explains the desire to keep a low profile. The hope is that the fewer people that know about our dark pasts working covertly for government agencies that don't appear in any directories or the more recent matters that we've successfully helped law enforcement bring to a close, the less the chance of an physics professor seeking to enlist our assistance in a "small matter" that ends up costing lives, possibly our own. Vinn and I have had long talks since our recent close encounters with our own mortality and we're firmly, irrevocably retired. All of our energies are now directed toward the legitimate employment that pays our bills and, more importantly, self-preservation. We'd like to stop adding to the scars that we count on each other's bodies while under the sheets at night, as entertaining and pleasurable as that can be.

As we slide into our chairs, the table talk instantly and awkwardly stops. Vinn's boss breaks the silence to greet us.

"Vinn, good to see you. I hope you're having a good time?" he inquires. "And, um...uh...you too. Enjoying yourself?"

Vinn to the rescue. "This is my friend Malcom Winters. And yes, Dr. Sanders, everything is lovely, thank you." She says nothing more, obviously on the same wavelength as myself. Don't give someone a hook to continue the conversation and maybe they'll leave. No such luck.

"We were just talking about you," he continues. Vinn sends me an "I told you so" glance as I mentally kiss my sawbuck goodbye. "I understand from chatting with the others here that you've had some interesting adventures outside of the academic realm." He pauses expectantly, clearly waiting for Vinn to fill in the gaps and regale him with wild tales of these so-called adventures. An uncomfortable silence follows before she realizes that he's not going to leave unless she says something.

"Well, yes, although I'm sure that much of what people have heard has been exaggerated," she tells him while casting a steely glare at the others in the circle. They all avoid eye contact as her glance makes its way around the table. "But that's all behind us now. The new semester is barely underway and all we want to do is concentrate on giving our students the best education they can get."

I almost choke and pick up my napkin to cover my grin. Each of us has always approached our teaching responsibilities seriously, even though I'm a complete fraud with no pedantic background, hired in a case of mistaken identity that I somehow have never gotten around to putting right. Vinn's credentials are legitimate, but acting as a cheerleader for the institution is as fake as I am. She'll hear about it from me later and she knows it.

"I see, glad to hear it," Dr. Sanders responds insincerely. "Well, it was great seeing you all but I have to move on. I see the main course is making its way out of the kitchen. Save room for dessert—I think it's candy rolled up to look like sushi—and of course take advantage of the open bar. Good night, all."

The quiet is overwhelming as Sanders strolls off, even after the waiter places our food before us and asks if anyone wants more wine. I reflexively count the seconds in my head as I chew my grilled pork cutlet and try to think of what I can say to cut through the tension. I also wonder what the topic of conversation was that makes them so hesitant to open their mouths in our presence. I've reached thirty-four seconds when it's Vinn who speaks first.

"Tell me, Dr. Thompson," she says sweetly to the bearded man on the other side of the table. "Are you working on any more articles about immunology?"

TWO

"It's not like we've posted pictures of our battle scars on the campus Facebook page," Vinn gripes as we sit in our customary spots in the cafeteria waiting for our first morning classes. My advanced seminar on the secular supernatural in modern literature proved so popular that it was moved from the afternoon to 8:00 a.m. to discourage students from signing up for it and to avoid complaints about a long waiting list. Vinn's freshman honors class in computational nuclear physics would be impossible for most people to understand at any time of day, so 8:00 is as good as any other.

"Are you still obsessing about the wedding?" I ask. I take a sip of the English breakfast tea I brewed at home since Manuel, who runs the cafeteria, refuses to stock loose-leaf teas of any sort mainly because he knows that's what I drink. A blend of black teas from China, Sri Lanka, and India, it's a little bitter for my taste but packs a powerful caffeine punch that will keep me from yawning for the duration of my class. "I'm sure whatever they told Sanders, he wrote it off as exaggerated gossip. Nothing will come of it."

"I wish I could believe that Mal," Vinn sighs. "I just have a bad feeling. Did you see the look on his face? It wasn't disgust, it was curiosity. As if we're a possible solution to a problem."

I pat her hand in support. I'm not concerned. If there's a weak link in our determination not to place ourselves in danger's path ever again, it would be me. It's a hundred to one shot that Sanders is involved in any such thing or would seek our assistance if he was, and

Vinn wouldn't hesitate to tell him to go to hell if he did. She would even use more colorful language, boss or no boss.

I watch Vinn for thirty straight seconds as she mashes the cranberry muffin she bought with a fork. The pastry never made it near her mouth, instead serving as an outlet for her frustrations still simmering from the wedding. It's not like Vinn to leave any food that sits before her uneaten, which might explain why my chocolate croissant was smaller than I remembered it being each time I picked it up.

Vinn inhales a roomful of air and sighs, absentmindedly looking in the direction of the clock on the wall behind me. The panic in her eyes causes me to turn as well, and without a further word we grab up our belongings and rush off to class.

Office hours in the first few weeks of a semester are always an adventure. I return from my mid-afternoon "Mystery Loves Company" senior course to a line of eight or nine impatient students lined up outside my door, each one looking like they were there on behalf of an older sibling. Freshmen. I nod in the direction of the first few in line, which was apparently interpreted as an invitation for all of them to follow on my heels as I opened my door. My office is only marginally larger than a broom closet, so even if it were appropriate to field all of the "why do I need to know anything about Shakespeare as an engineering student" inquiries at the same time, there's no room for more than two others at one time anyway.

I've barely begun getting irritated with the first

student when my office phone rings, which baffles me. No one ever calls me. It's rare that most of my fellow teachers even acknowledge me. Normally I would assume that it's bad news and ignore the call, but no matter what awaits me on the other side of the line, it has to be preferable to hearing any more whining about the unfairness of having to write a five hundred word essay the same weekend that an anime convention is in town.

I'm shocked to hear Vinn's voice in my ear, as she either texts or just drops in when we're on campus. She sounds distressed.

"Mal, I need you to come to my office right away. It's important. At least I assume it is. I'll explain when you get here. Did I say right away? Okay, good. See you in a few."

It's only when I hear the click of the receiver on her end that I realize I never said a word. Vinn is the epitome of calm under pressure, so whatever it is must be a big deal. I decide not to ponder if I should be insulted at the presumption that I'm at her beck and call until after I hear why I've been summoned. I glance back at the student across from me, who takes that as a key to start in again.

I hold up my hand. "Robbie, the assignment is ungraded and you can write about any subject of your choice. Be creative. Compare the battle readiness of Pikachu and Squirtle if you want." Robbie looks horrified. Are Pokemon no longer a thing? "Anyway, I need to go. Five hundred words."

I hustle him out the door, throw my business cards to the now-longer line of students, mumble something about sending me an email, and hurry off to meet Vinn.

"Dr. Sanders wants to see me. Us. You and me, I mean both of us, at least I think so," Vinn stammers. As amusing as it could be to see Vinn flustered, which almost never happens, her angst is contagious as memories of being summoned to the principal's office flood my brain. Now I'm just as nervous and I don't know if there's any reason to be.

"Any idea what he wants?" I ask.

"I've been in his office maybe twice in the entire time I've worked here," she responds as she pulls me into a hug. "I'm sure it's no coincidence that this is happening the first school day after his daughter's wedding. So either he wants our feedback on that horrid candy sushi, which is unlikely, or it has something to do with whatever the discussion was that we interrupted when we got back to the table. Mal, I told you before. I don't have a good feeling about this."

I squeeze her tight. "Only one way to find out."

We walk down the hall about thirty feet to Sanders' office and usher ourselves in. Unlike the cramped quarters granted to the teachers, his position apparently merits not only a large office but a secretary stationed in a smaller room adjacent to it. An ancient man in a suit almost as old as the school itself sits behind the outer desk. He eyes us suspiciously.

"We're here to see Dr. Sanders," Vinn assures him in a steady tone that belies how she's truly feeling. In response the secretary runs his fingers down a blank page in an appointment book, shaking his head as he does so. "He asked us to come here" Vinn adds, now obviously annoyed.

"Vinn, Morris, come on in," we hear from the next room. Despite her mood, Vinn snickers. Great. I'm not sure of the protocol. Do I correct Vinn's boss, risking alienating him, or become "Morris" for the rest of my tenure here?

Vinn rescues me by pretending not to have heard him, a good indication that she's back on her game. "Good to see you again, Dr. Sanders," she says firmly as she extends her hand. "It was a lovely wedding on Saturday. You remember my friend Malcom."

"Yes, of course," Sanders replies warmly. "I'm glad you were both able to come. Please, have a seat." Given how I'm feeling being on this side of the desk, I resolve to start treating my students with a little more compassion.

Sanders suddenly looks uneasy as we wait for him to tell us why we're here. His discomfort has the effect of magnifying our own with each passing second. He finally clears his throat, runs his hands through his thinning hair, and leans forward, elbows firmly planted on his blotter.

"I had a most entertaining, I should say 'intriguing,' conversation with the other members of the faculty sitting at your table," he begins. Vinn and I immediately sit up straight and stiff, on alert. Sanders notices and puts his hands up as if offering an apology. "Don't panic. Ninety percent of what they told me couldn't possibly be true. I'm interested in the other ten percent. Would it be accurate to say that you've both got some abilities, some skills, in the area of, um...solving crime, shall we say?"

Vinn glances at me and I nod, acknowledging that she's to take the lead on this and that I trust her to as to how much she wants to disclose. That trust probably wouldn't flow in the opposite direction, with good reason. Mr. Good Judgment I'm not.

"Each of us come from former jobs that allowed us to develop some experience in that area, yes," she begins slowly, choosing her words carefully. "But that was a long time ago. And the others you spoke with probably passed on that we've been drawn into a couple of investigations during our time here, but I'm sure that they exaggerated our role in them. They haven't interfered with our teaching duties, sir, and we've both resolved not to go any further in that direction."

"I'm actually counting on that not being the case, Vinn," Sanders replies solemnly, moving his eyes to include me in his assessment. "I've made a few calls to people I know in the police department and they confirmed much of what I heard on Saturday. It sounds like you two were invaluable in solving more than one murder, although it puzzles me why my sources didn't seem to be entirely appreciative. The word 'rogue' came up more than once."

Vinn starts to object but is cut off before she can say a word. "It's that word, that trait if you will, that made up my mind to reach out to you. That's just what I think is needed," Sanders continues, his voice wavering and his eyes losing their focus, seemingly gazing at a memory. "My brother-in-law, my wife's favorite sibling, was killed back in June and the police have gotten nowhere. I know I have no right to ask you to get involved, and it won't affect your job here if you say no, but as a personal favor to me and to my wife we'd appreciate it if you would consider looking into it."

Vinn's face drains of all color. Our vow to each other to avoid any involvement in circumstances that could put us in harm's way is about to be shattered barely weeks after we swore to stay straight. Someone once called us a "trouble magnet" and it's hard to argue with that assessment. Vinn looks at me with an expression of remorse and sadness. Both of us know that Sanders' promise that turning him down won't affect her job status may be true on the surface, but that he'll hold it against her nonetheless. I take her hand in mine and once again nod.

"Of course, Dr. Sanders," she says with more commitment than she's feeling. "We'd be happy to help."

THREE

"I'm so sorry, Mal," Vinn apologizes for the third time as we step outside into a blinding sun. "I figured that if anyone was going to breach our new policy of non-involvement, it would be you."

Clearly I wasn't the only one who thought that. Still, I find no comfort in the fact that I was able to last a few weeks without dragging us into what's sure to be a mess only to have Vinn do it for us. In reality, of course, nothing she did brought this on and she couldn't exactly turn down her boss without repercussions, facts that I've repeated as often as she's asked for forgiveness. Ultimately it doesn't matter which one of us was the gateway for trouble to find its way to our door. It's here and we just have to deal with it.

What concerns us most isn't the danger to our lives. That wasn't the reason either of us left our former jobs or even the biggest factor now. It's the slippery slope. Most of our adventures, both before and after we got together, at some point involve the use of violence, often fatal. Over time, you become immune to the emotional effect of holding a knife to someone's throat or putting a gun to her head, and it becomes easier each time to follow through. At some point you actually begin to relish the rush—the feeling of control and of power over another human being. The final step is to enjoy the kill and to look forward to the next one. Both Vinn and I were on that precipice, looking into that void, when we chose to walk away. Lately, with each investigation, the old feelings have begun to return. We're sliding back into our old mindsets. By the time you realize you've gone too far, it's too late. We don't want to tempt fate, yet here we are. Our greatest desire is that whatever we've gotten ourselves into, it won't necessitate the use of force. Or dying, which may not be at the very top of the priority scale but still ranks pretty high in importance.

Dr. Sanders wasn't exactly forthcoming with information about the murder of his brother-in-law, Brandon Mills. More than that, he flat refused to provide any details at all and seemed flustered and defensive when we pressed him. "You'll get all you need from the case file," was all he would volunteer before he clammed up.

"It's almost like he was embarrassed that his wife's brother died the way he did, which makes me wonder," I posit to Vinn. "Maybe he was found handcuffed to a bed wearing panties and a bra or was found in bed with a couple of sheep."

Vinn snorts despite her mood. "That's all I need," she says with a grin. "But it might come in handy the next time I ask for a raise."

Before we go by the police station to pick up a copy of the file, which Sanders told us would be ready tomorrow, we decide to drop in on our favorite campus cop, London Jenkins, to see if he can provide any insights. The low man in the department in terms of seniority, as well as the shortest and only one to look like he's starting high school this fall, he makes up for these deficiencies by working to be the most informed. He also dreams of transitioning to the big leagues, i.e. the Chicago Police Department, which explains the presence of a police scanner on his desk. He's well aware of our history and far from simply tolerating us, seems to thrive on any piece of the action we can throw his way. That being said he seems genuinely alarmed to see us cross the room to his desk in the far corner. We tend to have that effect on people.

"Whatever it is, I don't want to hear about it," he tells us when we're still ten feet from his desk. "Can't you see that I'm busy?"

No, not one bit. His desk, as always, is as neat as if it were on a showroom floor. "Oh dear, I guess we caught him at a bad time," I tell Vinn. "That pretty coed in Stukel Towers must have lost her keys again."

"My money's on the science lab's lizard escaping and hiding out in the women's room," she replies.

Jenkins throws his hands up in defeat as we move to sit in the chairs in front of his desk. "Officer, you should really dust these once in a while if they haven't been getting any use," Vinn comments as she pushes a finger across the arm of the chair and holds it up for him to see.

"Okay, okay, point taken," Jenkins says. "But the start of the semester really is busy. Lots of lost and stolen laptops. I can give you five minutes."

"Then we'll get to the point," I tell him. "What do you know about Brandon Mills?"

He can't hide his surprise, looks in the direction of the nearest detective sitting three desks away, then leans forward to speak in a conspiratorial whisper. "Please tell me you're not poking around in that," he pleads.

"Not by choice," Vinn responds. "Clearly you do know something about it. Spill."

"Not a chance," Jenkins says firmly. "I'm not high enough up the ladder to have been clued in, so if I know anything at all, which I don't, it would mean my job if any information you drag up is traced back to me. I will tell you two things. One, my boss and my boss's boss were on the receiving end of a loud and scathing tirade from some professor a couple of weeks back. Apparently he was hoping they would make inroads where the 'real' cops haven't." Jenkins uses his fingers to quote the word "real." His greatest annoyance is when people think campus police aren't true law enforcement.

"Second," he continues, "be prepared for a crime scene the likes of which you've never seen before. And that's all I'm going to tell you. Now scram."

After a few more minutes of not-so-gentle prodding from Vinn, it's clear that we've gotten all we're going to get out of Jenkins.

"Whose idea was it to drop by Jenkins to see what he knows?" Vinn asks rhetorically as we're clear of the station and heading toward the el. "Because to be honest, I feel even more hesitant to get involved now than I did before."

Back in my apartment, Vinn lets me know that her brain won't function until she makes her stomach happy before she flops on my couch with her eyes closed. I rummage through the freezer to find frozen scallion pancakes that we bought the last time we were in Chinatown then pull out the remnants of a block of chihuahua cheese from the back of my refrigerator. A quick pan-fry of the pancakes, sprinkle with a generous helping of cheese, then fold over and serve. A fast and tasty, if multi-cultural, taco dinner.

We're still chewing the first bite when a rhythmic beating at my door signals the arrival of my downstairs neighbor Ted, most likely in the form of his/her alter ego Rebecca given the knock that I'm supposed to recognize as a show tune. I begrudgingly desert my food to rise and walk to the door. As she makes her grand entrance flouting her latest frock, she frowns with disappointment at the blank expression on my face.

"'Waving Through a Window' from *Dear Evan Hanson*," she tells me sadly. "Really, Malcom. Ooh... excellent." Spotting first my unfinished pancake and then with a glance at the kitchen seeing the makings of another serving she walks over and lights up the burner. I return to my seat next to Vinn, whose grin and shrug of the shoulders affirms my own feeling that in this crazy and unpredictable world, in some ways it's comforting to have the steady presence of Rebecca in our lives, as maddening as that often is. We wait for the diva to return from the kitchen and grace us with her presence.

"I was counting on your being here," Rebecca says to Vinn between mouthfuls. She retrieves a few articles of clothing she draped over a chair on her way in. "Would you wear this top with this boho skirt or the three-quarter pants?"

After a thoughtful pause, Vinn answers. "Definitely the pants."

"Great, thank you," Rebecca says sincerely. "The skirt it is."

Vinn makes a face but truthfully Rebecca probably made the right call. A woman most at home in a ratty college t-shirt and sweatpants, no matter how beautiful, may not be the paragon of fashion whose opinion she should rely on. Rebecca brings her plate to the kitchen sink and turns to leave before pausing, studying our faces.

"You've got something going again, don't you?" she tells us more as a statement than a question. "How exciting! You know where to find me when you need me." With that, she struts toward the door, accenting her exit with a fashion twirl. We've reluctantly enlisted Rebecca's assistance previously and she's been instrumental in resolving a few cases, but the high maintenance required and jeopardy we've placed her in don't have me eager to bring her on board again.

Vinn turns to face me. "How does she do that? I don't know if our facial expressions reveal a mood of excitement or the sad anticipation of oncoming tragedy."

"Some of both," I concede. "And speaking of tasks that we'd rather not get involved in, what do you say we do a little research on our victim to see what we can find out before we look at the file tomorrow?"

In response Vinn pulls open her laptop and we snuggle close together, partly so that we can each see the screen but mostly because of our intuitive fear that if this investigation puts us in harm's way, like each other one in the past, we can't be sure when any chance to get intimate might be our last.

"Okay, Brandon," she mutters to herself as she presses keys. "Reveal yourself."

Our initial search for information on his death results in nothing but frustration as the details reported by media are sparse and useless. Other than the date he died and the fact that it wasn't a natural death, we strike out.

"How much of a big shot is your boss anyway?" I ask Vinn. "I don't want to read 'no further details have been released out of respect for the family's privacy' one more time. If his murder was as bizarre or salacious as we suspect, the press should be all over this."

"The fact that he can make a phone call and get us a copy of the cops' file is a pretty good indication as to his influence right there," she sighs. "So I guess we shouldn't be surprised at the coverup. I'll bet if we check the guest list of that fancy wedding the name of a police chief or two and probably a newspaper editor would be on it. We'll just have to go in cold on the details tomorrow. For now, let's get some general background on the guy."

More information is available about Mills' personal and business life thanks to the usual social media outlets, LinkedIn and Facebook, although his name also pops up in local news articles about his philanthropy or presence at an event. Married to his college sweetheart with two grown children, a son and a daughter, with a grandchild on the way. He seems to have made a decent if not affluent living as the chief executive officer of a small electronics company.

"An ordinary man living an ordinary life," Vinn sighs. "The only thing extraordinary about his guy's life seems to be the way he died, if the rumors are true. There's got to be more that we'll need to dig for, although if I want to keep my job we'd better be discreet. If he was a member of some kinky secret society, we need to keep that quiet."

As a last resort we navigate to his company's web page. "Motivon Electronics: We're Wired To Excel."

Vinn makes a face. Beyond the company's apparent fondness for puns, nothing stands out. High-end, custom small kitchen appliances, computer accessories, and the like for discerning customers with money. After several minutes looking for anything that would give us insight into the man or a motive for his murder, we reluctantly pull the laptop shut.

"I guess we start with a clean slate tomorrow," Vinn says. "I'm almost hoping for the extraordinary."

I glance at Vinn warily. Be careful what you wish for.

FOUR

By pure chance, both Vinn and I are done with classes early on Tuesdays this semester, although she's supposed to be supervising labs beginning at 2:00. An email from Dr. Sanders notifying her that the file on his brother-in-law's killing will be waiting for us at the Near North district station, though, led her to make other arrangements and have a teaching assistant take over halfway through. She correctly assumed that her department head would have no issues with her priorities. By 3:00 we're on the el heading north.

The 18th District police station is a modern but nondescript building that manages to emit an aura of desperation and despair which gets stronger the closer we get to its glass entrance. Instinctively we both pause briefly before stepping into the revolving door. Our treatment in various similar venues across the city triggers a survival instinct that explains our involuntary resistance to moving inside. Our eyes meet, we each shrug our shoulders, and we push our way into the lions' den.

No posse of cops with guns drawn greets our arrival. Instead, a bored desk sergeant with an attitude makes a call and reluctantly gives us passes to enter the inner sanctum with instructions to ask for an Officer Nelson. Thirty minutes later, with no Officer Nelson in sight despite being told several times to be patient, we decide not to be patient and to push our luck. We're probably close to being put in a cell by the woman we've cornered when a pimply-faced rookie cop finally makes an appearance.

"Here," he says, thrusting a thin, unmarked manila folder at me. I quickly flip it open to reveal a single-sheet incident report listing the name and address of the victim, the date of the murder, and the detective who caught the call.

"Wait!" I call to his back as he hurries away. "We were told that we'd get a copy of everything that you have. This is nothing."

Nelson slows and does a half-turn, his hand sliding down to the vicinity of his holster, his expression that of one who feels that his position makes him immune to any challenge and woe to anyone who thinks otherwise. My visions of a shootout on a dusty western street at high noon are interrupted when a voice to my left calls out.

"Officer," Vinn tells him with a slight smugness in her tone as she extends the arm holding her cell phone, "this call's for you."

Befuddled but willing to call Vinn's bluff, Nelson approaches and snatches the phone from her grasp. He's in the middle of an impressively creative string of profanity when he suddenly stops, color draining from his face. I can't tell who's on the other end of the call, but I can guess, and he'll need a throat lozenge after he gets done screaming at the top of his lungs at the hapless rookie. I almost feel sorry for Nelson. Almost.

The verbal harangue continues for at least two minutes before a loud click indicates the call was terminated with a slamming down of the receiver on the other end, a punctuation mark suggesting it was made from a landline in this very building. Nelson takes a few moments to look up before handing the phone back to Vinn. "Follow me," is all he manages to say. He directs us to wait in an interrogation room that smells of sweat, piss, and fear.

"Sanders?" I ask Vinn as I try to get comfortable in a chair whose legs seem to be cut to different lengths.

"At first," she replies. "I get the impression that he wasn't happy and may have brought a higher up at the station here on the line that had poor Officer Nelson quaking in his boots. Don't imagine he'll be in any hurry at the copy machine, though."

She's right, as usual. We're going on twenty minutes and I've resorted to making faces into the two-way mirror to entertain whoever might be watching us from the other side when the door opens. A large, imposing man with a nasty scowl and a much thicker folder in his hands fills the doorway as he enters.

"Mendez?" Vinn and I exclaim in unison. "I didn't know this was your case," I tell him.

"It wasn't until five minutes ago," he growls unhappily. "Someone in the upper reaches of the department has the false impression that the two of you and I successfully worked together in the past and make a good team, so he pulled some strings. I'm under orders to assist you. Ask me if I'm happy about it."

"By assist, you mean prevent us from getting too close to the investigation and to stay out of the way while pretending to help?" I suggest. Mendez' silence is all I need to know that my assumption is right on the mark. No wonder he's not pleased. His job is to babysit us.

Our history with Mendez is one of an unspoken mutual respect and outspoken hostility. He's firmly in the camp that criminal investigations, especially those involving a dead body or two, should be conducted solely by professional law enforcement. Not an unreasonable position. More importantly, he believes that there are certain rules that need to be followed in the pursuit and capture of the bad guys. This is where we part ways. While he appears vaguely aware that both Vinn and I at one point in our lives performed a similar role to his own in the shadows while being only peripherally sanctioned by the government, and perhaps even respects our experience, he strongly disapproves of our methods despite our perfect record of success. This is also reasonable given the chaos and multiple bodies that accompanied the prior two times we joined forces. Still, it's hurtful that we don't at least get a little credit for the points he's scored within the department for 'solving' some difficult cases.

"I thought we had an understanding," he snaps as he drops the file on the table with a loud thud, "that I do my job and you do yours. Which as I understand it, involves your teaching our impressionable youth and staying the hell away from me."

"First of all," Vinn retorts, irritation in her voice, "your memory appears to be faulty. That was a demand you made to which we never consented. That being said, we did agree between ourselves to stick to teaching. We were pulled out of our retirement by someone who wouldn't take 'no' for an answer."

Mendez' features soften as he grabs a chair, flips it backwards, and lowers his heavy frame into it. "Yeah, I get it," he admits. "The fact that you're getting this file is proof enough that there's some heavy weight behind it.

Enough for my boss's boss's boss to look the other way as to your involvement. But it's my ass that gets burned if you leave another trail of carnage in your wake."

"Never our intent," I state for the record. It never is, of course, but I can understand if blood and bodies are becoming our brand. "Now, what do we need to know?"

"I just got this myself, remember?" Mendez sounds annoyed. "How about I look on while you two go through it here in front of me?"

Vinn and I exchange glances and don't see any objection in each other's eyes. It may help to have him here in case we have any questions or want a third opinion. We open the folder to the cover page that we've already seen. Vinn pulls out an envelope of pictures and begins to spread them out over the table. Mendez circles around to look at them over our shoulders.

"Holy shit," he mutters. My sentiment exactly.

What used to be Brandon Mills lies prone and naked in a bathtub filled halfway up with water, his sole piece of clothing a striped tie with a small logo on it. I pick up the photo with the closest view of the tie. "Vinn, what was the name of his company?"

"Yeah, I thought of that too," she replies. "That's it. A company tie, I guess."

As odd as that feature would be on its own, it's the other details that have the scene crossing over to the bizarre. In one hand Mills' body holds a kitchen spatula with what appears to be a pancake duct taped to its flat surface while the other grasps a shaving kit. A comb is knitted into his thinning hair. A toothbrush is stuck halfway into his mouth. Dozens of pill capsules, partly dissolved by the bath water, float on the surface. A futuristic toaster floats half-submerged between his legs.

"That's not what killed him," Vinn tells me as she notices me studying a closeup of the toaster, which unsurprisingly was manufactured by Mills' company. She's reading the autopsy report. "Unlike what you see in the movies, dropping a live toaster into a tub of water is unlikely to kill anyone. The current disburses and the power source trips off." Thank you, Ms. Science. "He actually died of an overdose of sleeping pills and pain killers. Abrasions to his throat indicate he may have been forced to swallow them."

"He probably died in the tub," Mendez adds as he reads. "But most of what you see here would have been added post-mortem. The scene was staged after the fact. Someone was trying to make a statement."

"What's the point of making a statement if no one can figure out what it is you're trying to say?" I ask mostly to myself. Vinn and I look through the rest of the file and pass the paperwork down to Mendez, who by now has pulled his chair around so that we're all on the same side of the table. We read silently for several minutes.

"No marital problems, had enough money that the wife didn't need his insurance payout which wasn't significant anyway, didn't take drugs or gamble, no enemies that anyone could point to, obviously not a suicide, nothing was taken out of the home. In other words no motive, no leads, and this investigation has gone nowhere since Day 1." Mendez stares menacingly at Vinn and I. "Thanks so much for getting me involved in this."

"Happy to do it," Vinn says with a smile. "So, Officer, what's our next step?"

Mendez' next step, his next several steps in fact, were straight to the door of the room, which he swung open, stepped through, then slammed with enough force to rattle my shaky chair.

"He isn't wrong," I remark as Vinn puts the file back together the way it was first brought to us. "There's nothing that immediately pops into my head as to what to do next."

"That's obvious," Vinn tells me. "You choose. Sushi or barbeque."

FIVE

Back in Vinn's condo, appetites sated, we brainstorm over what we learned from our initial review of the official police file. We're forced to admit that if anything we're further from a solution now than we were when we were totally ignorant of the facts. Discussing how to proceed from here brings on a livelier debate.

"I say talk to his wife," I suggest.

"And ask what?" Vinn answers. "'Did your husband often make pancakes while taking a bath?' Remember that whatever approach we take with her will be relayed back to Sanders before we even back out of her driveway. We can't just go on a fishing expedition or do anything to reveal how clueless we are. We have to at least look like we're proceeding according to a theory of some sort."

"Which means that we need to actually develop a theory, which brings us back to where we started." My frustration clearly shows.

"Then let's come up with one, Watson," Vinn states. "Whenever I'm stumped in the lab, when an experiment defies all of my assumptions and predictions and I don't know why, I find it helps to make lists. That means write down what we know, try to categorize elements of the crime scene, list questions and the facts we need in order to answer them, propose crazy theories. Sometimes just having a visual aid helps brain function. Assuming you have a working brain to begin with," she adds slyly with a grin.

I don't take the bait. "Between the two of us, we should have the equivalent of two average intellects, however unevenly distributed." I walk into Vinn's bedroom and return with a legal pad and pen. She keeps them on her nightstand to jot down middle-of-the-night ideas on the assumption that she'll forget them by morning. I teased her about it for the first few months of sleeping over given how ridiculous most of her notes were, but eventually saw that for every ten nonsensical musings scribbled at 2:00 a.m., there were one or two brilliant insights. I now keep a pad on my own nightstand, although more for Vinn's use than my own. English professors rarely need to puzzle out solutions to scientific conundrums in their sleep.

Vinn begins by drawing a vertical line down the middle of the paper. "Let's start out slow. I'm sure you noticed from pictures of the scene that there were a number of discordant objects that fell into two general categories. Let's test our memories first then pull out the photos to make sure we don't miss anything."

"Right. Spatula, pancake, toothbrush, comb."

Vinn prints each word in her tiny, neat script in the left column, each on their own line. "Okay, then we have a necktie and toaster. Oh, and a razor with assorted grooming aids in the kit." She places the necktie and razor in the right column before pausing to look at me.

"I think I see a pattern, however unlikely," I say. "For now, move the razor into the first column. I'm not sure about the toaster. It kind of fits both sides with what I'm thinking."

Vinn nods slightly. "I think we're on the same wavelength. Scary if true; we may be spending too much time together." Without waiting for a reaction from me, she prints 'toaster' in the middle, straddling the dividing line before adding "company logo" on the right side.

I pull out the photo to see if we missed anything. We did. "Don't forget the pill capsules in the water, and we couldn't see it but the report said there was a nail clipper in the tub," I remind her. Vinn dutifully adds both to the left column.

Vinn flips to the second page of the pad and tears the bottom portion neatly across, then again in the other direction to make two pieces of paper of identical size and shape. She hands one to me. "First impressions are important," she tells me in her best professorial tone. "Write down what you think the objects in each column represent. Don't think about it too hard, just what went through your mind as we made the list. There are no wrong answers. Then fold the paper in half and put it on the table."

The left column is easy, but it takes me awhile to come up with the correct phrasing for the right one. I add my paper on top of Vinn's.

"Okay," she tells me, taking hold of her laptop as well as taking charge. I might take offense a little bit when she assumes control of an investigation as if I'm an idiot—there's a reason she called me "Watson" instead of "Holmes"—but I'm okay with it for two reasons. One, she's sexy as hell when in command. And two, she takes us in the right direction more often than not.

She types each of the words in the left column into Google then presses the return button. Instantly the screen lights up with links to online schools and employment opportunities. She scrolls down and moves through three pages of results, not bothering to actually click on the links since all of them are clear in the description as to the degree or job which they're advertising. The exact phrasing varies somewhat but the specified duties do not.

"Home Care Aide," Vinn states finally. "I don't think it would be useful to search for the righthand column, not enough words there to narrow it down. But if you and I truly are thinking alike, I bet we won't need to."

She reaches down and opens up both scraps of paper. On mine, I wrote "Personal assistant-health" and "Businessman." Vinn, "Caregiver" and "Business owner." I like her nomenclature better but we're there together in our thoughts.

"I almost put 'nurse,'" I add. "Except then I would expect a stethoscope and nurses don't prepare meals. But a caregiver makes meals, dispenses medication, helps with personal tasks like shaving and brushing teeth."

"Agreed," Vinn responds as she leans back and stares at the ceiling. "As a working hypothesis, and since both of our minds and Google went in this direction, let's assume that the killer wanted to convey those two occupations and not simply a home chef or someone's grooming habits. The logo on the tie and the fact that the toaster was manufactured by the victim's company may be referencing someone higher up in a company, not just a factory worker, which would also track with our initial impressions. We may be totally off base, but if our assumptions get us nowhere we can start over. Yes?"

"Yes. Is this really progress, though?" I ask. "We have no idea what this means."

"Not yet," Vinn replies with more enthusiasm than I feel. "But now, at least, I think we have a starting point as to what to ask the wife."

The Mills' home in the north shore suburb of Wilmette is a nicely appointed, two-story wooden structure with a large, meticulous lawn and a long driveway devoid of cars until we pull into it in the Honda Civic we had to rent from Zipcar under a false identity due to our history of not returning their cars in the best of conditions. The last one we had to abandon after being shot up and I'm not sure Zipcar ever found it, or wanted to.

Vinn assumed the lead in arranging the appointment with her boss' sister-in-law and will take point with the interview as well. I'm fine with this, not only in deference to the workplace politics at play here but because I'm still not entirely sure how to proceed. Vinn seems to have no such qualms.

We're greeted at the door by a trim woman in a light blue dress that wouldn't be out of place at dinner at the local country club, and she took the time to add a jeweled necklace and to do her makeup. Only the lines under her sad eyes and her forced smile as she greets us give away the strain that the last few weeks have put her under.

"Julie Mills," she says as she steps aside to allow us to pass through the door. We follow her into the living room and onto a designer couch. Pictures of children of various ages adorn the walls and the carpet is plush under our feet. Everything about Julie and the home itself says comfortable and tasteful without being ostentatious. There's some money here if that factors into the motive for the killing, but from what I can see not outrageous wealth.

Vinn introduces us and declines an offer of coffee. "We're so sorry to dredge up such an unpleasant subject, Mrs. Mills," she begins. "And I apologize if we ask questions that you've already answered a hundred times with the police. As your brother-in-law may have told you, we're just getting involved and are essentially starting from scratch. It's also important in bringing fresh eyes to the investigation to start at the beginning."

"I don't know why he thought it necessary to pressure me into doing this," Mrs. Mills responds, all of a sudden sounding adversarial. "We agreed to keep this within the family."

Vinn pauses for a few beats, then hearing no further complaints, continues as if we're still on friendly terms. "To begin, can you tell us about your husband? Who he was as a person, his interests, who his friends were. Include information about his company as well. We're just looking to get an impression of the man in general."

Mrs. Mills draws in a big breath and looks toward the ceiling. A brief expression of annoyance further betrays her feelings about our presence. "He was a wonderful man. Warm, kind. Never had a bad word to say about anyone. Everybody liked him. He was on the boards of several charities, we always made sure to donate both time and money to them. We shared the same friends, mostly neighbors and a few people we know from church. I don't think you need to talk to them."

The sharper tone she used with those last few words immediately raises the question as to what she's hiding that she doesn't want the neighbors to disclose. Or maybe she's worried that we'll reveal the odd circumstances of his death, which would provide fodder for gossip for years. Vinn chooses to ignore the command and gets the woman back on track. "All that we're looking for right now is background information, Mrs. Mills," she says calmly. "Any hobbies, other interests?"

"Nothing that would make someone want to kill him," she says angrily. "Golf once or twice a week— you kind of have to when you're in business, to take prospective clients out. He watched baseball and football. Liked to do puzzles. He said it kept his mind clear. Is this really necessary?"

"Tell us about his company, please," Vinn prods. "Did he start it himself, what did it do exactly, and was it doing well?"

Mrs. Mills glares at me for a moment before deciding to grace us with an answer. "Yes, it was his from the start. He was working for an engineering company when we were married but about five years later went out on his own and started Motivon. At first he focused on widgets and gizmos for the manufacturing trade. His idea was to make what other companies made but to do it better, to be top-of-the-line. It worked. Over time he expanded to items for the general public, like kitchen mixers, vacuum cleaners, toast—"

She stops suddenly, distressed. "Of course, we understand," Vinn says. "And was the company doing well?"

"Of course it was, didn't I say that?" Mrs. Mills snaps. "We weren't in financial difficulty if that's what you're implying."

Time to redirect her away from Vinn. "Mrs. Mills," I say as gently as I can. "Did your husband or anyone close to him have any connection with a caregiver, or did his company make any items of interest to the health care industry?"

I get the evil eye as she decides whether to answer. "I don't understand the question, young man. We're both in perfect health and can take care of ourselves. And no, he didn't manufacture anything for hospitals or the medical profession that I know of. Is that all?"

As tempting as it is to comment that her husband is not, in fact, currently in perfect health, I bite my tongue and remain silent. Vinn and I make eye contact and we're both on the same page. We're not going to get anything further here.

"Yes, thank you for your time, Mrs. Mills," she says, rising from the couch. "If we think of anything else I hope you won't mind if we call."

We get no answer other than a quick escort to the door. Back in the car, we sit for a few moments before I start the engine. "I'm not sure I understand the resentment. We're only trying to help. Hell, we were pressured to help," I comment as I back out of the driveway.

"I know," Vinn agrees. "She has every reason to be upset that her spouse was killed, but I felt like she was blaming us for his murder. I suspect her hostility is directed as us because she's angry with her husband for getting himself killed, especially in the way he did. Not sure she's going to be a source of any useful information."

"Neighbors?" I ask.

"I caught that too. But I think not. Within the hour word will be out not to cooperate with us or to hold back on whatever it is she wants hidden from public view. It may not have anything to do with his killing. There are lots of secrets in these communities that they'd rather keep quiet. It might be worth a discreet question or two with Dr. Sanders, though, just to be thorough. If you don't mind I think it would be best if you handled that. I don't want to be a pariah with the entire family, especially my boss."

We're quiet and left to our own thoughts as we head back into the city. It was too much to expect that we'd get something useful out of the wife, but only now am I realizing that it's the only lead we have.

SIX

I fulfill my promise to Vinn by probing Dr. Sanders to see what he knows about his brother-in-law and the neighbors but all I got in response was a depiction of the All-American success story with all glitter and no warts. Within the first six minutes it became clear that my trip to his office was a waste of time, but I had to endure fifteen minutes more of interrogation as to what we've learned and what our plans were from here on. Considering I have no more of an idea than he does as to what we're going to do next, it was an awkward quarter of an hour and I don't think I did Vinn a whole lot of favors with my stammering. For the next few days Vinn and I toss really bad ideas back and forth but fail to stimulate either's imagination in ways that lead to action.

I'm packing my satchel to head home for the weekend when a shadow crosses my office door. Looking up, I'm startled to see my own boss, Stuart Vanguard, hovering as he watches me toss the first batch of efforts from a creative writing class into the bag. Stuart should be proud of me as his prize hire since the evaluation scores from my students are always near the top in the university every semester, but instead my success only underscores his bitterness that he was duped into offering me a job due to a case of mistaken identity I did nothing to discourage. He's not one hundred percent certain that I'm a fake, but that hasn't stopped him from looking for an excuse to fire me.

"Going somewhere so early, Mr. Winters?" he snarls.

"I need to get home to prepare for the University President's white tie dinner party tonight," I reply. "I can never quite remember how to put on a bow tie and may need a little extra time. Maybe we can go together and you can give me a few pointers?"

I look on with my most innocent face as Stuart squirms. He's ninety percent sure that I'm lying but the other ten percent that I'm not rankles him, and a part of him is terrified that I'll tell the head of UIC that I'm late for dinner because he held me up.

"I had a previous engagement" he finally squeaks, playing it safe. He backs out of the door and is halfway down the hall to his office by the time I'm locking up. I marvel at the difference between Vinn's boss and my own. Equivalent positions filled by complete opposites. Which triggers a thought. Two different personalities in the same job. Two different careers represented in the same person. Maybe Mills' killer wasn't as interested in the jobs he or she portrayed with the items left on and around his body as in the difference between them. Top of the pile versus a more common or unremarkable job, at least as the world typically views them. Wealthy CEO of a successful company versus a poor home care worker who wipes her charge's ass. In the depths of my mind this line of thinking seems to be a breakthrough, but how or why still eludes me. Maybe what I need is to run the thought by a distinguished group of thinkers.

Maybe "drunken" is a more accurate adjective than "distinguished." I'm sitting in my usual chair in the kitchen of my tenant Leo, who occupies the garden unit. Leo is a gruff, taciturn, rough, hard-bodied old man who sticks to his story that he's in witness protection for having tried to assassinate Fidel Castro many years ago even though Vinn and I uncovered the truth about his past in the course of our last caper. We always knew he couldn't possibly be Cuban due to the questionable authenticity and verifiable inedibility of the food he prepares at his shack of a restaurant, The Kuban Kabana. But what his cooking skills lack he makes up for in his sourcing of rare, colorful, and undeniably potent liquors from south of the border. Which border is still up for debate.

Tonight's drinkfest consists of he, I, and Rebecca, who's pouting after the combination fashion show and food truck event in the parking lot of an Aldi she had front row seats for was canceled when one of the massive speakers lining the stage fell and wiped out the runway and an empanada truck. She's still wearing the sparkly blue faux Armani gown she hoped would draw attention her way. Vinn passed on joining us, claiming a headache. She's an infrequent guest anyway. While she can usually drink a posse of sailors under the table, the hooch Leo finds gives her a guaranteed hangover that amuses me so much she tries to avoid our get-togethers unless absolutely necessary.

The time is somewhere between midnight and morning and the room is spinning when I describe the crime scene and my thoughts on what the killer was trying to portray. Confidentiality isn't an issue because no one will remember what I said by the morning anyway. Rebecca stares at me as I talk then belches and passes out. Leo looks at me with reddened eyes that still hold an icy consciousness.

"Yur right," he slurs as he refills our glasses with a neon yellow liquid, "'bout differences. Thas' why yur lookin fur a woman. No man wuld tape pancake."

I don't know that I agree with his reasoning, but the thought that a woman is the killer as an added part of the dichotomy makes perfect sense to my addled brain. I head for the door, only tripping over Rebecca once, crawl up two flights to my unit, and the last thing I remember is writing "killer is a woman" on the legal pad next to my bed.

I awake to a steady patter of rain against my bedroom window, the lack of sun making it unclear if it's early morning or mid-afternoon. I count the number of painful throbs per minute inside my head and decide that they're spaced far enough apart that it's got to be just short of lunchtime. I then do what I could have done initially and grab my cell phone off the nightstand. 10:15 a.m. Still plenty of time in the day to ponder the meaning of life, more specifically my place in it and how and why I got thrown in the middle of an impossibly frustrating investigation. It's going to be a long weekend.

Replacing my phone, I notice the scribble I made on the pad last night before leaving the conscious world. For the life of me I don't know why I wrote "kilsitwoma." I stumble to the kitchen and paw through my tea collection searching for the bag of uji gyokuro green tea, which I'm pretty sure I haven't finished. The irony of trying to remember if I still have a supply of tea that supposedly stimulates the brain's neurotransmitters to improve memory recall and cognitive function isn't lost on me. With a cry of triumph I find the crumpled bag erroneously stored among the yellows and quickly begin steeping the last remnants.

Whether it's the effect of the tea, the gooey pastry I ate with it, or just the fact that my hangover is clearing up, I'm gradually able to reconstruct the conversation I had with Leo last night fully enough to decipher my handwriting as "it's a woman" or something close to it. Even sober I like the idea as a working theory. If true, it narrows our list of suspects down to half the world's population. It's a start.

I eagerly call Vinn to relay my thoughts. She's not as impressed as I had hoped.

"As much as I'd like to jump on board with the theory you pulled out of your posterior, and it does resonate on some levels, it's too early to narrow our focus," she tells me, choosing her wording carefully so as not to deflate my ego too much. "But speaking of being desperate to make progress, what's your opinion of profilers?"

Criminal profilers use their knowledge of how a criminal mind works, combine it with a huge database of offenses and the types of people who committed them as well as statistical probabilities, then apply their expertise to a specific set of facts for a particular crime or, in the case of serial killers, multiple incidents. While they've had some high-profile successes, I still see it as more of an art than a science, something to consider but not necessarily allow to 'narrow the focus' as Vinn would say. An aid, not a foregone conclusion.

"Um..." I begin before pausing to think how I want to put this to her.

"My thoughts exactly," Vinn interrupts. "But to say

we're stuck at the moment is an understatement and I'm willing to give it a shot. I know a guy the people I used to work with would use."

"Is he any good?" I ask, still unsure if I want to go in this direction.

"He's a total asshole," Vinn replies, an edge to her voice. "And he thinks any woman he meets either falls under his spell or is in denial that she's doing so. But yeah, as profilers go, he's as good as they get. Just ask him."

I sigh, resigned to a trip down this rabbit hole. "Okay, fine. At a minimum, it'll give you something to tell Sanders so that he doesn't think we're sitting on our hands. Do you have any idea how to find him?"

"Already did, and unfortunately he happens to be in Chicago on another matter, so a phone conversation isn't an option. We're meeting him at the Chicago Athletic Club at 3:00. 'We' as in you and me, so get your head cleared of Leo's hooch, take a shower, and get over here. Don't blame me if you're not around and I succumb to his charms."

Vinn hangs up without another word. I finish my tea and head for the bathroom.

Cindy's is the rooftop bar of the Chicago Athletic Club on Michigan Avenue in the South Loop, an 1800s-era gothic building that's been updated to a boutique hotel. Directly across from Millennium Park, it boasts an outstanding view of the park, the concert pavilion to its east, and Lake Michigan itself. Despite today's drizzle, tiny white sails are visible on the water as we approach the area where a tall, bearded man with thinning reddish hair awaits. He's seated at a table for two and a bottle of wine chills in a stand positioned next to the table.

Vinn diplomatically chooses not to sit at the sole open chair. "Barry, it's been a long time. This is my partner and co-worker Malcom Winters. We're working on this investigation together. Malcom, Barry Levin."

By this time the sharp-eyed maître d' has arrived to escort us to a larger table where a waiter has already transferred the wine stand. Levin arises wordlessly without acknowledging the hand I proffered and moves to the claim the middle seat, guaranteeing a place next to Vinn, who's rolling her eyes at me behind his back.

"It's great to see you again, Vinn," Levin says before glancing at me, a touch of annoyance in his voice. "I always thought that you preferred working alone."

"We've found that we each possess certain traits that mesh well with the other's, both professionally and personally," Vinn replies not too subtly while putting up a hand to stop Levin from pouring wine in her glass. He returns the bottle to its icy resting place without looking in my direction. Vinn sends a pleading glance in my direction.

"We're hoping to get your thoughts on the type of person who might stage a murder scene in an unusual way," I tell the back of his head. As I describe the scene, with Vinn throwing in a detail from time to time, Levin leans back with his eyes closed, either in concentration or to avoid looking at me. It doesn't take long to finish my narrative. Levin remains immobile and silent for several minutes before coming back to life. His first action is to turn his chair so as to better face Vinn.

"Definitely male, early 30's. He's in the health care field and is feeling frustrated about his job, the lack of status compared to the head of a business as well as the low pay. He's struggling financially. Almost certainly white or his anger would have been directed at someone of his race more successful than he. There was a certain level of premeditation at work here, he's been dreaming about this for some time, although not necessarily in this amount of detail. His staging took advantage of what was available to him. Unusual in that people in his line of work—caregivers, nurses, those underappreciated medical staff who do most of the work and gain little of the credit—have an emotional composition that inspires them to help those in need with less need of recognition than you would think. They feel a calling to assist. It's rare for someone in that position to kill unless out of compassion or in the heat of the moment. He may have been mentally ill."

As he speaks, Levin's hands move slowly in Vinn's direction, causing the rest of his body to lean forward in sync. As a scientist, Vinn puts into practice the theorem that for every action there's an equal and opposite reaction. She shrinks back in her chair and uses her feet to edge it further away from the table before standing up and motioning me to do the same.

"Thank you, that was very informative," she tells Levin in a tone that betrays her feelings that it was anything but helpful. "Enjoy your stay in Chicago."

"Well that wasn't too awkward," she spits as we make our way to the elevator. "And now I'm on board with your theory. This killer had damn well better be a woman as Leo posits. If not I'll make him one just out of spite. So much for the so-called experts. Time to put our noses to the grindstone and work this out the old-fashioned way. With sweat and street smarts. Now first..."

Vinn pauses mid-thought as we exit the revolving door of the hotel, tilts her head to the south, raises her nose slightly, and sniffs. Ten minutes later we're ordering cheeseburgers.

SEVEN

Monday mornings are a terrible way to begin my week, with three classes before noon starting with the secular supernatural class and immediately followed by my 9:00 a.m. snoozefest, "Too Cursory to be Thoreau," a study of nineteenth-century short poems. It's a sad sign when my students are more alert and interested in a subject than I am. As lunchtime approaches I'm looking forward to hiding in my office with a sandwich but know instantly that those plans are about to be trashed when I see Vinn pacing outside my office door.

"Sorry, Miss, my office hours are on Tuesdays and Thursdays," I tell her as I approach.

"Not funny, Mal," she responds testily. "Why don't you ever remember to turn your phone back on between classes? Anyway, we've been summoned."

That explains her mood. I don't need to ask who called us in or why. We walk slowly in the direction of Sanders' office, delaying the inevitable as long as possible.

"It's too much to hope that we're being fired from the investigation," Vinn muses. "So I assume he wants a progress report. What do we tell him? How do we explain that a lack of progress doesn't reflect a lack of activity? Dammit, I wish he didn't want to hear an update directly from me. You're much better at making complete bullshit sound like something tangible."

Vinn has a talent for making a compliment sound like the exact opposite. I decide to accept her comment as a positive thing as well as a request for advice. "We need to stress that we had a very long and productive meeting with one of the top criminal profilers in the country, leaving out his bedroom eyes. Stretch that out and tell him that it gives us a laser focus on the type of person we're looking for but that it's been too soon since we met to turn his information into action. That we have several theories but never give details at this stage so as not to raise expectations, but say it in a way that will make him think we're onto something. Use words with a lot of syllables to draw out your little speech. The key is to lead him to think that we know more than we do but are choosing not to reveal it."

We pause outside the big man's office. "Words with a lot of syllables?" Vinn asks me. "God help us if that's the best advice you have." We pull open the door, survive an interrogation by his ancient secretary, then find ourselves once more sitting like school children waiting to hear our punishment for using permanent markers on the whiteboard.

Vinn does her best to make nothing sound like something, and even I began to get optimistic about our chances of solving this thing by dinnertime by the time she's through. Her boss, though, doesn't seem to share my newfound attitude.

"You sound a lot like the lieutenant I've been talking with," he says sternly. "What I want to know is when you're going to identify the bastard that did this to Brandon. The longer this goes on, the less the chance of solving it, isn't that right?"

Great, he watches cop shows. I decide to step in to give poor beleaguered Vinn a break from Sanders' attention. "These things take—"

"Anyway," he continues as he stares down at Vinn, apparently deciding that nothing I say will contribute to the conversation, "I've arranged for you to meet with the team up at the 18th District. Maybe by comparing notes at least one of you can pull something out of your respective asses. I saw that your last lab today ends at 3:30. Your meeting is at 6:00 tonight."

Vinn sees the flash of anger in my eyes as my mouth begins to open, cuts me off with a curt "Thank you Dr Sanders," then takes me by the elbow to escort me out the door. Once in the hallway she exhales as she leans against the wall, looking like she'd just had a run-in with the front end of a truck.

"I'm sure you were about to say what I was thinking," she smiles, showing all is well between us, "which might not have been the best thing for my career. That being said, I've got to come up with a way of diplomatically telling him to butt out and let us do our jobs. Just because he forced this on us doesn't mean he pulls the strings." She pushes herself upright and we begin the short walk back to her office.

"I'm sure the cops are as thrilled to be forced into this meeting as we are," I say. "Maybe if we play our cards right they'll do what Sanders won't and get us off this case."

Vinn looks thoughtful. "Mal, whatever it takes, however it ends, you know how I feel. No more rogue investigations, no more walking on the wild side, no more risking our lives. We've come too close too many times to losing what we have with each other. Let's put everything we can into this one knowing it's the last time and wrap it up as soon as possible."

She pulls me through her office door and continues physically the passion she just expressed verbally. Sheepishly, but with a sparkle in her eyes, she kicks the door shut and leads me over to her desk, which unlike my own is totally free of clutter and perfectly prepared for what she has in mind. Another fantasy realized, and suddenly the prospect of being in the same room as a group of hostile police officers doesn't seem so bad.

My classes done for the day, I'm relaxing with a cup of Gyokuro and grading the first set of essays from a freshman class while I wait for Vinn to finish her lab. We plan to grab a quick snack somewhere before heading up north. Perish the idea of entering this meeting on an empty stomach. I'm just about to toss my pile of papers into the trash bin followed by a lit match when my cell phone chirps. Literally. It makes baby bird noises for calls from numbers it doesn't recognize.

"Winters," a gruff voice speaks softly, "Grab that lady partner of yours and get your ass up here."

"Mendez, the meeting doesn't start for a couple of hours. Whatever's going on you can tell me there."

"Screw the meeting, we won't be there. I may regret this, but since I'd probably be forced to clue you in down the road anyway, you might as well see the scene first-hand. I'll text you the address."

Mendez hangs up before I can ask for details. Clue me in anyway? On what? Did another one of Sanders' in-laws get killed? I notice that Vinn should be done by now and on the way to her office. I lock up and move to intercept her and to break the bad news that the snacks will have to wait.

The address Mendez directed us to in the Lincoln Park neighborhood shares a zip code with Vinn's condo but is a world apart in terms of affluence. The white cobblestone, three-story home on a shady, tree-lined block brushes to the edge of being ostentatious, but it's hard not to exude luxury when it must have cost its owners closer to eight figures left of the decimal point than a mere six. Half of the street is blocked by squad cars and crime scene tape frames the entire front yard of the home. Eight cops stand around trying to look like they're doing something useful. The one officer who does have a job, checking names of anyone wanting to enter against a list on his clipboard, is currently giving us problems.

"Let them through," Mendez shouts from the entryway. "Just put 'consultants times two' or some such nonsense and note that I authorized their presence."

We duck under the tape and walk slowly up the steps under the watchful and not terribly friendly stares of the idle men and women in blue. Mendez has already disappeared back into the foyer, where he waits impatiently tapping his foot while we put on disposable booties and hair nets. He blocks our movement further into the house.

"Don't get the idea that this means that I like you or welcome your role in police matters," he begins. "As you know I was compelled into taking over that investigation with the guy in the bathtub even though it happened outside the 18th. This one, though, happened on my turf. You'll know why I called you in when you see the victim."

Mendez turns and walks about four feet to a door on his left. We follow him down dimly lit stairs to the basement, where we find ourselves in a meticulous recreation of a 50s-style rec room, complete with fake wood paneling on the walls, short-shag carpeting, and a pool table in one corner. In another corner is a built-in bar with a shiny laminate surface and four tall stools. The wall behind the bar is lined with shelves containing a colorful array of bottles that puts Leo's collection to shame, glasses hanging from racks on the ceiling. A vintage neon Pabst beer sign casts an eerie illumination over the area. It looks like a fun and inviting place to kick back with friends and down a cold one if it weren't for the woman's body sprawled across two of the stools.

"Don't touch anything," Mendez warns unnecessarily as Vinn and I move in for a closer look at the scene. It's immediately obvious why he called for us. The woman is clothed, mostly, with a business woman's blouse and suitcoat on top and a pair of white men's underpants down below. Both our eyes and noses make clear that the underwear is heavily soiled. Her feet, clad in black pumps, rest on a wide stool. A hypodermic needle, plunged part way in, dangles from one arm. Coffee grounds are scattered over the bar and spill onto the floor, where they partially cover an orange peel. A paper take-out menu from a local restaurant is sticking out of the front pocket of her jacket.

What draws my attention most, though, is the stethoscope hung around her neck. Band-Aids are taped in no apparent pattern over her left leg. Peeking out from behind the menu in her pocket are several tongue depressors. A blood pressure kit rests on one of the unoccupied stools. I have a hunch.

"Mendez, how closely has she been looked at? Would there happen to be anything inserted into, um, her backside?"

"How in the hell would you know that?" he growls. "Yeah, a thermometer. I'm serious, I want an answer. How did you know that?"

"Just makes sense given some of the other implements here," I respond vaguely. "No, I don't have any idea what it means."

Mendez grunts, obviously not satisfied with my answer but unsure how to press further. "You don't want to get any closer than that," he tells Vinn as she leans into the body. "Initial thoughts are that she didn't die of a drug overdose. More likely poison."

"That's what I was looking at," Vinn tells him. "Her lips are a little blue. What do we know about the victim?"

"It's early, so not much," Mendez replies. "Sandra Summers. Lives alone. A divorce attorney for the rich and powerful is my understanding." He looks around the room. "She obviously wasn't doing so bad herself." He crinkles his nose. "Let's go upstairs and chat."

We congregate in the kitchen, where the air is indeed fresher. "I'm not saying that we have a serial killer here," Mendez says as he wipes perspiration from his face with a paper towel that he then sticks into his pocket, "but I've been doing this a long time and never seen anything like this. So two of them all of a sudden? Have to think that they're related, or at least keep it in mind."

"Who found her?" I ask.

"Cleaning lady, comes twice a week. She wasn't any help, too hysterical to even remember her name, but we'll circle back to her. So now that I got you here, tell me what you think. Same killer?"

Vinn and I exchange glances to make sure we're on the same page. "Hard to ignore the similarities," I reply. "The staging, the props. It could always be the latest fad on TikTok, but if you want my honest opinion, yes, these are related. Eighty percent the same person. Can you keep us informed on this one as well, copy us in on the reports?"

"I'll need to get the department's okay, but I don't think that'll be a problem," Mendez admits reluctantly. "But this is a two-way street. You come up with anything, you share." He tilts his head in response to a noise from outside. "That'll be the medical examiner," he tells us. "Time for the two of you to scram."

Once back outside and out of hearing range of the cops still lingering in the yard, Vinn turns to me. "Eighty percent? Was that your honest opinion?"

"No," I admit. "Maybe closer to fifty-fifty. Clearly a lot of similarities, but then again this one just felt different. A different attitude toward the scene I guess, but it's more a feeling that I can't pin down. Does that make any sense?"

"Absolutely," Vinn grins. "Because I felt the same thing but I think I know why. The first scene with my boss' brother-in-law was very straightforward, factual. The killer had something to say, whatever it was, and staged it to convey that message. This one, though, had something the first one didn't. A sense of humor."

"Ah," I say. "Yes, that's it. The legal puns. A lawyer at the bar. Her feet were resting on the bench. The menu, as if the judge were about to order lunch. Wearing briefs."

"And did you catch the reason for the coffee and the orange?" She sees my blank look. "Coffee grounds and an orange peel. As in grounds for appeal. Crude, but I kind of like that one."

"So," I summarize, "briefs, grounds for appeal, approaching the bench, order of the court, and an actual lawyer at the bar. Then we have more medical references."

"I don't think we need to Google those, do we?" Vinn nods. "This time I'm almost positive we have your nurse. A doctor's a possibility but they don't take rectal temperatures. So for now, let's assume a nurse and a lawyer. A home care worker and a CEO. Any thoughts that you chose not to pass on to Mendez?"

"Not a one," I admit. "But do you think it's too late to show up for our meeting at the 18th District station?"

Vinn hits me on the arm and her point is made. We head off to her place.

EIGHT

Vinn rinses dish soap off the last dinner plate and hands it to me to dry and stack before flipping a switch on her coffee maker, leaving it to me to start heating water for my tea. We knew our relationship had become serious when, unbeknownst to the other, she ordered tea from a discriminating and expensive online source to keep on hand on the same day I bought a fancy coffee maker for my place. I've learned to accept the fact that if the one trait about Vinn that drives me insane is her choice of caffeinated beverage, I'm doing pretty well. Vinn's list of my imperfections extends far beyond just one thing, but my love of tea and strong dislike of coffee is fairly far down the list and she tolerates it.

"Okay," she sighs as we slide onto her couch, "can we assume, or at least use as a starting point, that these two killings are related?"

"The very fact that Mendez called us to the scene of his own accord considering that he'd much rather ship us off to another continent far away from any investigation he's a part of speaks for itself," I reply. "But even beyond that, the bizarre staging, the confluence of exactly two professions, and the fact that they each took place in the same city close together in time makes it a near certainty. At the very least it helps us narrow our focus for now. If we're wrong, we start over. For me that's not the real question."

"Right," Vinn concedes. "I'm there as well. Did the same person murder both victims? Every factor you just listed would say yes. I'm having a hard time accepting that, even as a working hypothesis. My gut says no."

"As does mine," I agree. "I don't even think it's fifty-fifty anymore, more like seventy-thirty against. But if we agree the two incidents are related but not performed by the same killer, we're left with one of three possibilities. One, that the two killers know each other and are committing parallel crimes made to look alike; two, that there's a third person or persons behind them pulling the strings and coercing two unrelated people to kill and stage to his or her specifications; or three, that we're totally off base about these two murders being linked and they were done by different people without knowledge of the other. I don't list copycat because details of the first one weren't made public."

"Which means that before we move ahead assuming related killings by different people, we need first to convince ourselves that they truly are related." Vinn pauses, lost in thought. "We need more than a hunch, or in this case two hunches. We need to find something tangible that links them. What are the odds that Mendez will grant us access to witnesses, the crime scene, and everything that his team finds?" She reads my facial expression. "Right, stupid question. But we need to be able to do a lot of digging and the department has these two cases on such a tight lockdown that we won't be able to do a thorough job unless we can do it ourselves. We need to find something that Mendez will want so badly that we can barter. Information for access."

"So you're saying that we need the type of information to use to trade that we can't get without getting the access we need to trade for?" I ask with only the slightest bit of sarcasm. "Am I missing something here?"

"You give up too easily, honcho," Vinn says smugly. "I shouldn't tell you this because it'll ruin your opinion of me as being smarter than you, but I don't solve all of the scientific enigmas I face with pure brainpower. Sometimes a solution resists every trail of logic, every rational explanation, every test I design. In those situations I apply the ultimate strategy that works nine times out of ten. Okay, maybe four out of ten. I guess. I brainstorm crazy, nonsensical procedures to apply and try every one of them until something either works or gives me an idea of what else might. It's the 'give a hundred monkeys typewriters and eventually one of them will produce a Shakespeare-quality play by pure chance' approach to science. So c'mon, Bonzo, let's get to it."

I get up to retrieve my laptop out of my backpack, on the way back taking a detour to the kitchen where I grab a banana off the counter, cut in in half, and hand one piece to Vinn, who's already furiously typing away. She acknowledges my gift with a smile then goes back to her work. I don't have any idea where to start, so instead of opening Google, I lean back and close my eyes, floating into a half-awake state of consciousness.

I don't know how long I was out of touch with the world, but eventually the most obvious place to start pops into my brain, so clearly evident in its simplicity that I examine it for several moments longer before opening my eyes and my laptop simultaneously. I type five words into the search bar: home health, nurse, CEO, and attorney. Without looking at the results, I open a new search substituting "lawyer" for "attorney," then another using "executive" for "CEO," and then the various permutations, thinking to add "caregiver" as well. I end up with around fifteen open tabs and begin to examine them, my initial search first.

As I click and scroll, my concentration intensifies. After eliminating advertisements and come-ons from fake colleges offering fake degrees, one link repeatedly appears. Vinn senses my excitement, closes her own computer, and scoots closer, staring at the screen. Eventually I have seven pages open and without saying a word, move from one to another, staying on them only long enough to absorb their basic content.

"My god," Vinn finally says. "I really didn't expect this to work. If what we're seeing is what we're up against, this is truly terrifying. And it means the killer or killers aren't done yet, not by a long shot."

I close all but one tab and send its contents to Vinn for printing. It's an article from *Business Insider* referencing a book about the mindset of psychopaths and contains a simple set of two lists. The first itemizes, in order, the top ten professions most likely to produce a serial killer; the second the top ten least likely to do the same. At the top of the "least likely" list, home care aid is on top followed by nurse. The "most likely," CEO and attorney. Someone is either playing a game or sending a message or possibly both. Now all we need to do is figure out what and who before the when produces the next death. No problem, even a chimpanzee could do it.

Our relationship with Mendez has returned to normalcy in at least one regard, that he avoids being seen with us in front of his fellow cops as much as possible. We're sitting in a small coffee shop near a busy intersection in Lincoln Park where the painted brick walls are adorned with portraits of dogs in military-style uniforms. Vinn is the only one of our trio who's comfortable in the meeting place she suggested, being perfectly at home ordering an iced horchata latte with the establishment's "secret recipe" of espresso, rice milk, vanilla syrup, chai, oat milk and cinnamon. The look Mendez and I received from the young man behind the counter when he ordered a black coffee and I an iced tea, no sugar or other additives, made me think Vinn is the only reason we weren't asked to leave for the crime of being too boring.

Mendez shifts in his chair and glares at us. "Now what's so important that you had to see me right away? If you tell me you solved these cases I'll eat my hat. Or better yet," he looks up at the menu on a chalk board hanging from the wall, "go back up and have them add a double shot of doppio, whatever that is. Now spill because I have places to be."

Vinn seems to have been transported to a coffee-drinker's nirvana, so I take the lead. "What would you say if I told you that we're certain there are more similar murders to come and that while we can't identify the killer and victim by name, we do know what jobs each of them have?"

Mendez's eyes narrow and twitch as he stares at me without saying a word, then transfers his gaze to Vinn. "Is he serious?"

Vinn nods. "We think we're onto something. Of course, if this were a scientific study, our results wouldn't mean much because the sampling is so small. But I doubt that you'd prefer that we wait for the bodies to pile up before we brought what we've found to you. We did promise to share."

She pauses to take a sip of her drink, causing Mendez to drum his fingers impatiently. "And Mal did overstate our case in one regard. We're confident as to the occupation of the next victim, less so what the killer does for work. That's more supposition, and you'll need to catch him or her before we fully commit. We were only able to make this deduction because of the access we had to the file on the first case and your thoughtfulness of inviting us to the scene of the second," she continues. Mendez's lips tighten. He's not dumb. He knows that Vinn's patronizing complement and the information she's about to share will come at a cost.

Vinn proceeds to recap the items found on or around both victims, our joint opinions as to what each collection of items represented in terms of a job, supported somewhat by various online sites, and then jumps into the two lists. She conveniently ignores the fact that we only got to those lists by a combination of chance, guesswork, and hunches, leaving Mendez to assume that our conclusion was the result of superior brainpower.

"So the staging in both cases clearly reference two occupations, one of which fits the victim," she concludes. "What would the purpose of the items identifying a second career be if not teasing the occupation of the killer? Add in the job descriptions of the two lists, and how they're ordered, and it seems a near certainty."

Unsurprisingly, Mendez doesn't leap up from the table in joy and offer us medals. If anything he looks more miserable than he did ten minutes earlier. "Okay, I'll bite," he finally says. "What's number three on those lists?"

"If we're on the right track," I jump in, "a therapist will kill someone in the media, specifically television or radio."

"So what am I supposed to do," Mendez moans, "send out a bulletin to all of the radio and tv stations in the city warning them to avoid shrinks? Proactively arrest everyone with a psychology or psychiatry license and ask them if they plan to commit murder any time soon?"

"I'm hurt," Vinn responds in her best pouting tone. "We bring you an important step forward in a pair of investigations that are going nowhere and all we get is attitude."

"Yeah, yeah, I get it," Mendez concedes. "So I assume that you've got an idea of what you want to do next, and need me to set it up. Tell me I'm wrong."

"Well there is one small favor we'd like to ask," I say deferentially, "if it's not too much trouble. We'd like access to the second victim's home and computers, including laptop. And if we have a question for the wife of the first victim, it might be best to pass it on through you. Okay, that's two favors."

"Our guys already went through her computers. Nothing there to see. No death threats, no sketchy social media contacts, no love letters, zip. They're so useless to us that we didn't even save them in the evidence room. They're back in her house. I'll arrange to get you a set of keys." He frowns. "Not that you need them, but I don't want to get a call in the middle of the night due to an observant neighbor. And return them when you're done."

Mendez's willingness to cooperate is a sign of

just how desperate he is. I offer to pinky swear, which only motivates him to get up and stalk out of the shop. Mission accomplished. Now we just need to hope that we find a breadcrumb where an entire police department did not.

NINE

A special messenger arrives at my office the next day with an envelope bearing keys but no return address and no note. Being the sharp detective I am, it only takes me three and a half minutes to figure out where it came from and whose front door it opened. Given the unlikelihood that the CPD's budget allows for such extravagance, I assume that Mendez went out of pocket both to make a copy of the key—not cheap given the brand of lock—and to have it delivered in person. I'm not sure if he's being nice or dipping into his 401(k) to assure that neither Vinn nor I will show our faces at his workplace.

"He sent a key?" Vinn asks, crestfallen. "Dammit!" She suddenly realizes that there are other people eating lunch in the school cafeteria and looks around sheepishly. There was no need to worry about being overheard. People stopped sitting within two tables of us long ago.

"Let me guess," I tell her. "You wanted the challenge of picking the lock." Among the many skills at which Vinn excels, not to mention performs far better than me, is getting past the best security money can buy. She loves to show off her talent, although given the illegality of the task her audience is generally limited to only me. My contribution is the pricey set of lock picks I bought her for Christmas, in her eyes the most romantic present I could have given her.

"Getting past that lock is a given, I've done it before," she says with a smile. "I just wanted to better my personal record of..." she pulls out her phone and taps a few buttons, "three minutes and forty-two seconds.

I don't suppose..."

"In that neighborhood in broad daylight at the outside door of a murder scene? Not a chance. A neighbor would see to it that Mendez is the least of our problems. So when do you want to do this?"

"I've got a department meeting tomorrow night. How's Thursday?"

"Need to grade freshman essays. I promised them by the end of this week and of course never miss a chance to ruin their weekends," I reply. "Do you have plans for Saturday?"

"Are you asking me out on a date, Professor?" Vinn squeals in her best coquettish voice. "Will that help my midterm grade?"

"It'll bring it up to a 'C.' You'll need to do better than that to ace my class."

Vinn giggles. "Okay, then, Teach. A sleepover it is. I have Friday afternoons clear this semester. Come on by when you're done with your classes. Bring vittles."

It took physical force, in this case a less than gentle nudge, to get Vinn through the front door of the second victim's home without giving her the chance to use her lockpicks. We pause in the spacious foyer to get our bearings and to listen to any clues the house may be sending us as to where to begin.

"Let's save her computers for last," she suggests, "that way if our search of the rest of her home is a total washout we won't be too depressed because whatever she has stored electronically is our best chance to strike gold. Office or bedroom?"

I opt for the office and continue down the hallway

as Vinn heads upstairs. I wander through the kitchen, pause to admire the six-burner stove and double refrigerator, then find myself circling back to the front of the home through a mahogany-paneled dining room before I find the door to the office. It might measure large in raw numbers, but it's claustrophobic due to the rows of file cabinets lining the walls, the uppermost drawers above eye level. The top of each cabinet is filled with a disarray of messy piles of paper reaching almost to the ceiling. What may be an expensive Persian rug is barely visible beneath knee-high stacks of cream-colored files. Going through each file to look for a disgruntled client or opposing party would take forever and is probably unnecessary. That would be the first job given to a rookie cop and if they found anything useful, Mendez never would've willingly given us access to the home.

I start opening drawers of a large antique desk. In contrast to the disorder all around me, each drawer is neatly organized, free of clutter, and equally devoid of anything even remotely useful. Out of habit I tap on wood looking for false bottoms and feel beneath each drawer for anything taped out of sight. I've just moved on to the bookshelf, randomly flipping pages in various volumes of law books, when Vinn enters the room.

"Nada," she says without prompting. "And from the number and variety of self-pleasuring devices in her nightstand, along with the lack of condoms, I'd say looking for a jilted lover may be a waste of time, at least for now. How are you making out? We're ignoring the files, correct?"

I nod. Vinn disappears for a few moments then returns carrying a dining room chair, which she plops next to the desk. Together we page through an appointment book and a desk calendar, seeing nothing that piques our curiosity.

"When I passed through the kitchen I stopped to take a look at the calendar hanging on the side of the fridge," Vinn comments as we put the desk calendar back in its place. "And unless this woman kept all of her personal appointments on her phone, which I assume the cops still have, she not only had no time for romance, she didn't have any friends she socialized with either. Every evening and weekend completely blank of plans. Not even one '7:00—drink with the girls.' Or with one of the other victims, for that matter. All work and no play and look where it got her."

"Maybe a lesson in there we should look at as well," I grumble. "I'm sorry we forgot to ask Mendez for her phone, but we may be able to pull up most of what it would have on there off of the cloud. So are you ready to dig into the computers?"

"Yep. I don't suppose Mendez gave us her passwords?"

"Too much to ask," I reply. "But this sticky note taped to the monitor labeled "password" might be a place to start. Thank goodness her memory was as bad as mine is. Do you want to see if she used the same one for her laptop?"

"Bingo," Vinn tells me after tapping a few keys. I'll work on this one and you can have the desktop. Anything even remotely inexplicable or odd and we stop. Agreed?"

We work silently for thirty minutes, then forty, until with each rotation of the second hand of the clock on the far wall my desperation mounts. The good news is that passwords for all of her accounts autofill, preventing the necessity of having to crack them or outsource that task to someone more qualified.

I've viewed about six months' worth of her checking account statements when I lean back in my chair, sigh, and stare at the ceiling. "I hope you're having better luck than I am," I tell Vinn, "because she had to be one of the most uninteresting people in the universe, or at least the most antisocial. About the only interest she has outside of the law seems to be puzzles, the kind that she can do by herself. She subscribes to several sites that send daily or periodic puzzles to her inbox or have them online. In March there was an exchange of a few nasty emails with someone from a group called 'Puzzlers Anonymous.' Apparently she was an absentee member who joined but never attended meetings and that rankled an officer in the group who argued that if she wasn't going to show up, it was tantamount to not belonging at all. He also implied that by staying home she was using her computer to help solve puzzles during competitions. I can't imagine that that has anything to do with this or that someone would kill over a silly dispute about attendance and puzzle contests, but if they're local, maybe it's worth checking out since we have no other leads at the moment."

"Looks like they're based in Chicago," Vinn says without missing a beat. "And yes, they do have monthly meetings in person as well as a chat room that currently has four members in it. If I knew what to ask I'd join in using Summers' account, but let's wait until we think we have a reason to do it. I mean, if this is the best we've got we might as well quit. And it fits with the one thing in her bedroom she has more of than sex toys, which is puzzle books and magazines. I didn't mention it earlier because I didn't see any relevance to them. Still don't."

Something is tickling the back of my mind and I close my eyes in an effort to retrieve it. By the time I open them, the first thing I see is Vinn staring at me with an expectant look on her face.

"What am I missing?" she asks.

"Probably nothing," I respond, meaning it. "But I'm ready to grasp at straws. Think back to our conversation with Julie Mills, the wife of the first victim. Before she shut down on us. One of us asked about his hobbies, or what he did outside of work, or something like that. Do you remember what she said?"

"Golf is what I remember," Vinn replies. "Wait, and there was something else." She bites her lip and stares off into space looking for the answer that hovers there somewhere. She must find it, because her eyes grow wide. "Oh shit. Puzzles. Golf and puzzles. The puzzles kept his mind clear. You don't suppose..."

I already have my cell phone out. "Mendez, it's Mal. No, we're still as up a tree as you are, which explains the following request. Can you please call Julie Mills and ask if her husband belonged to a group called 'Puzzlers Anonymous,' based in Chicago? And if so, did he attend their meetings? No, I can't give you a reason because we don't have one ourselves beyond that it's a long-shot hope and a prayer, and I doubt you want to tell her that. Fine, you have my number.

"I wonder if his mother knows he talks like that," I tell no one in particular as I consider disinfecting my phone. Vinn smiles and returns to the laptop.

Forty-five minutes later we both concede that our time here has been a bust. I shut down the desktop computer, Vinn closes the laptop, and we lean back in disappointment and exhaustion. We're both rising out of our chairs when my phone sounds the melody of "I Fought the Law," the Cricket's original version.

Vinn gives me her "Are you kidding me?" look as I shrug my shoulders and answer the call. It's a short conversation which I terminate after being accused of withholding evidence followed by more profanity.

"You're much more creative than he is when you swear," I tell Vinn. "You should give Mendez lessons. Yes, Brandon Mills belonged to Puzzlers Anonymous. Unlike our lawyer, he regularly attended meetings, an apparent sore point with the wife. She knows nothing about the group or what they did there or why he found it necessary to spend time away from her with a bunch of eggheads. Her word, Mendez claims."

Vinn's eyes brighten. "Well, it's more than we had when we woke up this morning. A place to start even if it we may be reading more into the link than is warranted just to feel like we found some sort of connection. Let's grab some chow and then see what we can find out about these 'eggheads.'"

"One more thing," I tell Vinn as we head for the door. "The initial speculation that Mills overdosed was confirmed by the coroner, although it appears the medication was not only forced down his throat but also administered by means of an enema."

Vinn makes a face. "Could've gone without that information right before lunchtime, Winters. Let's concentrate on the puzzle aspect rather than anal purgatives at the moment, if that's okay with you."

No problem here. We head off to her condo, by way of a nearby hummus shack.

TEN

I emerge from the bathroom just as Vinn hangs up her phone. "That was our friend Barry," she tells me, the distaste obvious. "In his not-so-humble opinion there's no way that both a caregiver and a nurse would commit two similar murders, or even a single murder of this type, their psychological profiles just don't allow for it. He now claims the killer has to be someone outside of those professions who's mentally ill and probably had a bad experience with someone or multiple someones assigned to take care of him in a facility, perhaps a mental hospital. Oh, and you apparently are completely the wrong match for me."

"What I've been telling you all along," I grin. "So do we believe him? About the killer, I mean. Not sure I buy into his analysis, although we haven't exactly kept him up to speed. Would you like me to do it?"

Vinn makes a face. "Thanks, but I'll have to suck it up and do it myself. With where we are now, any informed opinion even if it's from Barry couldn't hurt. In truth, though, I don't buy into his theory either and that smug son of a bitch makes me even more willing to think just the opposite. For now let's stick with our hypothesis that these are the work of separate killers who either know one another, know of each other, or are acting under orders of a third party. And if that last one is the case, we can totally forget the usefulness of profiling because the person we're really after isn't doing the actual killings. Before we entangle ourselves in that morass, though, let's go down a different path for a while."

"Way ahead of you," I say as I look up from my laptop screen. "We have a couple of options. The local branch of Puzzlers Anonymous is the obvious choice, but I don't see dates for any upcoming meetings on their website and there's no direct contact information for whoever's running it. On the other hand, if we want to delve into how the mind of a puzzle addict works, there's a meeting tonight of the Chicago League of Puzzlers."

"CLOP?" Vinn says with a grin. "Sure, why not? What do we have to lose?"

The address for the CLOP meeting turns out to be a German restaurant in the Lincoln Square neighborhood. The hostess directs us to a back room, leading us past tables of diners digging into schnitzel, wursts, and overflowing steins of beer. Given the sophisticated nature of CLOP's website, we're a bit disappointed to see only seven people scattered around several tables, each one so focused on the papers before them that it's several moments before our presence is noticed. There's a notable absence of laptops, which I assume prevents cheating. A dark-haired woman with a broad smile eventually approaches us, several sharp pencils tucked neatly into her bun.

"Sorry, I didn't see you," she greets us warmly. "Once we get started on the evening's puzzles it's hard to pull ourselves away. I've never been very good with anagrams, though, so I'm happy for the distraction. My name's Marla. Are you here for the puzzle group or are you looking for the restroom?"

"We're actually hoping to talk to whomever leads the group," Vinn tells her. "My name's Vinn Achison and this is my partner Malcom Winters. We're investigating a series of crimes that may be connected by the victims' interest in puzzles, so we're hoping to get a general idea of the kind of person who likes this kind of thing. Frankly, we're pretty much fishing at this point so I can't give you any more detail than that."

Marla's face falls as she realizes we're not going to add to the group's membership or give her the opportunity to solve crimes for us, but she recovers and leads us to a nearby table. I guess we're still preferable to the dreaded anagrams. It never ceases to amaze me how willing people are to open up to strangers if we use the magic word "investigate."

"I'm not sure I can help you. As you can see, we're a pretty small group and our members don't have a lot in common beyond the enjoyment of having our brains challenged and the satisfaction of solving a difficult problem. Joe there is 82 years old and a retired pipefitter. Angie is our youngest member, never asked her age but I'd guess about 35 and she's a stay-at-home mom. I work in PR. I don't think we'd run in each other's circles outside of our monthly meetings."

Her description of the group is exactly what I expected from the moment we walked in, but I'm still disappointed and decide to give her a nudge. "Are there any other local groups that you might be able to direct us to?" I ask.

She hesitates. "Well, the largest one in the city is Puzzlers Anonymous." Her tone is akin to describing the taste of spätzle made with rotten eggs. "They actually require that you pass a test to join. Pretty snooty group; they would use the word 'exclusive.' I think they're more homogenous than we are. What they have in common is arrogance. Arrogance and a focused sort of brilliance," she grudgingly adds.

"What do you want to bet that she failed that test?" I say as we leave the room, having gathered exactly nothing useful.

"Several times is my guess," Vinn replies. "But I don't think this was a total washout. "We have a most basic beginning of a profile for members of PA. Brilliant and arrogant, maybe to the point of being insufferable. Could be a motive for killing. People have done it for less. I suggest we infiltrate the group and start asking around about our victims. The responses we get will hopefully provide insight about both the victims and the group itself."

"Sounds good," I say before realizing that Vinn just proposed that we take a test requiring more than a modicum of smarts. If this is what the investigation is relying on, God help us all.

"Leo, maybe lay off the booze for the next hour," I suggest as I watch him pour a healthy dose of some sort of purple liquid into a glass. "You need to have your wits at full capacity." Leo glares at me and places the bottle on the floor at his feet, but not before draining what he'd just poured in one healthy gulp.

Vinn, Rebecca, and I round out the group spaced out around my living room, an impromptu gathering of would-be puzzle addicts. A quick visit to the membership page for Puzzlers Anonymous revealed a lengthy diatribe disguised as an FAQ as to the rules for taking the qualifying exam, including several warnings about cheating by having someone assist in finding a solution. Supposedly each test is different and every answer requires showing your work on a makeshift tablet, which is then run through an analytical program which analyzes handwriting, logical tendencies, and the like to identify multiple submissions by the same person under different names. The penalty is denying membership to every such entry and a lifetime prohibition against trying again. The apparent speed at which questions need to be answered also discourages copying notes scribbled by someone else or working together.

After proposing then vetoing several work-arounds, Vinn finally admitted that while she could probably beat the system, it wasn't worth the risk of having both she and I banned from membership. What was unspoken was the assumption that I would be the one copying answers from her. It was her suggestion to bring in Leo and Rebecca to pad the chances of getting a companion for herself at the meetings. If it seems like Vinn's level of confidence that she would pass the test borders on the type of arrogance that would fit in well at PA based on Marla's description, I have to say that her opinion about her brainpower is fully justified and my opinion of her level of vanity is better left unsaid.

I circle the room to give scratch pads and pencils to everyone for those times when they don't want the program to see how their thought processes work by using the tablet. Vinn naturally sets hers off to the side, Leo scowls as he accepts his, and Rebecca immediately neatly prints her name at the top accessorized by hearts and flowers.

"Okay, everyone, I've uploaded the start page to each of your laptops and filled in the personal information for you," Vinn tells the room. "You should see a big yellow start button. Press it when you're ready to go."

The test has a one-hour time limit after which it immediately shuts down, automatically saving and sending in the answers. Vinn finishes in forty-two minutes with a satisfied sigh. She strolls around the room looking over our shoulders until she gets growled at for being annoying and distracting. That reaction didn't come from Leo. All of us are still working when, one by one, our screens go blank. I turn to Leo to tell him he's free to go back to his hooch but notice that the bottle at his feet is already empty. It was two-thirds full when we started the test.

"It can take up to twenty-four hours to get the results," Vinn announces as Leo and Rebecca rise and head for the door.

"There, that wasn't so bad," she continues once they've left, "but did you have the one about the farmer and his sheep? I almost stumbled on it until I saw that the clue itself was an acrostic. After that it was easy."

I bite back any number of replies, put my fingers to her lips, and lead her to the bedroom where a different kind of skill set brings its own rewards, which doesn't include being in a room full of smart people.

"You have got to be kidding me," I say for the third time, albeit only the first time without a string of profanity thrown in. "You and Leo? English isn't even his native language. I'm not even sure it's in his top five."

"Maybe if you'd partaken in his bottle of unknown origin," Vinn smirks. "It must have powers to stimulate the brain." Vinn accepted her own passing score as a given. What makes her attitude insufferable is the glee with which she greeted the news that Leo also got in while I did not, putting me in Rebecca's company. Only the fact that the email simply gives a pass or fail without revealing what was likely her perfect score prevents me from leaving the room. I can also at least pretend that I missed the cut by a single point.

The email from Puzzlers Anonymous rejecting me made clear that I could try again in six months' time, although its tone discouraged any such attempt, implicitly denigrating anyone requiring more than one test as unworthy. That limitation also makes any attempt to have someone else take the test for me impossible except under a different name, and getting around the group's stringent method of verifying identity would be too time consuming and expensive considering how little information we expect to gather from our infiltration anyway. Even given all of that, the main reason we don't make a second attempt is Vinn's acceptance of Leo as a perfectly viable substitute for me. That'll have to be a discussion for another time.

My focus on my own apparent ineptitude almost makes me miss the fact that Vinn is continuing to speak, having moved past the issue of the test results much quicker than I have.

"My email included a schedule of meetings, and the next one is on Friday night," she tells me as she reads the information off of her laptop. "And it includes a short orientation for new members before the main event. The email is short on details as to what happens at these meetings, so we'll have to play it by ear as to how to approach getting information out of them. What we can do in advance is determine what we hope to learn from them. We went into that first group's meeting unprepared expecting to get nothing and that's what we got. We need to set our sights higher this time."

"I agree, although I'm not sure that we can come up with a checklist of facts that we hope to learn. All we have at this point is that the sole connection between our two victims besides the bizarre staging of the scenes is affiliation with this puzzlers' group, even if one never showed her face there. And when I say that's all we have, I mean it. Beyond that, we're clueless as to which direction to take our investigation." I pause. "No, putting it that way makes it sound like we've got more than one direction to choose from. We basically have nothing else but speculation."

"Thanks for that perspective, Mr. Optimist," Vinn responds. "But of course you're right. I understand that this is a fishing expedition and we don't know what to use for bait, so let's start instead by identifying the fish." Vinn seems puzzled by my baffled expression and inability to decipher her metaphor. She sometimes fails to remember that mere mortals can't always follow how the mind of a genius works. "What I mean is let's work our way backwards, writing down what information would help us move forward, then come up with questions to see if they elicit that information. If not, we were trying to land the wrong fish. If we identify several options designed to hook different species, hopefully one of them will be the right one."

"I get it now," I admit, "but I think that wedding at the Shedd that started this whole mess has infiltrated your brain. Let's agree to leave any reference to under the sea creatures out. I'll go first with the most obvious link. That both victims made a common enemy within the group by doing something so offensive to he or she that they were motivated to kill. Maybe won a competition or cheated on something or won the wrong person's affection."

Vinn smiles. "That's exactly what I meant, Winters. And I agree that's the most likely scenario. Let's also consider the flip side. That the killer was the one who was discovered and maybe even called out for breaking a cardinal rule, perhaps an infraction so serious they were kicked out of the group. And they blamed the victims. So we want to ask about friction within the group, issues between members, how well people get along, what it would take to be forced out and if it's ever happened, that kind of thing."

"It's a start," I tell her. "But let's say that those lines of inquiry don't bear fruit. We need to find someone that knew one or both of the victims and have a longer conversation with them outside the parameters of a puzzle meeting. People they knew, who they hung out with, controversial views, that kind of thing. The link may not be related to puzzles at all but to something happening with Brandon or Summers in their personal lives."

"I guess I could pose as a friend of one of them, or maybe Leo could say that Summers is his lawyer, that he can't get in touch with her, and that he knows she belongs to the group. Maybe she wasn't as much of a recluse as we think and hung out with one of the members online even if not in person. Good idea, we'll work that up. But we have to consider that things aren't this simple."

"Right, especially if we really believe that there's more than one murderer. That the killer or killers, whether members or not, is a psychopath and the staging of the scenes is just the working of a deranged mind. Or maybe the killers weren't members or crazy but were put up to it by someone who is. I'd be thrilled if you can get names of members who have a reputation of being odd or unstable."

"That could be all of them," Vinn says sadly, "but I see where you're going with this. The likelihood of getting all or even most of this information from a single meeting is low, and we don't have the luxury of time to draw it out over several weeks or months. At least that clarifies the main goal, which is to befriend the club gossip or whomever has their ear to the ground and then pick their brain outside of the meeting. That also has the advantage of getting you in on the face-to-face."

It's nice to finally have my usefulness acknowledged. We set up a night to prep Leo, agree to brainstorm ways to identify our target individual, and call it a night.

ELEVEN

I stare wordlessly at yet another freshman engineering student as he enters the seventh minute of a whining rant about the lack of value in knowing proper grammar in the modern world of text-talk, rampant use of acronyms, and grammatical illiteracy among the nation's so-called elite, but most importantly the irrelevance of words in designing a space shuttle or creating special effects for the next Marvel movie. I've heard it before and to keep from yawning design a game inside my head giving myself points for predicting key phrases or arguments the kid will use in support of his position. I don't know what a winning point total is, but I probably surpassed it long before I hit a big score when he got to "who cares if words are spelled wrong if people know what I mean."

Apparently that's the culmination of what he came to my office to say, but if he expects me to acknowledge his brilliant insights and demand that the administration modify the curriculum, in particular the rule requiring English 101 class for all first-year students and especially engineering students, he's about to be disappointed.

"I don't suppose this has any relation to the 'D' you received on the assignment asking you to write five hundred words about any topic you choose," I begin. "I confess that I debated long and hard about that grade." I avoid telling him that the debate was whether to create a new letter grade further back in the alphabet than 'F.' "But ultimately the fact that you used no punctuation at all, misspelled over twenty-five percent of the words, and ended by using the same profane word fifty-four times in order to reach the five hundred word threshold makes me think you haven't been paying attention in class or reading the assignments. If you'd taken a look at the syllabus I passed out in the first class you'd know that every student can rewrite and resubmit an assignment to try to get a better grade. I'll be looking for it from you at the next class. And maybe pick a topic this time instead of copying definitions from an online dictionary."

The subtle extension of the student's middle finger on his left hand doesn't go unnoticed as he storms out the door, nearly running into Vinn as she enters. She makes no attempt to hide her broad grin that no doubt is the result of eavesdropping outside my office for the past ten minutes.

"He does have a point," she tells me as she lowers herself into the chair just vacated by the student.

"Of course he does," I admit, "and he'll pass the class if he simply tries." I sigh and run my hands through my hair. "Did you come to debate the usefulness of basic English or to whisk me off to a seedy hotel room for a quickie?"

"Neither one, I'm afraid, although there are some words I'd like to try out in that hotel room someday. I just wanted to let you know that I've arranged to meet Leo at your place tonight for some prep work, and to offer to escort you home by way of that deli we've been meaning to try to pick up some pastrami on dark rye for dinner."

"Okay fine," I reply. "Just give me a minute to pack up these student essays I need to grade tonight if I can face them without calling the suicide watch hotline."

Vinn can sense the frustration in my voice, so she rises, walks around my desk, gives me a hug and pats me on the back as if I were a child coming down from a temper tantrum.

"There, there," she says, although knowing her, she was really saying "they're their" just to shove the knife in deeper. I clasp shut my briefcase and we head for the door.

If there was ever living proof that one can thrive while barely using words at all, much less correctly, it comes in the form of the large, gruff, old Bolivian sitting across from Vinn and I in my living room. Vinn has explained what we hope to achieve from his and Vinn's attendance at the puzzler's meeting, but his barely opened eyes and near total silence since he arrived make me wonder if he heard or comprehended anything she said. Vinn appears to be thinking the same.

"Leo," she begins tentatively, "do you have any thoughts on how to achieve our goal? We need to identify one or more persons who knew either or both victims well enough that they may have some information that'll help us, and to gain their trust to an extent that they'll be willing to meet with us outside of the meeting."

"Got it," Leo grunts. An awkward silence of several seconds follows before we realize that's all he intends to say, a conclusion that's confirmed when he rises and lets himself out my door.

"God help us," I mutter as I stare at the door in disbelief. "The only saving grace is that he's your responsibility at that meeting."

Vinn's barely opened her mouth, probably to place the blame for this whole affair on me, when she's silenced by the ringing of my cell phone. The ringtone changes our mood instantly to one of curiosity, hope, and concern.

"Yes, Detective?" I say as Vinn looks on, her face clearly bracing for more bad news. "Okay, fine, we'll be there. I appreciate the invite."

"Nothing bad," I start with to quickly put Vinn out of her misery. "Maybe just the opposite. Mendez claims that they've caught the killer. He wants us to come up to watch the interview so that, in his words, we can see 'the results of real police work.'"

"Color me skeptical," Vinn says as she reaches for her shoes, "but I hope that he's right. Anything to avoid going to that puzzle meeting with Leo."

I don't know that I've ever seen Mendez smile, but the smug grin on his face is close enough and cuts as deeply as if he were outright laughing as he launches into a clearly rehearsed preamble to our observation of the interview with his suspect. We're seated in a dingy interview room that still smells of the sweat of whomever the cops last interrogated while waiting for her to be brought out of her cell.

"Fingerprints and hard-nosed grunt work," Mendez begins. "None of this fancy goose chase through puzzle clubs and consulting with psychics or whatever else you two think will magically produce an answer. We collected hundreds of prints from the scene and it just took time to organize them, clear up some of the smudges, and run them through the system. In this case, more than one system. We pulled this thumbprint from the back of a doorknob leading into that lawyer's basement. Wasn't in the database for past arrests, but from the records of the agency that manages nurses. They need to be printed as part of a routine background check before they can get their license."

"So she was a nurse," I remark, glancing at Vinn as I speak. "Interesting."

"Yeah, no," Mendez cuts in. "Don't even think about going down that road with those lists you pulled out of the air that makes you think there's a pattern here. Serial killer my ass. We have a crazy broad that decided to take out her frustrations with the world on a couple of innocents. We found her, we booked her, we'll keep her locked up, and we'll get her thrown behind bars where she belongs. End of story, end of killing spree."

He might have gone on, but the door opens and a uniform sticks his head in, mumbling a few words that must mean that the woman is ready to be questioned. Mendez nods before sliding a thin manila folder across the table. Vinn scoots over as I open it up.

"Vanessa Chalmers," Mendez says. "Thirty-eight, divorced, her ex has full custody of their son. Works at Loyola Medical Center in the cancer ward, has for the past eleven years. No priors other than a few tickets. Now follow me."

We move down the hall a few doors and follow Mendez into a cramped room on the transparent side of the two-way mirror that overlooks a room identical to the one we just left with the exception of its occupant. The woman fidgeting restlessly in the chair while handcuffed to the table is gaunt, her eyes red and encircled by telltale bags indicating a lack of sleep, her hair greasy and unwashed as it falls across the left side of her face. She looks nothing like the alert, defiant individual in the mug shot from her file that must have been taken just yesterday.

We wait several minutes in silence until a tall, thin black man in a crisply cut suit enters the room, followed by a short, stout white woman in dress pants and wrinkled cream-colored blouse. The man drops a file on the table and draws his chair in close in while the woman flips her chair around, taking a seat backwards as she leans onto its back. Neither speaks at first.

"My name is Detective Williams and this is Detective Bishop," the man begins, his voice low and authoritative. "And we have a few questions for you. First of all, do you know why you're here?"

Chalmers doesn't respond, instead looking down to avoid eye contact as a small tear makes its way down her cheek. Williams waits a moment before continuing.

"You're here because we're good at our job. You see, we've been investigating the killing of a lawyer in Lincoln Park. A woman who kept to herself, who had few friends and never invited anyone over to her house. A woman who would never let someone like you into her inner circle. And yet your fingerprints are all over the murder scene. Now why would that be?"

Chalmers remains silent but draws her shoulders in and begins visibly shaking, sobbing while at the same time not making a sound. Tears begin to flow more freely. Vinn looks irritated, most likely at the extrapolation of a single fingerprint into "fingerprints all over the murder scene."

Williams leans forward, his face less than a foot from that of his suspect. "And there's more. We sent a team to your apartment. Guess what we found?

Arsenic matching what killed the victim, bandages identical those we found at the scene, coffee of the same type that was scattered on her floor. You're not very good at this, are you Vanessa? You couldn't have made it more obvious if you tried."

A quick glance at Mendez reveals a repeated tic at the corner of his mouth and a pissed-off expression in his eyes. Either he wasn't made privy to this additional evidence or Williams is making it all up. Either way, while she hasn't said a single word during the interview, Chalmers' body language would convince even the staunchest skeptic that she's at the very least involved in the killing in some way. But Williams isn't done.

"You don't need to talk, that's okay, the evidence had done all the talking for you. But that lawyer wasn't your first victim, was she?" Bishop hands him another file, which Williams opens to what appears to be photos of Brandon Mills' body. He slides the file across the table in front of Chalmers, whose eyes open wide at the gruesome pictures.

"This was your first try, wasn't it Vanessa?" Williams tells her in a matter-of-fact tone. "It has your MO written all over it. Now, we've already got you down cold for a life sentence for the lawyer, why don't you make things easier on yourself and admit to this one as well."

At these words, Chalmers begins thrashing back and forth in her chair, finally speaking, but only to shout out "No!" over and over before dissolving in a fit of tears as she lowers her head to the table. Mendez' look of confidence is clearly wavering. He bites the corner of his lip as he rises and leaves the room for a few minutes.

Williams continues to push Chalmers to admit

to the first murder, while she steadfastly shouts "No" to everything he says. Mendez returns to his seat looking concerned. The browbeating we're observing moves on with no admission from Chalmers. The door opens and a young kid in a cheap suit, probably a newbie detective, hands papers to Mendez before closing the door and leaning against the wall to await further orders.

Mendez reads the documents, opens a file stashed under his chair, then stares at a paper there as well, moving his head back and forth between the two, his face growing darker by the second. He swivels his head to the cop behind him.

"Did you call and confirm?" he asks, to which he receives a brief "yes sir."

"Shit," Mendez mutters as he throws the file against the mirror, papers scattering. The newbie scrambles to pick them up. Mendez turns to us. "She didn't do the first one. Worked a double shift that day. She—'

Before he can finish the thought, a uniformed cop pushes open the door and enters in a hurry. "What is this, Grand Central Station?" Mendez growls.

"Sorry to interrupt, sir," the cop stammers, "but I thought you should know. There's been another one. Like the first two, I mean. Just discovered but probably happened late last night. They want you at the scene."

"Last night?" Mendez shouts. He and I simultaneously reach for the Chalmers file. I get there first, take a quick glance, then shake my head at Mendez."

"She got picked up yesterday morning," I tell him. "Couldn't have been her."

Mendez glares at me, ready to erupt. He storms from the room, not inviting Vinn and I to follow, although I expect we'll hear from him soon. Vinn's been quiet during the entire exchange but looks uneasy.

"Dammit," she finally says quietly. "Looks like I have to go to that puzzle meeting with Leo after all."

TWELVE

I'm staring woefully at the plastic cup of some sort of vile beverage that sits before me, courtesy of my grabbing a table at this Wicker Park coffee shop while Vinn handled the ordering. Not owning a car didn't prevent us from catching up to Mendez's filthy Ford sedan shortly after he left the station. Divvy bikes are everywhere in the city and it only took a quick swipe of a credit card before we were mobile on two sets of two wheels. Traffic in Chicago being what it is, it took all the effort we had not to pass him up. It wasn't a long ride, somewhere short of three miles, before his driver was waved under police tape stretched across a quiet, tree-lined street a few blocks away from where we now sit. We could see the medical examiner's SUV still parked in front of a brick two-flat, meaning the on-site investigation is in its early stages. If we're to be invited to view the scene, it may be a while.

"The board says it's tea, and it sounded interesting," Vinn explains as she tries to justify the abomination she set in front of me. "The barista said it's very popular."

"Cascara 'tea' is just another way coffee aficionados try to pull tea drinkers to the dark side," I tell her. "It's made from the skins or peels of the coffee fruit, essentially the waste left after harvesting the beans. It has a light hibiscus scent and isn't unpleasant to smell, but one sip and it's clearly not tea. But I appreciate your attempt to expand my horizons."

"Hmmph," Vinn pouts. "Here, I'll make up for it. Have a bite of my muffin." She pushes a napkin full of crumbles that moments before had been a blueberry muffin across the table.

"Actually, that was my muffin," I remind her as I push the remnants into a pile. "You had the donut, remember? Anyway, were you able to get the address of the house before we were shooed away? Your eyes are better than mine."

"It was either 1344 or 1346. So many official vehicles they spanned most of the block." Vinn pulls out her phone and connects to the Wi-Fi. "Maybe we can find out who lives in those homes and what they do by searching social media, especially Next Door. Garage sales, open houses, requests for recommendations on window blind cleaners, that kind of thing. While I'm doing that, go back and confirm the occupation of victim number three to see if we're right about the two lists."

Vinn's memory is such that she knows perfectly well what the occupation is. Giving me this task is a way of keeping me busy so that she can do her own research in peace as well as allowing me to save face by looking up the information to fill the gap in my own terrible memory. It takes me a few minutes. I look up to see Vinn peering at me over her phone.

"Media. More visual and verbal, like television and radio, than print," I tell her. She nods and moves her attention back to her screen. I pick impatiently at the pieces of muffin while I wait for her to finish. It's taking so long I'm tempted to take a sip of my faux tea.

"I might have one possibility," Vinn finally announces, "assuming that we're right about the crime scene address. Charlene Phelps. It appears from pictures she posted on Facebook over the past few years that she works seasonal retail, mostly in the women's departments at various high-end department stores."

I feel a heaviness in my chest. "If that's true, then our entire theory about the pattern based on the two lists is completely wrong and we're back to having absolutely no idea as to what the killings are all about or how to approach our investigation. If Mendez calls us at all, it's going to be to gloat about our half-assed ideas."

"Not so fast, honcho, you didn't let me finish," Vinn tells me as she continues to scroll on her phone. "There's a reason I focused on her. She hasn't updated her TikTok profile for over a year, but she did upload a number of videos of herself modeling dresses and putting on make-up. The style of her videos and commentary gave me an idea. Hold on a second while I check something out."

It's a lot longer than a second and my patience is gone. I'm about to suggest she continue her search from my place when a satisfied smile passes over her lips. My spine tingles and I lean forward in anticipation.

"Bingo," she says with not a small amount of pride. "I just joined her Patreon page. We'll need more time and privacy to go through all of the material here, but it's clear that our Charlene is—or was, if the victim is her—a budding influencer. There must be over a hundred videos here involving her trying on dresses, or unboxing makeup, along with a few scattered restaurant reviews and the like. The few I looked at, she's the center of attention, the star of the show so to speak."

Vinn hands me her phone and I study it for a few minutes, forgoing the temptation to watch a few videos. That can wait. "She has almost 75,000 followers," I note. "Not bad for a relative newbie. And at least in my opinion, that qualifies as video media."

"To anyone under the age of thirty, it's more popular than television," Vinn agrees. "Before we get ahead of ourselves, we still don't know that it's her but that's the best I can do on my phone," Vinn replies. "So I guess all we can do now is wait to hear from Mendez or read about it once details get leaked. In the meantime, do we continue to hang out here or go back to your place?"

In response I stand up and take satisfaction in dumping my drink in the trash. Vinn takes the hint and rises to meet me as we head out the door. We're in the process of getting settled on our baby blue bikes when my phone rings. Vinn and I instantly freeze.

"Yes, Officer?" I answer, trying unsuccessfully to keep any note of excitement out of my voice. "Sure. Uh huh. All right, if you insist. See you in a little bit."

Vinn grins as we both saddle up and begin to peddle. It's only then that I realize Mendez didn't bother to give me the address. He must know us better than I thought.

We have to wait nearly twenty minutes for Mendez to come out to the tape and escort us past the cop keeping curious onlookers away. The difference in his appearance from just over an hour ago is startling. He looks like he hasn't slept in weeks and the scowl he maintains whenever we're in his vicinity is deeper and more threatening. If it weren't for the combination of wanting to see the crime scene and my assumption that he needs us more than he's willing to admit, I'd be apprehensive to be in his company.

"This way," is all he says before turning his back and walking back in the direction of the house. We quicken our pace to keep up with him, nearly bumping into his rear when he stops at the outer door to don booties and gloves. We follow suit as he leads us up a set of stairs to a second door of what appears to be an apartment. "You can look but keep your opinions to yourselves," he says softly. "Lots of ears in there and I don't need word to get out about a possible serial killer. Doesn't look like this fits your theory anyway, but I wanted you to see that for yourselves."

He precedes us through the door and I'm imme-diately assailed with the sights and smells of a murder scene. For whatever reason I expected to be led to the bedroom, but a woman's body lies prone on the living room couch not even ten feet from the door. A chair is drawn up next to the couch positioned so that its occupant would be looking directly into the eyes of the victim. She's blonde, in her twenties, and has a face Vinn and I have seen just minutes before. I feel guilty at having to temper a feeling of elation that the two-list supposition is still in play.

"Charlene," I whisper to Vinn, who nods. Mendez must have overheard me, as his head snaps in my direc-tion with a nasty glare and a growl. He begins to speak but catches himself. I can sense his blood boiling and his urge to question me at my mention of the victim's name.

The cop photographing the scene moves to get into a better position, revealing a tripod with a video camera standing next to the couch facing the victim. Another stand behind the victim holds a large ring light, giving an eerie vision of a halo surrounding her head. The poor woman holds a pen in one hand and a small notebook in the other. A larger notebook sits open on the chair containing writing which I can't get close enough to read. A silver chain with a pocket watch attached rests on Charlene's chest. I move around Vinn and crouch down to get a view of its face. Both hands appear to be stopped, each permanently pointed at the ten. What appears to be a soft-sided lunchbox rests on the back of the couch.

"Do you smell that?" I ask Vinn, leaning my mouth close to her ear.

"Lavender," she replies, nodding her head in the direction of the breakfast bar separating the room from the kitchen. "Essential oil diffuser." Next to the diffuser sits a small potted plant and a tall glass filled with water. On closer inspection, I notice a goldfish floating on top of the water. Strange how viewing the woman's body seems almost routine but the sight of the dead fish turns my stomach.

"Time's up," I hear from behind me at the same time a firm hand grips my shoulder, forcing me to turn in the direction of the door. Vinn gives me an almost imperceptible nod, indicating that she's seen enough for now, and maybe affirming my own conclusion. There's no question that this one is related to the first two and that our theory has gone from "likely" to "virtually certain."

As we descend the stairs, the echo of a third set of feet follows us. So much for sneaking away and keeping our impressions to ourselves.

THIRTEEN

"Two observations and a question," Mendez says gruffly as he leads us to a spot next to a rose bush, out of earshot of the myriad of cops hanging around in the front yard. "First, I admit the staging might connect this one to the first two, although I'm not giving up on the idea that there's some weird challenge trending over the dark web that encourages this kind of thing. Copycats, suggestible psychos, whatever. Second, and this is the one that I want you to pay special attention to, the victim here did not work in television or radio." He reacts to my raised eyebrows. "Yes, I remember what you told me earlier and even double checked your lists on the way over here. Her paystubs show that she worked retail, and even then not that often."

Vinn and I exchange glances, each of us wondering if we should burst Mendez's bubble now or wait until we've had the chance to digest what we've seen more thoroughly. Before a tacit decision is made, Mendez continues in much more of an authoritative cop voice.

"And now I want to know how in the hell you knew this woman's name. That hasn't been released to the press. In fact, only about three of us in the squad know it as of this moment. Spill."

I sigh, our decision having been made for us. I take the lead since Mendez loves me so much. "I hate to disappoint you, but there's nothing mystic or illegal in how we knew who the victim was before we got here. We had never heard of her prior to an hour ago either. We got her name from what you would call 'nuts and bolts police work' if one of your subordinates had done the same. We took note of the possible addresses of the crime scene from our vantage point far outside the tape and used Google, social media, and Vinn's ingenuity to come up with a few possible names. We narrowed it to Charlene Phelps because of what she did outside of work."

I stop, waiting to see if Mendez rises to the bait. His face turns purple, his fists clench, and he starts to lean into my personal space. I'll take that as a yes. "She's a vlogger, Detective," I say quickly as I take a half step backward. "An influencer who's posted a large number of videos online recently covering her opinions on fashion, food, and any number of other topics. And she appears to be popular based on the number of her followers and views. We knew her name because we recognized her face. Now is there anything else?"

"Shit, shit, shit," Mendez says as he looks at the ground. A few uniforms look our way, probably ready to shoot one of us for upsetting the boss. "Get out of here but don't leave the city. Stay where I can reach you."

We watch him stomp over to one of the younger cops, most likely assuming he has familiarity with vlogs and how to find them, gives his orders, then heads back inside in a huff.

We head back to the land of civilians.

"He didn't seem terribly grateful for our insight," I tell Vinn as we retrieve our bikes. "In fact I'd say just the opposite. And I may not be a Constitutional scholar, but I don't think he has the authority to restrict our movements."

"Difficult for him to deny that these are all connected now, no matter how hard he tries," she says. "And that won't go over well with the higher-ups at the precinct. The serial killer shit is about to hit the fan. I'm guessing the next time we hear from Mendez, which will be shortly after he reports back to his boss, it'll be to tell us to keep our traps shut."

"Something to look forward to. Anyway, are you ready to dissect what we saw, Professor?"

"Not entirely," Vinn replies. "Ideally I'd like to have a little time to digest the scene. But first impressions are important too. You start."

"I think this time it's pretty easy. Not as much imagination as the other two, but let's come back to that. Obviously set up to look like a therapist's office. Charlene is the patient on the couch and the chair next to it is meant for the shrink. Then we have all of the trappings you see in a psychologist's office. Or so I assume."

Vinn gives me a sideways glance and a smirk as she wheels her bike around a deep crack in the sidewalk. "Not from personal experience, Winters? God, at first I was forced to undergo counseling after every, um, incident in the old job. If you weren't forced to do the same thing, I think that explains a lot. Which means I have a little familiarity and I doubt it goes out of date too quickly. Let me make a list while the scene is fresh in my mind. Are you going to write this down?"

We pull our bikes off to the side directly outside of a Korean barbecue joint. I know Vinn well enough that I can't discount the fact that our stopping point was planned. I take a scrap of paper out of my back pocket, unfold it, and get a pen at the ready.

"Let's start with the therapist's props," Vinn begins, her eyes closed and nose scrunched in concentration, "beginning with the items on the breakfast bar. The essential oil diffuser. That's a trend in therapist-land from what I understand. Supposedly the scent puts the patient at ease. And lavender is supposed to be relaxing, soothing. I know that from the couple of times I've gotten a massage. Personally, I prefer fresh air and find it annoying."

"I can't speak for therapists," I contribute as Vinn gets lost in the apparent memory of a smelly massage, "but my dentist and at least two doctors had fish tanks in their waiting rooms. There is something hypnotic about watching them swim around that I guess could put people at ease."

"Not much swimming going on in that glass of water," Vinn replies with distaste. "And we have to consider if the fish died on its own or if the fact it was dead was meant to send a message. What that would be is anybody's guess, so let's not get into that for now. The potted plant? Cliché for almost any type of office. Moving on. The notebook on the chair, of course. Standard therapy tool. Could you see what was written on it?"

"I could barely see that there was writing at all. All I could make out were blue scribbles. We'll have to think of what we have that we can trade with Mendez for a photo of that page. He won't part with that willingly no matter how much he's being pressured to cooperate with us. But speaking of the notebook, that links us to the smaller notepad on the couch. Have we finished with therapist crap?"

"The pocket watch," Vinn notes. "Any guesses?" She smiles triumphantly at my blank stare. "I'm sure you noticed the position of the hands. Ten minutes to the hour. Hour-long sessions are actually fifty minutes. This was the killer's way of saying that the patient's session was over. Permanently in her case."

"All right, I've got to give you credit on that one. I assume the cops will figure that out themselves. Half of them are probably in therapy themselves, or should be. The rest of the props are references to Charlene's being a vlogger, right? The notepad and pen for taking notes, although from what little I know about influencers they prefer to give their initial impressions live on camera."

"From what I've seen, yes," Vinn agrees. "Might not mean anything, but it also may indicate that the killer is older, ignorant, or simply not into the vlogging scene. Forgive me if I don't rush off to ask our neighborhood profiler. The tripod and camera, the halo light, both standard photography references but again, I don't think many influencers use that kind of lighting on site. They use a selfie light ring if anything. So the tripod and camera certainly, but not the light. That's more photography than video. Maybe the killer gathered these props in advance to track the still picture theme, then was forced to use them even though they didn't quite fit Charlene's niche."

"Which in turn could mean that she wasn't the original target, or at the very least that she wasn't singled out far in advance. So not a whole lot of planning went into this one. It may have been rushed, or..."

"Or," Vinn jumps in, "our theory about each one being different killers just got bolstered. The lack of creativity, the rush job, poor planning. Not the same vibe given off by the first murder scenes. This killer didn't put the thought into staging that the other two did, especially the second one, either due to lack of time or they just weren't all that bright."

"My thoughts exactly. But since we know killer number two couldn't have done number one, if one and three were also different killers, that raises the number of possible bad guys to three different people, one for each crime. I'm discounting Mendez's dark web idea of independent killers influenced by something they see online, but then again he may not be far off. Not an anonymous web page as the trigger, but a single person or group behind all three. Which we were already leaning toward."

"Which again brings the puzzler's group into play as our top lead. We need to get into Charlene's apartment, Mal, to see what link if any we can find. Barring that, Leo and I will somehow have to bring her name up when we're at the meeting to see if anyone there recognizes it, and that risks exposing our real purpose."

"I guess we have one more favor to ask of Mendez and it might require Dr. Sanders making another call to use his pull. I'm not sure that I want to deal with either one of them, but that's where we are for now. Because if we're correct about Mendez getting marching orders to keep us quiet, our silence might be exactly the right thing to trade in return for a look inside the apartment and a photo of the page from the notebook."

"Maggie would still be on campus, right?" Vinn asks, referring to a journalism student that assisted us in a prior investigation by placing articles in a couple of papers that we used as bait.

"Probably editor of the school newspaper by now given her ambition," I say smiling, recalling the mile-a-minute whirlwind speech pattern of the then freshman eager to do anything to see her name in a byline. "An 'inadvertent' dropping of her name might be just what we need to get our way with the cops."

"Do it," Vinn tells me. "Are we done with the props?"

"Depends. Was that lunch bag filled with Charlene's sandwich or was it something the killer brought for us to see?"

"Lunch bag?" Vinn seems puzzled, then her face brightens. "Oh for god's sake, Mal. That was a softbox. They're used by photographers to diffuse light and minimize shadows. I almost forgot about it because again it's more for still photography and doesn't really fit video. Another reason this killer seems a bit less, shall we say, in tune than the first two."

I realize I stopped taking notes about three seconds into our conversation, so I stash my pen in my front pocket and my paper in the rear. It appears we're done noting our first impressions, but if history is any indication we'll have much more to discuss as to what we saw with the passage of time as our subconscious brains puzzle over the scene. I move to get on my bike but Vinn stops me.

"As long as we're here..." she begins.

We lock our bikes and follow the smell of garlic and fermented soybeans into the shop.

FOURTEEN

Virtually on cue, Mendez calls later that evening just as Vinn and I are settling in for the night, me reading a book on the psychology of killing that Vinn claims will help us see into the mind of whomever is behind this bizarre string of deaths, rendering Levin obsolete, and Vinn playing games on her laptop that she insists are priming her brain for her upcoming initiation into the world of puzzlers. That also serves as her excuse as to why she isn't reading this book herself.

"Yes, Officer?" I say politely. Vinn doesn't look up from her screen, clearly immersed in her research.

"I just came from a meeting with the brass, so that you know this isn't only coming from me," he begins. "And while the official position is that the three killings are similar in style, there's no evidence that a single person is behind them. In simple words, Winters, no serial killer, nobody pulling three sets of strings. Got it?"

"You say that's the official position. What about your unofficial take?"

His immediate reaction is to clam up until the silence on the phone makes me wonder if we were disconnected. His voice is hesitant when he comes back on. "Let's just say that I'm keeping an open mind. Open mind, but a closed mouth. That's the second part of the message from up above here. You and that smarty-pants sidekick of yours have been commanded to keep mum about any details of any of these cases, and if you mention the word 'serial' at all it better be in conversation about what you ate for breakfast. In fact, for your own benefit, I'll make this clear and simple. Not one fuckin' word about any of this. Period. Comprende'?"

"Yes and no, Mendez. I understand what you're asking. What I'm a bit unclear about is why this sounds like an order rather than a polite request." Vinn must have been listening because now she looks up, interested at last. "Did I miss the ceremony where we were deputized by the Department?"

"Now look here," Mendez begins, his voice rising. I decide to play my trump card before he hangs up on me and sends a squad car over instead.

"Don't worry," I say calmly, "discretion and cooperation are our middle names. I'll let you guess whose is whose. But if we're going to be subject to the edicts of the Chicago PD, we need to be treated like one of the team. To start with, we need access to the latest victim's apartment, free of any supervision, and we need to see the crime scene photos. That means all of them, not a curated selection. We're especially interested in a closeup of the notebook that was resting on the chair. Tonight would be nice. Vinn seems to have nothing better to do."

I'm rewarded with a middle finger from across the room and a heavy sigh from across town. "Fine," Mendez finally says. "I figured that would be your response. I'd do the same. If it were up to me, I'd let you take over the entire investigation. Couldn't do any worse. Arresting that mope for number two did more to set us back than move us ahead. Good for statistics, but it puts us back at the beginning for the other one. By the way, Chalmers confessed to offing the lawyer. Developed a drug habit by skimming her patients' medications at work. Her addiction threatened visitation with her boy. She got counseling to pull her life together so she wouldn't have the one good thing in her life taken away. Counselor promised to help her out and put a good word in with the court if she would do one little favor."

"You're kidding me."

"I know, right? She was desperate and her brain still addled on pills. And before you ask, we haven't been able to find the counselor and Chalmers has clammed up. Anyway, back to the subject at hand, this latest killing and the crime scene photos. You said 'start with.' What else are you after?"

His openness about his frustrations do work to generate some sympathy on my part, so I tone down my snark. "Don't give up all hope," I tell him. "We both feel that something will come out of this puzzle line of inquiry. Fortunately it's our resident genius that's taking point on that one. I know you think we're stretching it, and you may be right, but if there's anything to the puzzle link we'll find it. So I might as well ask. Did you find any evidence that Charlene was into puzzles?"

"Didn't look for it," Mendez admits. "So go for it. If anything develops on that front, it was my idea. Otherwise, keep it to yourself. You'll have the pics in your inbox within the hour, keys dropped off by tomorrow."

He hangs up abruptly, preventing any more witty banter or questions that only remind him of how hopeless things look at the moment.

"What did he say?" Vinn asks.

"Most importantly, he called you my 'sidekick,'" I say proudly. "Which makes me the superhero. At least he got something right. Other than that, they've got squat. He already had the photos ready to send tonight and we'll get the keys tomorrow."

"Okay, Superman," Vinn replies. "Fetch me a drink and let's see what that notebook has to say."

As it turns out, the notebook didn't have much to say at all, or more accurately at first glance appeared to be total gibberish. At second and third glances it still looked like gibberish. If we stared at it all night, which in fact after thirty wasted minutes we were close to doing, it still wouldn't make sense. If we were expecting a note identifying the killer and his or her motive, all wrapped up in one or two neat sentences, we had set ourselves up for disappointment.

"What the hell," Vinn says. "'GSVTZNVRH-ZULLG3425.' Saying it out loud doesn't help reveal its meaning, damn it. We've been working under the assumption that killer number three may not be at the top of their class, but I doubt this is a misspelled word. Can we discount the idea that this may be just random letters that were scribbled in there just to put something in the notebook and that they actually have no meaning at all?"

"Not entirely," I answer. "But I'd say no for two reasons. First, the fact that there are numbers in there as well as letters. If I were just going to quickly write something in there to simulate therapist's notes, even if I didn't take the time to use actual words I don't think I would add numbers to the letters. I know, not the strongest argument but it just seems that the numbers are out of place in that scenario. You'd use all letters or just unreadable lines and squiggles. Second, they were printed with care, almost fanatically neatly. That indicates to me that it was written into the notebook ahead of time, not at the scene. Most anyone who is in the same room as the body of someone they just murdered wouldn't take the time to be so persnickety."

"Agreed on both counts, although I'll keep open the possibility that whoever is behind these killings thought it'd be amusing to leave a clue that actually isn't a clue at all just to play with the cops. But there's a third reason that for me is the most convincing. Even though we still haven't taken a look at the scene to search for a puzzle connection to this victim, isn't this a connection in itself? If the mastermind wants to play games with the cops, and puzzles are the link, then this must be a puzzle too."

"Are you suggesting we spend tonight trying to break the code?" I ask. I had hoped for time of a more romantic nature.

"The whole evening, no," Vinn responds with a smile, showing her thoughts are on track with mine. "But either it's so complicated that we'll need to run it through a computer program, which we don't have handy, or it's meant to be easy enough that even a cop of average intelligence can solve it. Either way we should know after a little effort."

Resigned to a night of attempted code breaking, I grab a couple of pads of paper and some sharp pencils. Vinn demurs, preferring to do everything on her laptop. I find much greater success organizing my thoughts by writing them down by hand. I copy the clue, if that's what it is, across the top of my page.

"Let's start by brainstorming together before we try to solve this individually," she suggests. "Thoughts?"

I stare again at the combination of letters and num-bers, this time from the perspective that they're meant to be a puzzle to be solved. I start out tentatively. "If it's crafted to be too difficult to solve without running it through artificial intelligence, we're wasting our time. So let's work on the assumption that we—mostly you—are meant to figure it out on our own. If that's the case, it's probably a basic cypher, something not overly complicated. A simple code."

As usual, Vinn's way ahead of me. Pulled up on her screen is a website that lists twenty-five codes used through the ages for messaging secrets, ranging from grade-school level through the Enigma code used in World War II.

"We can eliminate most of these," she says. "They don't use letters at all." After a few more minutes, she sighs with clear disappointment. "We can actually eliminate all of these. Nothing quite fits."

"Then let's use our brains. How many words do you know that have eighteen letters, fourteen if we drop the numbers? Doesn't it make sense that these are multiple words run together?"

Vinn sits up straight, warming to the task at last. "So if we break these up in the correct way, then use probabilities based on typical letter frequency and commonalities in relative positioning, this should be easy, right?"

"Um," I begin, not wanting to admit that she lost me halfway through. "Sure. You start."

"The first thing that stands out is the double L near the end. Those could be consonants, but then G would have to be either an S or a Y or a vowel based on probability. I'm going to start by assuming that the L is a vowel. If I'm wrong we'll start over but let's see where it leads. Not sure I know any words with two 'U's or 'I's or 'A's. So let's think they could be 'E's or 'O's. Tweet? No, can't be because the T doesn't match up on both ends."

I'm behind but need to try to contribute something. "What's one of the most common words in the English language? 'The.' Can we just for kicks assume the first three letters are 'the'? Just to see where it goes?" As soon as I say this, an idea kicks in, but again Vinn is a fraction of a second ahead of me.

"Wait, Mal. If that's the case—"

"And we remember the numbers at the end—"

"Exactly," Vinn says as if we had actually expressed our thinking. "The numbers signal the length of the words. Then if the first word is 'the,' the last word is five letters long ending in either 'eet' or 'oot.'"

Times are rare that I not only keep up with Vinn but get a step ahead. I quickly write out the alphabet in two columns on my page first forward, then backward directly next to it. I now know what the message says.

Vinn senses something and looks up from her screen. "What are you grinning at?" she asks suspiciously. She leans over and glances at my page. "Well I'll be damned. We were making things way too complicated."

I pause to consider if she just called me a simpleton. Even so, I'll take my victories where I can.

GSV TZNV RH ZULLG
THE GAME IS AFOOT

"Sherlock Holmes?" Vinn asks rhetorically.

When I'm on a roll, which isn't often with Vinn, I take the opportunity to rub it in. I am, after all, an English professor albeit a fake one. "Actually Shakespeare before that. King Richard IV, Part I." The students in my Introduction to Shakespeare class last year may not have learned anything, but apparently I did.

Vinn closes her laptop and we both lean back on the couch. "Is there any doubt at all now that these killings are being directed by one or more people who don't do the actual hands-on work?"

"Not in my mind," I agree. "And that puzzles or puzzlers link all three killings together. Do you want to tell Mendez or should I?"

"You," Vinn answers emphatically. "Because he's used to getting news he doesn't like from you and may not be as willing to kill the messenger. But not tonight."

Vinn takes me by the hand. We work well together in our investigations because our minds work in very different ways that merge to find solutions to complex problems. Where we're headed now, we come together even better.

FIFTEEN

Procrastination has a made a bad name for itself, but in my mind it can be a key to survival. I choose to hold off notifying Mendez of our discovery in the hope that the cops will discover it on their own, thus saving me from having to deliver the bad news and wrongfully take the blame for what it reveals. A couple of days pass with no word from the men and women in blue, so either they're still in the dark or they've decided to keep it to themselves.

"You've got to tell him," Vinn reminds me as we sit in the school cafeteria early on Friday morning. "Not that I care too much about keeping our promise to share what we find out—they're not living up to that on their end either—but because it might just enable them to solve this mess themselves. This isn't a competition, Mal. The sooner it ends the better, even if it means we don't get the credit. Dr. Sanders is getting impatient and even more insufferable, if that's possible."

"I know, I know," I admit begrudgingly as I pour the tea I brought from home. Today it's a rare pu-erh tea that supposedly was aged in a cave for twenty years which I found fallen behind the back of my kitchen cabinet. For better or worse I guess it was also aged there for another year or so. It's good, but not worth the price or the hype. "I decided to wait until after I go through Charlene's place. I may find more links to puzzles so he might as well hear all of the bad news at once. Are you sure you don't want to come along?"

"Sorry. I have a rescheduled lab this afternoon then I want to fit in a short nap before going off to that Puzzlers Anonymous meeting tonight. Need to be as sharp as possible. Besides, that code in the notebook pretty much establishes a connection. Anything you find will just be gravy."

"Understood." I'd much rather have her company, more to speed up the process than with the expectation that Vinn will see something I don't. For a routine search like this, we're both capable of going solo but the less time I spend in a room where a dead body has been just days before the better.

We each have a class to get to, so we gather our papers, confirm what time Vinn will be picking Leo up, and go our separate ways. With luck, the next time we see each other we'll both have a story to tell.

I duck under the crime scene tape as I make my way into Charlene's apartment and am immediately assailed by the lingering smell of death and the odor of too many sweaty bodies that entered in its aftermath. I'd already decided to make this as quick as I can without sacrificing thoroughness and now I'm doubly motivated to get in and out fast.

It's unlikely that she knew that she was being targeted or that she had reason to hide secretive information that would implicate her killer, so I give a quick once-over to the living room, lifting the couch cushions to look beneath them but not pushing my hand inside to feel around. Thankfully the room is sparsely furnished with little clutter, so within less than ten minutes I'm on to the kitchen. That takes slightly longer only because of all of the cooking and eating materials and the food containers in the cabinets, but again I decide that there's no need to pour out the cereal or sift through the bag of flour. The bathroom is a brief pass-through.

Which leaves the bedrooms, my main target all along. The guest bedroom looks like it's used less for guests and more as a walk-in closet and storage space with clothes jammed onto hangers and boxes stacked three high on the closet floor with more under the bed. Each drawer of the sole dresser is filled with women's winter clothes. Out of habit I walk to the master bedroom to compare clothing sizes and confirm that the warmer items belonged to Charlene and not some unknown house guest. I sit on the bed, pulling boxes out and resting them beside me as I search.

The task is tedious and unproductive. High school yearbooks, which I admit were entertaining to read until I forced myself back on track, plastic bags containing tangles of unlabeled cords and chargers, fitness DVDs, half of which were still in vacuum packed plastic, and assorted personal items which were she alive she would be embarrassed to know a stranger is pawing through. Nothing, however, of any relevance.

One room to go, admittedly the one most likely to yield results if there are any to be found. I deliberately begin with the closet and dresser drawers, leaving the nightstand for last. Not expecting to hit paydirt, I'm surprised when I feel a small spiral notebook hidden inside the laces of a corset and stashed deep inside her underwear drawer. Easy to miss on a casual search, explaining why it's not sitting in the evidence room down at the precinct. Pulling it out, still wary of what it might contain, I'm pleasantly surprised to find it contains a list of all of her usernames and passwords for various sites. My spine tingles when two-thirds of the way down the list I see an entry for "PA."

I reluctantly set the notebook on the bed while I continue my search. After twenty more minutes the only significant things I've discovered are her penchant for collecting travel brochures to exotic locales and a cryptic crossword paperback in the drawer of her nightstand. My excitement is tempered by the knowledge that crossword puzzles are so common that it doesn't really put Charlene in the category of an addict or add anything that we didn't already know.

Her laptop sits on top of the nightstand, filthy with fingerprint powder both outside and on the keys. I assume the cops have been through it, although their focus may have been so myopic that they didn't bother to open its contents or, if they did, didn't find anything they considered important enough to keep the laptop. Surprisingly the charger dangles from its side, letting me plug it in to make sure I have the juice to look around inside.

The first thing I do is scroll down her bookmarks, and while not surprising I'm still thrilled to see Puzzlers Anonymous among her saved sites. One click and I'm at the home page, where I quickly fill in her username and password and hit enter. Instead of bringing me inside the website, my efforts are rewarded with a pop-up message telling me that the account has been deactivated. My computer skills are too limited to know how to find out how long that message has been there, but if she let her membership lapse I would think I would simply be denied entry. The aggressive deactivation message leads me to believe that this was a termination of an active account, possibly due to the fact the member is no longer alive. A bit of a jump, but I find the pop-up slightly mystifying and more than a little suspicious to a brain wired to distrust everything odd.

I move to her gmail account and once again luck out. It takes me scrolling back nearly six weeks to find, but there's a not-too-genteel exchange of several emails between Charlene and a Charles Broden, whose signature line states that he's the "Vice President and Puzzle Master" of the group and whose name rings a bell from Summers' similarly toned emails with the group. The subject seems petty, a debate about whether the wording of a puzzle handed out at the May meeting was misleading, allegedly making it impossible to solve without inside information. Without actually saying the word, Charlene is accusing Mr. Puzzle Master of cheating. The conversation ended when Broden stopped replying to her emails. Did he have a role in cutting off her account? Would her accusation be a sufficient motive to murder? On the one hand, slow down, Winters, you're jumping to conclusions. On the other hand, people have killed for less.

I spend twenty more fruitless minutes scrolling through emails and peeking into folders with nothing to show for it. Before I leave the apartment, I call Vinn.

"Have you left yet for the meeting? Good grief, Vinn, let him bring the bottle if he thinks it helps him. Anyway, I confirmed that Charlene was a member, at least until recently. When you're there try to innocently work her name into a conversation with a man named Charles Broden. A Puzzle Master, whatever that is.

No, I'm not going to tell you why. I've already leaped to conclusions way beyond what's justified and I need you to have an unspoiled mind so that we can compare impressions. Okay. Good luck."

With that done, and after one more glance around each room just in case, I lock up and head for home.

I often silence my phone when conducting a search. I tell others that it's out of respect for the deceased, but in reality my attention span is equivalent to that of a hyperactive toddler so that when I'm interrupted in the middle of going over the scene of a murder, half the time I forget what I'd already done and end up searching a room twice. The upside is that I get done more quickly and I'm more thorough. The downside is that I frequently—meaning every single time—forget to take my cell off silent after I'm done.

Which explains the three missed calls followed by a frantic and unkind voice mail from Mendez that I first notice around 8:00 p.m. He leaves me his personal cell number, which indicates a level of desperation I wouldn't expect from a seasoned detective. He probably regretted giving it to me the moment he hung up, thinking I would abuse the privilege of having access to a ranking member of the local constabulary around the clock. Smart man. I decide to test the number out, half expecting to be connected to a phone sex hotline.

"Where the hell have you been?" he roars after picking up before the echo of the first ring leaves my ears.

"Officer, not all of us are slaves to our phones. I had the ring off while I conducted some important investigative work. Now what can I do for you?"

"You can open your damned door. I'm on your landing."

My mind immediately rushes into panic mode, wondering what happened to Vinn. Within two seconds, I'm going against instinct and experience by letting a cop into my home. I can't read his face because it always looks like he's come from an Irish wake. I show him to a chair and sit nervously opposite.

I'm confused as Mendez doesn't immediately reveal the purpose of his visit, instead running his fingers through his thinning hair. His features relax a degree and the tone of his voice softens.

"The three killings took place in three different districts," he begins, his gaze focused on a point behind me. "Earlier tonight, I was called into a meeting with three commanders, a deputy chief, and the chief of detectives. The Superintendent was on speakerphone. And guess who the focus was on? Me. To no one's surprise, there's been a leak and the details of the three murders are now in the hands of a reporter, so we expect a front-page, sensationalized story as soon as tomorrow morning. That wasn't unexpected, it happens all the time. The difference here is that we've made zero progress on two of them and can't explain how the one killer we caught is connected to the other two, if at all.

"So the Superintendent is going to be front and center at a press conference tomorrow morning to try to get ahead of the story and he asked the room what he can say to show that the department is on top of the investigation and that the public can expect another arrest soon. Everyone looked at me and all I could do is disclose that we know there are at least two different killers and beyond that we've got zip. You can imagine how that went over. He gave me until 10:00 tomorrow morning to come up with something he can tell a roomful of hungry reporters without looking like a fool."

He stops and for the first time looks me straight in the eyes. I'm slow on the uptake. "And the reason you're here is...?"

"You're going to make me say it?" he growls. "Fine. I need your help. I need to know what you found in that apartment tonight. Yes, I know you were there, we have eyes on the place. I need to hear your theories, no matter how farfetched. It's no secret that you and your partner see things in a different way than cops do. I need something I can tell my boss's boss's boss by morning. Hopefully something we can spin."

"Even if what I tell you will in all likelihood make your head explode?" I ask hesitantly, edging back in my seat.

Mendez eyes me with a mixture of apprehension and suspicion, clearly pondering whether he wants to hear what I have to say. He finally gives in. "Hit me," he says.

I get up and retrieve the notes from my code-breaking session with Vinn, laying them on the coffee table facing in Mendez's direction, keeping silent to let him review and digest them at his own pace. As it turns out, I don't need to explain a thing.

Mendez continues to stare at my notes, but his eyes are no longer in focus. "Shit, shit, shit," he mumbles. Seems to be his go-to expression of dismay.

"There's more," I finally tell him. "Charlene,

Victim Number 3, belonged to the same puzzlers' group that the other two did. That's the group that Vinn is infiltrating. Tonight, in fact." I choose not to reveal the existence of the emails or the name of Charlene's antagonist in the group. The last thing we need is for a swarm of cops to descend on him before we get our crack.

"So," Mendez says slowly, "we have a clear connection between all three murders beyond the bizarre crime scenes and that's their interest in puzzles and membership in this group." He looks up at me. "But that's not all, is it?"

"No, sorry," I respond. "And the news doesn't get any better. It's our firm belief that three different killers are involved and that one or more people not doing the actual killing are behind the scenes pulling the strings."

"Yeah, I got that from the message too," Mendez says sounding depressed. "So we have a psycho serial killer who thinks this is all a game and is taunting us to catch him. Plus a couple of actual murderers on the loose. Thanks a lot, the Super will be thrilled with that information."

"It'll definitely test the department's ability to spout a lot of encouraging words without saying a thing," I say, hoping that Mendez got what he came for and will be leaving now. "But maybe Vinn will get a nibble at tonight's meeting. I'll let you know."

"Correction," Mendez says as he settles more deeply into his chair. "She'll tell me herself. What time do you expect her back? And do you have anything to drink?"

SIXTEEN

Mendez dozed off at 9:18 p.m. and Vinn inserts her key into my door at 9:43 p.m. I know the exact times because I've been looking at the time on my laptop roughly every ninety seconds for the past hour. Mendez thanked me for the beer I brought him, after which we fell into absolute and complete silence devoid of any theorizing about the cases or small talk. It was beyond awkward but still preferable to forcing a conversation.

Vinn begins to greet me but stops, startled, when she notices the large man slumped into my chair. I mouth the words "not my choice" and she nods, instantly grasping the situation. We move into the kitchen.

"If you grab him under his arms and I take his legs, do you think we could carry him outside without waking him up, then run off to Milwaukee or something?" she asks, only half joking.

"There'd be an APB out on us before we made it three blocks," I reply. "Do you want to tell me what happened tonight before we wake him?"

"Nah, I'm tired and would rather not have to repeat myself," she says with a sigh. "Besides, there's not that much to say. And if he can discern a thread from what went on at the meeting that helps him capture whoever's behind these killings, I'm all for it. There is one possible thing I need to run by you, but you'll need the full background first so it can wait."

I return to my seat while Vinn heads back to the door, which she opens then slams shut with force. Mendez jumps with a start, clearly disoriented. He quickly regains focus, remembering where he is, then turns his head to confirm Vinn's presence.

"Officer Mendez," she says sweetly. "What a pleasant surprise. Did Mal offer you something to drink?"

"Hhmph," he mumbles as Vinn takes a seat next to me. "So what happened tonight? I want details and don't leave anything out."

"Right to the point," Vinn says calmly. "I like that about you. I'll do the best I can but if you have any questions or want more detail, please feel free to interrupt.

"New members are asked to get there thirty minutes early for an informal orientation to the group. Leo and I were apparently the only newbies this time. We were met by Charles Broden, who introduced himself as an officer and tonight's official greeter." Vinn squeezes my hand tight when she feels me react to the name and I immediately bring myself back under control. Mendez doesn't seem to have noticed. Total cooperation is taking a hit, but we're not ready to share our hunch about Broden yet.

"One of the first things he asked was how we heard of Puzzlers Anonymous. I told him that I introduced myself to Charlene at a Starbucks when I noticed her working on what appeared to be an interesting puzzle, something I hadn't seen before. She told me about the group and suggested I take the entry exam if I was interested." She stops when Mendez emits a low growl. "I hope that wasn't too forward," she quickly adds. "Then I asked if she would be coming tonight. All he said was that they never knew in advance who would be attending but that she was a regular. I didn't notice any unusual reaction. I told him that once I decided to take the test, I asked Leo to try as well so that I would know someone here, as I'm not very good at meeting strangers.

"After that, he asked about our jobs, particular puzzle interests, backgrounds, that kind of thing. I did most of the talking but Leo contributed where necessary. Then he went into detail about the group, stuff like attendance policies, dues, special events, and what a typical meeting was like. I don't imagine you care about any of that." Not getting a response from Mendez, she continues.

"By that time people began to filter in. He introduced us to a few then left us on our own to meet them while he prepared to run the meeting. Leo and I started out together but as attendance grew split up in order to interact with as many members as possible. There were probably about thirty-five total, which apparently is about average. I dropped Charlene's name when I could but she seems to have kept to herself mostly. Leo said he met the club nosy body, a man who seemed to be very familiar with the backgrounds of each member, so he probed a little to try to lead him to mention Brandon, but got nowhere. We didn't want to be too obvious so after that we stopped."

Vinn pauses to go to the kitchen for a glass of water. Mendez's expression has been slowly transitioning from passive to irritated. So far Vinn has given him nothing.

"After a few announcements, Broden passed out the night's puzzles. He put an electronic timer in plain view of each table and set it for an hour. There were five puzzles total. The first couple weren't that difficult then they got harder. I was still working on the last one when time ended." She turns to me. "Another ten minutes and I would have had it.

"Obviously there was no talking allowed for that hour, but afterward there were snacks and a short time to mingle before the meeting broke up. Understand that the members are there to be mentally challenged, not to socialize. I got the impression that this is the world's greatest collection of introverts and loners. That being said, I did get the names and emails for a few. I think one more meeting—the next one isn't for a month—and I'll be comfortable reaching out to one or two for a more private conversation where I can be more direct."

By this point, Mendez looks deflated. "So you got nothing that will help us?"

Vinn feigns offense. "What did you expect for one meeting, Officer? If you know of a way that would have rendered immediate results, I'd like to hear it. We couldn't exactly constantly bring up the victims' names without everyone wondering why. I thought we pushed pretty close to the line as it was."

"Yeah, yeah," Mendez concedes. "I expected nothing and that's what I got." He rises slowly, his shoulders slumped.

I actually feel sorry for the man. "You can tell your boss that we've successfully infiltrated a group where there's a strong reason to believe the mastermind is hiding," I offer. "As you know, these things take time."

My last few words are spoken to Mendez's back as he makes his way to the exit. For moments after he's out of sight, Vinn continues to stare at the door, her face troubled. I ask what's wrong.

"I'm sorry, Mal, I couldn't do it," she says mournfully. "I mean, be completely open with a cop. Years of habit I guess but also out of fear that rather than solve the damned case, they'll screw up any lead that we turn up. I wasn't completely honest. Okay, I outright lied by omission. That group is the key to solving this thing. This evening wasn't the total loss I made it out to be."

"In my defense, I did fill Mendez in on the facts fully and completely," Vinn asserts ten minutes later as we sit on stools at Leo's rickety kitchen table, glasses half-filled with a smoky liquid of undetermined color at our elbows. After a short debate, which consisted mostly of Vinn arguing both sides with herself, we decided to move downstairs to include Leo in the extended version of what happened at the meeting since he was there as well. Up until this moment, his contributions have consisted of two grunts and a belch. "What I left out was more of an impression and a longshot lead which may amount to nothing."

She takes a sip of Leo's booze, grimaces, then shoots him an accusatory look as if she had been poisoned. He remains impassive. "First off, there's no doubt in my mind that Broden reacted when I mentioned Charlene's name. He immediately went still and his eyes flashed, then it took him a moment longer than necessary to respond. He seemed to be uncomfortable after that and rushed us through our orientation, although I admit that may have been my imagination. I know that's not exactly conclusive evidence and you can guess how Mendez would have reacted to that if I had mentioned it, but I'm positive Broden knows something. Leo agrees with me."

I look over at Leo just in time to see an almost imperceptible nod. I'm hoping that his affirmation isn't the only reason we're here. Vinn takes another sip of her drink, this time without the face or the glance at Leo, then continues.

"As I said earlier, we had very little time to interact with the other attendees, so when it came to our goal of isolating someone who'd appear open to further conversation outside of the meeting, I struck out. Leo, though, came through big time. Leo, do you want to take it from here?"

The big man shakes his head, utters a word that may have been "you," then pours himself another drink. Vinn sighs, shrugs her shoulders at me, and fills me in.

"I'm not sure how he did it," she says softly, as if Leo weren't sitting a few feet away. "Because I don't think he said more than three words in my hearing all night. But somehow he charmed a pretty young thing, by far both the youngest and most attractive woman there, to agree to meet with him for lunch tomorrow. Maybe it's a case of opposites attract. I hope that's the case because we need her to be not only knowledgeable about the workings of the group and familiar with both Charlene and Mills—Summers would be a bonus—but a regular chatterbox ready to talk. And talk and talk until she says something useful."

Without further prompting, Leo pulls a business card from an inside pocket of his shirt and pushes it across the table in my direction. It's an eye-catching, multi-colored card advertising the woman's services as a life coach. It's her name, though, that draws my immediate attention.

"'Megan Vixen?'" I say incredulously before repeating it. The corner of Leo's mouth twitches slightly, the closest thing to a smile I ever see him make. I turn the card over, where she wrote "Bongo Room

12:00" in purple ink, with a hand-drawn heart for good measure. I hand the card back to him.

"Not sure she expects us to crash the party," Vinn says. "But the more the merrier. I'm sure Leo will be able to smooth things over with his date afterward. So that's the other thing that I didn't tell Mendez. My guess is that waffles and coffee will open her up more than being browbeat by a couple of sweaty cops in an interview room. And it may be that she won't be of any help to us, in which case Mendez doesn't need to know about her at all.

"Now I want to return to Broden," Vinn continues. "We didn't have any interaction with him after the orientation until we were getting ready to leave, when he went around the room handing out what the members call 'DGPs', or Departure Game Packets. They're puzzles to work on between meetings. They also get posted on the members' section of the website, but from what I can tell a lot of members prefer paper copies. When he got to me, he stressed how much he hoped I'd take the time to work on them, and twice he said 'all' of them with emphasis on that word. That struck me as odd. I looked around at the packets everyone else had and noticed that they were held together by the standard silver paper clip. My clip was green. My suspicions were and are raised. Leo, do you have your packet?"

While Leo stumbles away from the table to retrieve the papers, Vinn takes out her ever-present laptop and types away. When Leo drops the papers down, she grabs them quickly and starts paging through them, every so often glancing at her screen. After a few minutes she hands the packet back to Leo.

"The puzzles in Leo's packet match exactly what's on the website. Now for the moment of truth." Vinn pulls her own packet, green clip and all, out of her laptop bag and repeats her actions of a minute before. When she comes to the end, she goes back and does it again. By this point, both Leo and I have our eyes glued on her. She doesn't disappoint.

"Just as I thought," she says, a twinge of excitement in her voice. She holds up a single page. "I have a puzzle that Leo doesn't and that isn't on the website. As careful as we thought we were, we've been made, Mal. Broden just sent us a message."

SEVENTEEN

We retreat to my unit, where I make copies of the puzzle, store one in my desk drawer in case we lose the other nineteen, then make the trip back down to Leo's to drop one off with him in case he wants to work on it when he's not at his diner, which is almost always. He neither thanks me nor jumps for joy.

When I return, Vinn's hunched over the puzzle at my kitchen island, pencil in hand and laptop at the ready. She reluctantly closes her computer and puts the pencil down once I join her.

"Sorry, Mal, I just can't focus tonight. It's late and I had a busy day to cap off a long week. I really want to tackle this as soon as possible and may not be able to get my brain to stop dwelling on it enough to sleep, but I'm not up for it. You can get a start on it without me if you want."

As she utters the last few words, her eyelids droop heavily and her elbows slide sideways, lowering her head to the counter. Her brain must have made the decision not to dwell on the puzzle long before letting her conscious self know, as heavy, regular breathing sounds reach my ears. I carry Vinn to the bedroom, settle her in, then return to the kitchen. Even as sleepy as she is tonight, Vinn working at twenty-five percent intellectual capacity would still exceed my own abilities working at full tilt. I only make the effort in the hope that something immediately clicks in my mind and I can look like a genius to the woman I love.

At first glance, what I see is a whole lot of nonsense. Near the top of the page, neatly typed, is what appears to be a quotation, beneath it two sets of numbers:

"Death's hand has been called upon more than the run of the. Retreat and move the beginning of hell, or all shall be lost." *As You Like It [V, 1, 2217]*, *William Shakespeare*

32 81 42 21 62
53 63 81 73

Second and third glances also see only nonsense, and I begin to understand why Vinn decided to push any effort in solving it until she was well rested. I'm about to follow suit, but to the English professor in me, fake as it may be, the quotation doesn't sound like Shakespeare. While the introductory class I taught didn't cover *As You Like It*, the rhythm of the language is off from the plays we did study. The missing word or words at the end of the first sentence bothers me as well, so before I can join Vinn in slumber and let my subconscious mind work it out, I pull out my computer and find a searchable text of the play.

Nothing with the key words from the puzzle's quote pop up, so I type in the line number. Immediately blood rushes to my face and my anger rises as I read the true text of the reference.

"The fool doth think he is wise, but the wise man knows himself to be a fool."

Damn it. We're being taunted and it's game on, so to speak. I'm going to make sure that whoever's behind these killings just picked on the wrong set of fools.

In all of the excitement about the extra puzzle in Vinn's packet, I'd forgotten about Leo's lunch date until Vinn reminds me as I slide half a panful of steaming hot chilaquiles onto her plate before topping them with slices of ripe avocado, queso fresco, and a fried egg. No sense describing what I'd found until she's at least semiconscious, and there's nothing like food to bring her alive in the morning.

"I figure we'd let Leo go in first," she tells me, "since Ms. Vixen isn't expecting a crowd. He can sweet talk her, exchange lovie dovies, and look deep into her eyes before we appear and break the magic."

The imagery she's invoking almost makes me lose my appetite, but not for these tasty, soggy chips. "I guess that's only fair to him," I concede as I sprinkle on additional cheese, "but let's not wait too long. I'm not sure what she sees in him, but after more than ten minutes one-on-one it's even odds whether she's going to stick it out any longer. We need to catch them during the honeymoon period while she's still more likely to cooperate."

As we eat I tell Vinn of the message Broden inserted into the puzzle. To my surprise she doesn't react as I did and seems very casual about being called a fool.

"Can't say that he's wrong," she states calmly. "It's not like we've unearthed anything so far that's brought us closer to a solution, other than an unprovable assumption that he's involved in some unknown way. All we have is a bunch of 'un's modifying our adjectives at this point. If we want to demonstrate our wisdom, we have to up our game."

We still have a couple of hours before we need to set off to crash Leo's rendezvous so we each grab a copy of the puzzle. Vinn stays at the island where she can have easy access to her laptop as well as to a notepad and the different colored pencils she arranges in a neat line while I sprawl out on my couch with only a single pencil and legal pad. Out of habit that's become tradition, we tend to work on certain aspects of a case individually to see what our different approaches can mine before talking it out together if neither of us reaches a solution.

Ninety minutes later, I throw my pencil across the room in frustration. I spent the bulk of my time attempting to discern the meaning of the text on the assumption that it was a necessary precursor to solving the numerical clue. Failing at that, I played with the numbers, trying to substitute letters for them in any number of ways, but I always ended up with gibberish. My patience ran out, leading to the number two projectile.

Vinn swivels on her stool to look in my direction when she hears the pencil hit the wall, closing her laptop as she turns.

"You too? I've tried using any number of computer algorithms, code-breaking programs, and simple brainpower with no result. Let's take a break then start from scratch by throwing ideas back and forth." She looks up at my clock. "But that'll have to wait. Let me freshen up and then we can take a slow walk to The Bongo Room. We can discuss our approach to this woman on the way."

We consider three or four different ways to draw information out of Meagan Vixen before we default to our usual "wing it." Some women will open up better to other women, but not all, so Vinn will start by playing the sisterhood card and if that doesn't work, let me take over. Ideally we'd prefer that Leo take on the key role here but neither of us considers him reliable and we're not convinced he has a firm grasp on what we're looking for. Not that I do either, this is a pure fishing expedition, but I may have a better chance of stumbling across it along the way.

It's 12:15 as we approach the restaurant. Vinn's eyes begin to glaze over as the smell of breakfast food permeates the air and I have to tell her to focus. We stop just inside the door. Vinn scans the room for our prey while I find the hostess for what turns out to be a pricey chat. Vinn tilts her head in the direction of the table while I nod slightly to confirm that my side mission was successful.

We hold hands as we saunter toward Leo and his date, nearly bumping into the table as we come up alongside.

"Leo, is that you?" Vinn exclaims in mock surprise. "And, I'm sorry, I don't remember your name but I believe we met last night. How great to see you."

"Meagan. Megs," the vixen squeaks out. I give her a close once-over. I don't see her as the beauty that Vinn described last night, but there's something indescribably seductive about her that makes me want to not only keep staring, but to whisk her away with me to a private island to live out our lives together. I have to break my gaze and get back to the reason we're here.

"What a delightful coincidence that we all decided to eat here today," Vinn continues, a wave of relief washing over her face as she sees the hostess approach.

"Would all of you like to sit together?" the woman asks, then goes on without waiting for an answer. "A table just opened up near the back. Let me help you move and I'll get Andre to bring additional menus." Neither Leo nor Meagan—Megs—has a chance to object as she grabs their plates and walks swiftly away. Vinn and I take their coffee cups and silverware and follow. We don't need to look behind us to know that the two diners will be trailing behind.

"Wasn't that nice of them," Vinn says brightly as we settle in. I'm still full from breakfast but agree to share Vinn's order of a chorizo, potato, and avocado omelet. Typically, there's no decent tea on the menu so I settle for juice.

After a few minutes of awkward small talk, to which Leo contributes nothing, Vinn shifts gears and I tense up as I know what's coming.

"Meagan," she begins, any note of cheeriness gone from her voice. "I could dance around and keep trying to steer our conversation in a certain direction but you impress me as a woman who appreciates straight talk. Running into you today wasn't an accident. We need your help."

I watch nervously as Megs turns to Leo with a questioning and accusatory look. He merely shrugs. It's obvious that Vinn decided to lay our cards on the table, not a first but certainly unusual for us. I can't say I disagree with her strategy. Since Broden has already seen through Vinn and almost certainly surmised the true purpose of her presence at the meeting, there's nothing to lose in confiding in a member. After a few seconds of uncertainty, Megs chooses to stay pat, looking up directly into Vinn's eyes. Vinn takes the cue, pausing only momentarily as the waiter brings food for the happy couple.

"You may not be aware of this, but three members of the Chicago chapter of Puzzlers Anonymous have met with unusual and particularly gruesome deaths recently. They were murdered, and we can say with some degree of certainty that their killings are not only connected but orchestrated by the same person or persons. And we believe the answer to who's behind them also lies within the membership of PA."

Megs' eyes grow wider with each sentence. I have to resist the impulse to reach over, pat her on the hand, and tell her that Uncle Malcom will make sure that everything will be okay. Apparently Vinn can read minds, as I'm brought back to reality with a sharp jab in the ribs.

"We're hoping to learn what you know about two things," I say, stumbling over my words as Megs turns her gaze on me. "First, the victims' names are Brandon Mills, Sandra Summers, and Charlene Phelps. They—"

"Charlene? Not Charlene!" Megs cries, drawing stares from neighboring tables. "But I just saw—I mean she was fine—I mean how could..."

"What can you tell us about her?" Vinn inserts quickly, trying to get the distraught woman past her shock and on topic. "Did you know her well?"

"Not really," Megs replies as she dabs the corners of her eyes with a handkerchief Leo produced out of nowhere. "It's not like we saw each other outside of the group. But we sat together at most of the meetings and got to know a little about each other. You know, girl talk. She was smart, really smart. She even caught the Puzzlemaster in an error once. He didn't like that."

"By the Puzzlemaster, do you mean Charles Broden?" I ask.

"Yeah, that's him. That's what he calls himself, I don't think it's an official title. He runs the meetings and thinks he's God's gift to puzzling and to the world. He's not well liked in the group but does a good job with organizing everything, which no one else wants to do so we tolerate him. Kind of a necessary evil, you know?"

"Does he associate with anyone there or keep to himself?"

"Funny you should ask. There's a couple other members, a man and a woman, that hang together with him. I don't remember their names offhand because we all avoid them, but I'll look at the roster and text the names to you. Behind their backs we call them the 'Terrible Trio.' They think they're better than everyone else, smarter and better at solving puzzles. About the only thing they've shown themselves to be better at is alienating the rest of the group."

Vinn takes over again. "Is there anything else you can tell us about Broden?" she asks.

"Not really. Like I said, I avoid him." Megs pauses and her mouth drops open. "Wait. Do you think that... maybe he and those other two..."

"We don't think anything at this stage," Vinn tells her. "We're just gathering information. And as long as we're on the subject, please don't tell anyone else that we're looking into this." Megs nods, but her eyes are starting to glance toward the door. We've about exhausted her patience. Vinn must sense the same thing.

"One more question if you don't mind," she says. "How well did you know Brandon Mills?"

"Not at all, really," Megs replies. "Except that he didn't seem to fit in with the group. I don't mean that in a bad way. He was quiet, but also not very good at solving the puzzles given out at the meetings. I overheard him once say that he felt too much pressure with all of the other people around him being so smart. Broden didn't think he belonged and publicly accused him of having someone take the entrance exam for him, but that was a long time ago."

Vinn and I thank her, she takes Vinn's cell number, and we remind her to look up the two members who Broden associates with. She rises out of her chair then takes two steps toward the door before turning back to us.

"Leo, aren't you coming?" He quickly exits the table and follows her without saying a word.

EIGHTEEN

We're barely back at my place when Vinn's phone signals an incoming text. "From Leo's phone," she tells me. "Probably Little Miss Vixen's way of telling us she doesn't want us to have her phone number and to leave her alone. I don't blame her, not wanting to get in the middle of the investigation, especially since she knows we're looking into Broden. I'm not sure she can add much to what she's already told us anyway, but if she thinks we can't track her down with or without Leo's help she's mistaken."

She forwards the text to my phone. It ignores customary pleasantries and consists solely of two names, Gretchen Connors and James G. Upton III. I scribble their names in my notes as Vinn pulls her laptop open and starts typing.

"'Gretchen Connors,'" she says out loud. "Fifty-four years old, an insurance company executive, married to an airline pilot. Two children, both at Ivy League schools. On the boards of a couple charities. Lives on the North Shore, beach access." Vinn pauses and wrinkles her nose. "I don't like her already. Everything screams 'snob.' Anyway, let's see what else we can find."

Over the next several minutes, as Vinn moves through the usual array of social media sites and random Google searches, nothing out of the ordinary stands out. Connors, at least to the public eye, is a woman who's made her way comfortably in the world and established herself as a socialite who would be on everyone's guest list for the usual circuit of galas and parties. If she has a side hobby of arranging to kill innocent people, she's kept it well hidden.

It's more of the same with Upton. Or should I say, Upton III. My innate prejudice against anyone with numerals after their last name is only bolstered by what Vinn turns up in her search. A plastic surgeon, his profile ticks off every box on my list of prototypical entitled rich people and he makes Connors look like a vagrant by comparison. Mansion on the lake, not one but two boats, vacation homes in the Florida Keys and Vail. He manages to get himself in front of a camera at every must-attend event in the city, always with his trophy wife draped over him and leaning forward to give a clear view of her rather impressive assets. Vinn isn't pleased when I ask her to enlarge the image of the happy couple on their yacht.

"Research," I mumble as she reluctantly complies.

"Into what law of physics keeps that bikini top in place?" she asks. "Seriously, Mal, not that rich people aren't subject to the same primal urges as the rest of us, but do we really believe that these two people teamed up with Broden to commit murder, even if through a third person? Not once, but three times so far? Wouldn't they rather be spending their time counting pennies in their vault or having dinner with the Governor? And don't forget, our overly-friendly pain-in-the-ass profiler insists that whoever's behind this doesn't fit in with everyday society and is most likely a pathological loner."

"In my experience people with that kind of wealth often feel that the laws that govern the rest of the population don't apply to them," I respond. "But even taking that into account, there's no hint of Connors running down the homeless with her car or Upton battering his wife or anything that suggests violent tendencies.

Vinn, I'm petty enough to want these people to be involved so that we can bring their worlds crashing down, and just as eager to prove Barry wrong, but if they're involved we're going to have to discover that a different way."

"Which brings us back to the puzzle Broden gave me," Vinn sighs. "I guess we've been putting it off long enough. Yesterday's waste of time makes me hesitate to get back into it just because I don't want to feel the same level of frustration I felt then. It's clear we need to solve this thing—we're stuck otherwise—so if we can't do it then I'll really be pissed."

I grab Vinn's hands and pull her to her feet before leading her to the kitchen. She grinds coffee beans while I sort through my stash of teas, finally settling on a green tea from the Yunnan province of China which has a slight sweetness that I'll bring out by adding fresh honey. While it's brewing I slice three varieties of cheese and a little summer sausage, bringing them out to the living room. When I return my tea and Vinn's coffee are ready at the same time and we each pour them into tall thermal containers to keep them warm for hours if necessary.

We look at each other, steel ourselves, and move to the couch. Game on.

"Okay, first thing," I announce, going first not because I have something significant to contribute but because someone has to. It's understood that when Vinn and I brainstorm, we really are encouraged to say anything that pops into our heads without risking ridicule, at least out loud. That rule leads to a lot of really dumb ideas but has also resulted in one of us saying something that triggers a barely related thought in the mind of the other that, once fleshed out, turns into a significant finding. "Can we discount that this isn't a coded message at all but a purposeful jumble of nonsense? That Broden or whoever put it together wanted us to waste our time trying to solve something that can't be solved, and that's how we look like fools?"

"That thought didn't occur to me," Vinn says with a frown. "Although I have wondered if once we decipher this—and we will—we'll have some sort of message like 'Go fuck yourself,' or something that won't help us at all. But I don't think so. Given the elaborate staging of the murder scenes that were teases to see if law enforcement could figure them out and catch on to the two list idea, I think whoever's behind this enjoys a game of cat and mouse, giving us just enough to stay two steps behind, testing how well we can play the game. It's plausible that this clue was going to be left at a future murder scene as an additional taunt, but I was too transparent in what I was after at the meeting and they changed tack and gave it to me instead. Besides, for now we don't have a choice but to proceed on the hope that this puzzle means something. It's not like we have any other paths to follow."

"When you put it that way...All right, let's get started. Are we agreed that the reference to *As You Like It* was put there solely as a taunt and that we can ignore it?"

"Yes and no," Vinn answers thoughtfully. "The reference itself, yes. The fact that it's italicized, no. Most people would use quotation marks or nothing at all, but this is the accepted way to cite a play. That shows at least some level of education, so if for any reason we need to abandon our assumption that the extra puzzle was placed in my packet by Broden, we keep that in mind in searching for someone else."

I'm a bit irritated as the English professor here that it took a scientist to raise that point, but I can't deny that she's right. Time to move on quickly rather than dwell on my mental deficiency. "When I tackled this yesterday I worked on the assumption that the text needs to be solved before we can understand the message found in the numbers, but I got nowhere. Is it possible that it's the other way around, and we need to decode the numbers first for a clue for breaking the code of the two sentences?"

"I thought the same thing as your initial impulse, and still do," she replies. "The fact that we were unsuccessful in solving the word portion of the puzzle doesn't mean that we're not right. I'm not ready to abandon the idea that it's the first thing we need to figure out. Are you okay with that? Good. Let's take it piece by piece. First up, 'Death's hand.' Go."

I don't take time to think and just say the first thing that pops into my head, which is the way this process works. Hopefully. "Death has to refer to the murders, that's obvious. 'Death's hand' I would think refers to the killer. Or killers, although it's singular."

"But it could refer to a group of two or more people, which would explain the singular even if more than one person is involved," Vinn says. "And when you hear that something is done 'at the hand' of someone, don't you think it leaves open that they may be the driving force but not the actor itself? I know it's a bit of a leap, but it also feels right. That 'Death's hand' means someone pulling the strings of the actual killer."

The fact that we don't ridicule ideas doesn't mean we can't challenge them. "I don't know, Vinn," I tell her, "I think you're trying to fit the code to our standing theory."

"True," she admits. "But can we keep it that way for now? Besides, either way we're in agreement that the first two words refer to the killer or the person or persons directing the killer, right? Let's keep going. 'Has been called upon.'"

I draw a blank at first and admit it. "I don't know. The killings have been ordered by God? That the killer sees this as a calling?"

Vinn makes a face. "Maybe. Or maybe we got 'death's hand' wrong and it refers to someone doing the killing on behalf of someone else who called them to tell them what to do. I don't know, Mal. This is where I got stuck last time. Can we skip it and come back?"

"No problem here. That brings us to 'more than the run of the...'" I look up and Vinn is grinning. "What?"

"You're so stuck on the fact that it's not a complete sentence, Mr. Grammar, that you're not zeroing in on the missing word itself. Start with 'run' and say it out loud."

I do so. Dammit. "'Run of the mill.' So obvious that I missed it. And then I assume that the word 'more'—"

"Means plural," Vinn interjects excitedly. "Mills. Brandon Mills, the first victim. So someone was called upon to kill Mills. Is it possible that the numbers give us the name of his killer?"

"Too much to hope," I say, trying to temper my own enthusiasm. "Let's work on the second sentence and see how that fits."

This time, two minds don't have any greater impact on a solution than one. Breaking the sentence into pieces, saying it out loud, running words groupings through search engines, nothing seems to help. Forty-one minutes later, we're ready to give up.

"Just to save face," Vinn says, "let's now work on the theory that the second sentence doesn't become relevant, and therefore remains unsolvable, until we know what the numbers are telling us."

"Sure, why not," I agree. "But first let's take a breather."

We watch a few YouTube videos, do twenty pushups, drink our tea and coffee, and eat some cheese. We both feel invigorated if not entirely optimistic.

"Number codes can be virtually impossible to solve without a decoder," Vinn says. "But we're working on the assumption that we're meant to solve it. So while it may not be easy, it's got to be something that we can do without a key. Unless the key is found in that second sentence. Read it to me."

I comply. "'Retreat and move the beginning of hell, or all shall be lost.'"

Vinn remains silent for a moment. "Are you sure that's what it says?" she asks with a puzzled smile. "Okay, maybe it's a red herring. Do you have any ideas or can we ignore it for now?"

"I've got nothing," I admit. "Not even a stupid idea to throw out there. On to the numbers, then?"

"Yep," Vinn says. "First impression: If it were one word, it would be set out in a single line. The fact that there's one set of numbers over the other to me suggests two words."

"Agreed as a working hypothesis which we're free to toss out later. Second impression: There are nine groupings of two numbers each. It's not likely that the message consists of nine two-letter words, so either the spacing isn't relevant and was placed that way to throw us off, or each grouping of two represents a single letter so that there are two words total, one five-letter and one four-letter."

"My thoughts exactly," Vinn says, warming to the task. "And if, as we speculated, this is in fact a name, we're looking at a first and last name."

"Vinn—" I begin.

"I know, I know," she interrupts, "I'm guilty of molding the puzzle to fit what I want it to be. A cardinal sin in science, but we're not in a lab. Can we run with it for now? Besides, whether the two words are a name or not, we'll still approach it the same way." She doesn't give me any chance to object before moving on. "So two words, two numbers for one letter. I don't suppose if we count from the beginning of the alphabet... I'll take the top one, you take the bottom."

I quickly write out the alphabet while Vinn races ahead by doing the calculations in her head. We finish about the same time.

"AKCU," I say. "A, K, C, U."

"I guess that could be a last name, but for a first name I got FCPUJ. Shall we try starting to count from the end of the alphabet?"

We get about two letters in before abandoning that idea. For several minutes we stay silent while I absentmindedly stare at my page, letting my mind wander. Without conscious effort, my eyes keep going back to the middle of the first sentence. An idea strikes me. I circle a word with my pencil and pull out my cell phone. Vinn stops what she's doing and watches me.

"My god, Mal, could it really be that easy?" she says, implying that if someone with my limited brainpower could come up with a solution, it couldn't have been complicated to begin with.

The word I marked is "called," and I copied the keypad from my phone, both the numbers and the three letters over each one. For the first set of two numbers, "32," I go to the number 3 on the keypad and jot down the second letter there. "E." "81" brings me to the letters "TUV," so the first letter is "T."

"Go faster," Vinn mutters, in the excitement forgetting that she could help out herself. Less than a minute later, I'm done.

"'Ethan Lots,'" Vinn reads. "That has to be it. Hold on, though." She opens her laptop and types in a few commands. "It's called the 'telephone cipher,' or at least a variation of it. So it's a legitimate and fairly well-known code. This has to be it. We did it, Mal! We have the name of Brandon Mills' killer."

"Slow down, Vinn," I caution. "That's one interpretation, albeit a pretty valid one. If this person is the killer, even an amateur one, then we need to turn his name over to Mendez. Remember, we agreed not to put ourselves in harm's way again. You can take the credit with Dr. Sanders, but let him make the collar."

Vinn frowns. "I get it, okay," she pouts. "Whatever it takes to get him off my back and to slide into retirement from the crime business." Suddenly her mood brightens. "We need to celebrate! Let's go out for gelato, then we can call Mendez."

We head for the door, hand in hand, moods elevated for the first time in days.

NINETEEN

"It doesn't hurt just to check," Vinn whines as we sit at a table outside the shop, Vinn finishing off her cup of goat cheese gelato with cashew and caramel and me nibbling at my malted vanilla with pretzel, which I had put in a cone to lessen the chance of Vinn's spoon making its way across the table. "Aren't you the least bit curious?"

I see that no reply is necessary as Vinn is already typing "Ethan Lots" into her phone. Her eyes quickly dim and a frown erases any joy she felt from her sugar rush and the prospect of putting the investigation behind us. I wait impatiently as she checks results for several minutes.

"There's an Ethan Lots subdivision in Arizona where you can buy land to build a home, sewer hook-up included, for the low, low price of $19,500.00," she finally says. "And an Ethan Plots cemetery in Iowa. The only actual person who turns up is somebody in India who has an empty Facebook Page. Damn it to hell."

"Don't get too discouraged," I tell her. "Not everybody is on social media, and Mendez should have access to nationwide databases from cops, the FBI, the military, and who knows what else. It's possible that our Mr. Lots got fingerprinted as a new teacher so that he's in the system even if he isn't addicted to Instagram or trolling TikTok. Or maybe it's a known alias for someone with a different name. We'll turn our information over to him and let the department do our work for us."

Vinn doesn't appear mollified, although her discontent may have more to do with the fact that she watches as I push the last bit of my cone into my mouth. We offer our seats to a harried mother with twin toddlers and a baby in a stroller and head back to my place.

Vinn leaves it to me to summarize our findings in email form and send them off to Mendez. I'm in the middle of typing a text to tell him to check his email the next time he's on duty when my phone rings.

"Hello, Detective," I answer. "How are you doing on this fine day?"

"Fine day, my ass," he says, louder than necessary. "Before I unleash the resources of the department on this guy, how sure are you?"

"Confident but not certain," I reply as I look to catch Vinn's eye. She nods in agreement. "I mean, the decoding appears sound and it's clearly a reference to Mills from someone who knows something. At the least, it's a better lead than nothing. And before you bitch, we didn't know about the extra puzzle until this morning. We figured we'd work on it a bit and wait to send it to you in case you were out on the golf course."

All I hear for a few moments is Mendez breathing into the phone, then the connection is cut off abruptly. I look at my phone in surprise. "I'm sure he meant to say thank you," I tell Vinn. "Now all we can do is wait."

Neither one of us is good at waiting and our attempts to distract ourselves by reading and online shopping are complete failures. Stomachs still sated from the gelato and stressed from having nothing to do, we eat cold cereal for dinner. By 8:00 p.m., it's clear that we won't be hearing back from Mendez tonight. It's a warm and enticing Saturday evening, so we agree that I'll walk Vinn the couple miles back to her place.

We're not far from the DePaul campus when we're startled by the ringing of my phone. The ringtone tells me who it is, so before answering we find a quiet place under a tree away from traffic and I put the call on speaker. I barely punch the button to answer when a string of profanity fills the air around us.

"The next time you decide that you've solved a case, take it to the papers and leave the detecting to professionals," Mendez screams. "I asked if you were sure and you told me yes."

"I didn't exactly say—" I begin.

"As far as we can tell," Mendez interrupts, "and my people are pretty confident on this, there are exactly three Ethan Lots in this country. One is on a ventilator in Florida and has been since he turned eighty-four five years ago. One has been in jail in California on an assault charge for the past seven months. The third guy is thirty-four years old and actually lives in Rockford so he's within spitting distance of Chicago. Imagine his surprise when ten cops break down his door and charge in, nearly knocking his wheelchair over. And yes, he also has an ironclad alibi for the time of the murder so he didn't roll himself into the crime scene."

Vinn and I sit in shocked silence. I feel I have to say something. "Mendez, I'm so sorry," I say, and I mean it.

"Screw you," he yells before hanging up, or at least that's what I assume the long string of mostly unfamiliar words he shouted mean based on context. I'm sure he wished he had made the call from the station to get the satisfaction of slamming down the handset.

We stay under the tree, absorbing the news for several minutes, each lost in our own thoughts. I finally get the nerve up to look Vinn in the eye, and we stare at each other waiting for the other to be the first to speak.

"Oops," Vinn finally says.

Her reaction causes me to snicker and soon the tension is broken as we both dissolve in a fit of giggles. I wipe tears from my eyes, offer Vinn a hand to bring her to her feet. We turn around and begin walking back to my place.

Knowing we may have a long night ahead of us, both Vinn and I head to the kitchen as soon as we cross my threshold, she to blend beans she'll use to brew a strong coffee that'll have her bouncing off the walls, me to dig through my cabinet searching for where I last stored the matcha I sourced from the Uji region of Japan. Even though matcha's fine green powder boasts one of tea's greatest concentration of caffeine, it's still only about half that of coffee. It's very high in I-theanine, though, which reduces stress and improves cognitive function and clarity. I may fall asleep before Vinn does tonight, but hopefully not before I contribute some profound insights with total calm.

"So what did we miss? Where did we go wrong?" Vinn asks as we get settled. "I have a hard time believing that we were completely off base with our decoding. I'm not ready to abandon the telephone keypad idea quite yet. It just made perfect sense. Still does."

"Obviously not perfect," I retort. "But I know what you mean. What are the odds that we came up with a name if we did it all wrong? Do you think the cops missed someone in their search or maybe he's in their system with an alternative spelling?"

"Doubtful. When the lead we provided turned sour, that made Mendez look bad. I'm sure he tried everything he could think of, or that we would think of, to save face. No, Mal, we need to admit to our own error and give up on Ethan Lots."

"I'll concede that the name is a dead end, but not that our methodology was wrong," I reply. "I'm not ready to throw out the phone cipher idea yet either, so let's start from scratch, go back and look at each step to see if we turned left when we should have turned right?"

Vinn sighs and makes a point of taking a large sip of her coffee. "Sure, I guess. As a scientist I'm never quick to discard a process even where it doesn't result in the answer I expected. We do it over several times before going back to the beginning. Just keep in mind that this is your idea, so if I burn through this coffee sticking to the telephone code theory and we're no closer to a solution by morning, it'll be on you."

"Fair enough," I respond, although I'm not sure I mean it. We first check that we read the phone keypads correctly the first time, then switch words to check the other's work. Even though we were both certain that wasn't where the error lies, it's still disappointing to come up with 'Ethan Lots' again.

"I'm almost relieved that we didn't discover that we were just sloppy," I tell Vinn. "Now let's work on the assumption that 'Ethan Lots' is what we were supposed to get. One thought is that whoever's behind the puzzle gave it two solutions, just to make us look foolish if we focused on the wrong one. Let's not go there yet because it was hard enough to come up with this one.

Is it possible that 'Ethan Lots' isn't the end result, but an intermediary step? That there's more we need to do with that name?"

Vinn slaps her own forehead. "Of course. We're morons, Mal. We were so excited to see that name come up that we forgot about the second sentence of the puzzle. 'Retreat and move the beginning of hell, or all shall be lost.' We didn't either retreat or move hell and look where it got us."

"Retreat. Move backward," I muse. "We tried to go through the alphabet backward and ended up with nonsense."

"Stick with the plan here," Vinn tells me. "That was for a different part of the puzzle. What do we get if we reverse 'Ethan Lots?'"

I write it out. "'Stolnahte'? Not sure that helps."

"Let's keep the words separately. Do it that way," Vinn suggests.

"'Nathe Stol.' Sounds better, but I'll guess there are even fewer people with that name than with 'Ethan Lots.'"

Vinn says nothing but is grinning widely as she sits back in her chair. I know that look.

"Dammit, Vinn. You've got it. Tell me," I say irritably.

"Look at the rest of that sentence, Winters," she says patronizingly. "What's at the beginning of hell?"

Vinn is never more annoying than when she knows something that I don't, especially the enjoyment she gets watching me squirm under her gaze. I'm about to throw a pillow at her when it hits me. So obvious that it's embarrassing not to have seen it earlier.

"The beginning of 'hell' is the letter 'h,'" I say. "So we move it from the first name to the last. So not 'Nathe Stol.' We get 'Nate Stohl.' I may be slow Vinn, but I got there in the end. Before we tell Mendez—"

"Way ahead of you," Vinn says as she turns her laptop in my direction. "Guess who lives less than three miles away."

"Great! What do you say we pay Mr. Stohl a visit in the morning?" I take two steps toward the bedroom.

"It's morning now," Vinn notes. "1:32 a.m. to be exact. And I'm so full of caffeine I won't sleep. There's no time like the present. Grab your shoes and let's go."

TWENTY

Going isn't as easy as getting shod and walking out the door. With a real possibility of meeting and confronting a murderer, some further preparation is prudent. For me, that means trying to remember which secret compartment in my kitchen holds my revolver of choice, while for Vinn it means adding a few sharp implements she stores here to those she carries on her as a matter of course. I have a couple of sets of dark clothing for just such an occasion and loan the extra one to Vinn. We debate renting a Zipcar but veto the idea. In the event something goes south, we don't want our movements to be traceable.

It's well after 2:00 a.m. by the time we set off on foot for what we hope is the residence of one Nate Stohl in the western reaches of the Logan Square neighborhood. Vinn's proclamation that his home is "less than three miles" from my own is accurate, but not by much. By keeping a good pace, it'll still take us nearly forty-five minutes to get there, more if we choose to avoid streets where we'll be clearly visible to any passersby. Even at this time of morning, there are enough cars and dog walkers around to make me wonder who these people are and what's so important that being up and out is more important than sleep. I assume there aren't many others wandering the streets sharing our chore of stalking a killer.

"It says here that if we continue straight west from his place we'll run into the birthplace of Walt Disney," I remark to Vinn as I check the GPS on my phone.

"I doubt they'll be open now or happy to see us," Vinn grumbles in response. "If you see an all-night sushi place let me know, otherwise just shut your trap for a while."

She's right, it's time to put on our game faces and take seriously what we might encounter once we get there. With each step, our experience looking for Ethan Lots raises doubts in my mind about whether this is just another false lead. As we draw near, I'm convinced that there's a fifty percent chance that we'll be waking up a grandmother or a family with young children. I also start to worry that grandma may have a shotgun on her nightstand.

Our plan, if you can call it that, is to casually walk by the home to evaluate points of access or observation, ideally an open first-floor bedroom window, where we could do a minimal reconnaissance before deciding on how to approach Stohl. The trees on his block, however, are too skinny and far apart to allow any sort of stealth should we need it. The houses are mostly small, many only one story, and are close together, increasing the odds of being sighted and reported by a neighbor with insomnia. We retreat to a school we had just passed and crouch down beneath the shadows of a slide.

Vinn pulls up a picture of the house on her phone. "It should be about a third of the way down the block on the north side of the street," she reports. "Single-family home, so at the very least we can see if his name is on the mailbox. But we really didn't come all this way in the middle of the night and arm ourselves just to do that, did we? If we do no more than pass on the name and address to Mendez, what are the odds that he'll act on it after the Lots fiasco?"

"I've assumed all along that we're going to break in, Vinn," I say. "After we check the name on the mailbox. It's what we do once inside that we need to discuss."

"Once we close his door behind us we're all in," she responds. "And whoever's in that house has the legal right to shoot to kill. First thing we do is find and disable any and all residents to take that threat away. And it's not like we can do that without waking them up, so we might as well take our time and have a look around afterward to see what we can find. Whether or not we find something significant, a serious discussion with Stohl is in order when we're done browsing. Mal, there's nothing I want more than to bring this thing to a close and to shut the door on any more of this cloak and dagger crap. In short, we do whatever it takes to make that happen."

"Got it." I check to make sure I remembered zip ties for the hands and feet and rags for the mouth, then instinctively pat myself down to feel where every weapon I brought should be. We crawl out from under the slide and move swiftly toward our target. Vinn takes the front steps two at a time while I run down the gangway between houses to investigate the back. I rejoin her in less than a minute.

"The back door appears to lead to the kitchen, but there's a bedroom right there. If he's a light sleeper, he'll hear us working on the lock."

Vinn nods. "More bad news," she whispers as she points to the front door to reveal a mail slot in the door. "No mailbox, no name."

She immediately gets to work on the lock, a cheap brand not worth buying at any price and no match for her prime set of picks, and within seconds is turning the knob agonizingly slowly. She frowns as she meets minor resistance while pushing the door open but continues. With a sigh of relief and a feeling of anxiety, we pull our balaclavas over our faces and step inside.

The first thing we see is the cause of the resistance, a pile of mail on the floor beneath the slot. Not a good sign. It's only seconds later that a familiar odor reaches my nose. Vinn obviously smells it as well.

"Shit, shit, shit," she mutters, mimicking Mendez, as we rush down the narrow hallway, ignoring all precautions. We pass one bedroom with its door wide open, which at a glance reveals it was being used for storage. The door of the bedroom adjacent to the kitchen is closed. The stench here is overwhelming. For a moment we do nothing. We both know what we'll see on the other side of the door and are in no hurry to view it.

I finally reach around Vinn and use my knuckles to gently push on the door, releasing a wave of stagnant, pungent air. I move behind her and look over her shoulder at the mutilated and decaying body of a man spread out over the bed. For a moment neither of us speaks.

Vinn finally breaks the silence. "Sorry to intrude," she says to the room. "Nate Stohl, I presume?"

As our eyes adjust to the dim light, details of the scene begin to emerge. It doesn't take long to recognize the detailed staging reminiscent of the first three murders. Having expected to encounter Brandon Mills' killer, I'm surprised and confused to instead find another victim. Were we wrong about the message of the puzzle we were so proud to solve?

Vinn speaks as if she's reading my mind. "This doesn't make sense," she says calmly. "I was so sure we were being given the identity of the first killer, not another victim. Are we being led on a chase, where we're given a coded clue as to who the next victim will be and have to race to get to them before the killer does?"

By this time, I've had time for first impressions to set in. "That would be my guess," I tell her, "except for the reference to Mills and the fact that you were just given that puzzle about thirty hours ago. You've seen enough dead bodies. How long do you think this guy's been gone?"

"A lot longer than that," she admits. "Okay, it doesn't make sense to stand here and postulate. We have several hours before sunrise and need to be long gone by then. Let's hustle and see what we can find."

We step back into the kitchen and put medical gloves on our hands. I find plastic food bags under the sink, which we slip over our shoes. I use my handkerchief to wipe down any surface that we may have touched, including the front doorknob. Vinn meets me in the foyer and stoops down to examine the stack of mail.

"Well, the good news, if you can call it that, is that all of this mail is addressed to Nate or Nathan Stohl. So we got that right." She carefully picks up several envelopes by the edges and turns her flashlight on them. "Some of these were postmarked five or six days ago. Local, so even assuming poor mail service he hasn't collected his mail since Wednesday at the latest. Do me a favor," she asks as she brings one piece closer to her eyes.

"Look up 'We Care Health Partners.'They're in Skokie."

I pull out my phone and type slowly, my gloves making precision difficult. The third entry down appears to be the company's website. "It looks like they're a health care supplier. Not medical equipment so much as office furnishings, home health necessities like bed rails, post-operative bandages, bed pads and adult diapers, home blood pressure kits, and the like. A lot of information here, so we'll have to look into it in more detail later. Why do you ask?" A thought strikes me before she answers. "Wait, are you saying—"

"It appears to be a paystub. Yeah, he probably worked there. And if I recall our two lists accurately, the first killer's occupation, the one opposite the CEO as victim, would be a care aide, correct? Do you remember what the fourth job on the victim list is?"

I don't and it takes me awhile to bring up the information on my phone. "Victim number four would be a salesperson. Killer, a craftsman. Sorry, crafts person."

"Are you thinking what I'm thinking?" Vinn asks. "We need to pin down this guy's job quickly, take pictures of the scene, and scram."

Ten minutes is enough to know that there's no information in either the tiny living room or spare bedroom that will give us what we want. We skip the bathroom and kitchen, which brings us back to the bedroom with the body.

"We need to risk the light," I tell Vinn and she flips the switch as we enter the room. I begin taking pictures on my phone while Vinn provides commentary.

"Salesperson items first," she states. "See that case in his hand? We can't risk opening it, but I recognize it from Antiques Roadshow on tv. It's a traveling salesman's case from the 40s or 50s. Probably has brushes or fence samples or something in there. Get a shot of the encyclopedias on top of the dresser, and the vacuum cleaner in the corner."

"Train ticket sticking out of his shirt pocket," I add. I check my phone. "Time's growing short. Move on to the crafts. Hopefully Mendez will let us back in here so that we can give it more time."

"Okay. I think the case can count on that side as well. Expert craftsmanship. A couple woodworking tools resting on the pillow. Victim is holding a leather wallet, probably handmade. We need to think of crafts outside of just wood."

We hear a dog barking and a shout. Vinn immediately shuts off the light. "Damn it," she curses. "That's all we're going to get for now."

"Not yet. I have a hunch. Use your flashlight. You look in his closet, I'll do the drawers. See if you can find scrubs."

Vinn strikes out, but it takes me less than a minute to locate several pairs at the bottom of a drawer. Just as I'm closing it back up, Vinn whispers excitedly, holding a book up from the nightstand.

"Look at this," she says. "'Effective Sales Tips from Experts Who Know.' I see where you're going. You think Stohl was a home health care aide, thus the scrubs, who moved or wants to move into sales of the stuff he used. A natural progression, probably the potential for more money and fewer sponge baths."

"Exactly," I reply. "So Broden, or whoever's behind these, did a twofer. Stohl as an aide killed Mills, then got silenced as the fourth victim, a salesperson. There's a certain amount of ingenuity in that."

"And brutality," Vinn reminds me. "It's an intriguing theory, but one that will have to await better proof than a couple pairs of scrubs and a book. For now we need to get our butts out of here."

Rather than move, though, Vinn remains in place, lost in thought. "Mal, I know this will sound insensitive in the presence of Stohl's body, but can we look at this development as a good thing? For us, if not for him? We're only involved in this mess to find out who killed my boss's brother-in-law and to get him off my back. We just did that, and I'm sure he'll be thrilled to learn that the killer was on the receiving end of what he dished out. We can finally retire as unofficial investigators and start that new, quieter, and safer life we've been striving for. Leave the ultimate solution for Mendez and his crew to figure out."

In the rush of affirming our solution to the puzzle, and the morbid fascination with the new murder scene, the fact that we had accomplished our mission never occurred to me. A sudden wave of calmness unexpectedly descends upon me.

"You're absolutely right," I tell Vinn, taking her by the hand. "Of course we'll need to lead Mendez to the conclusion that Stohl killed Mills, but that shouldn't take much doing. And maybe a little prompt will get them to discover the body sooner rather than later."

We exit through the rear door, listen for any evidence of human activity, then slide quietly into the alley and head for home and a date with our pillows.

TWENTY ONE.

I'm rarely one to sleep late, even when getting to bed at 5:30 a.m. as Vinn and I did this morning, so I'm surprised when I fumble for my phone in a semi-comatose state and notice that it's after 10:00. It's a call I expected to come much later in the day.

"Mornin' Mendez," I mumble as I watch Vinn roll over and pull my pillow over her head. "You working Sundays now?"

"Where were you last night?" he roars without preamble, forcing me to hold the receiver end away from my ear. I hear muffled cursing from the other side of the bed.

"Not that it's any business of yours, but Vinn and I worked late into the night here at my place on that puzzle. We're pretty sure we solved it for real this time but given what happened last time thought we'd do a little more follow-up before giving you another name to check out. That's on the agenda for later today after we catch up on our sleep. Why do you ask?"

"Someone called 311 early this morning to report a noxious odor coming from a house on the near northwest side. About ninety minutes ago a patrol car found time to go check it out." He pauses, voice rising when he returns. "Funny thing is, they had to be right up next to the back door to catch even the slightest hint of a smell. Funny thing number two: the call came from a pay phone. Who in the hell uses a pay phone these days and do you know how hard it is just to find one? And why be anonymous just to report an odor? An odor you probably wouldn't notice unless you were either looking for it or were inside the house. You wouldn't happen to know anything about that would you?"

I don't make any attempt to keep the irritation out of my voice. If anything, I try to accentuate it. "Mendez, what's this about? Does this have anything to do with... Vinn, what's that name we came up with?" My question is rhetorical and for Mendez's benefit only, since I well know the name and Vinn has managed to fall back into a deep slumber. I feign reading. "Nathan Stohl?"

A moment of intense silence is broken by the loudest shouting I've ever heard through a phone. "You need to get here right now! And I mean now! I'm sending a car." The connection ends. I go to the kitchen to start up the coffee maker and to put on water for tea before waking Vinn.

The poor rookie cop who was tasked with picking us up tried to play tough but got flustered and backed down when Vinn told her in her most professorial voice that she needed to "do her face" and that it would take a few minutes. In reality she went back to bed after getting dressed to sneak in a few more minutes of sleep. Vinn doesn't wear makeup. Once the "few minutes" neared twenty, I pulled my reluctant and crabby partner out of bed and we made our way to the squad car.

It takes significantly less time to be driven to Stohl's house than to walk. Figuring it would add to Mendez's suspicions if we remained quiet, we ask the cop questions about where we were going and why, followed by mumbles of complaint just loud enough for her to hear. Once convinced we'd played the role of ignorant and offended citizens long enough, we lapse into silence.

Mendez is pacing inside the crime scene tape blocking off the front yard as we approach. He signs us in then immediately pulls us aside. While offering no apologies for his attitude during the phone call, he's now decided to treat us civilly, which can only mean that he wants something from us. Luckily we came prepared.

"The medical examiner has the room, which gives us time for you to explain how you came up with that name," he says. I start to say something but he holds his hand up to stop me. "All I'm going to tell you now is what you've probably guessed already. Yes, there's a body in there and yes, his name is—was—Nathan Stohl."

Vinn's decoding notes from last night are on her laptop, which she didn't bring for fear that Mendez would seize it, which leaves my nearly indecipherable handwritten scribbles to show him. I leave it to Vinn and her analytical mind to briefly but completely describe our thought processes that led to the correct answer to the puzzle, being careful to also express surprise that Stohl is the victim, not a captured killer. She also notes that she went to her members' page of Puzzlers Anonymous and verified that he wasn't a current member.

"I guess whoever's behind this exhausted the list of members he had a grudge against and has moved to the general public," she tells Mendez, citing the conclusion we made in the early hours as if it were something that just occurred to her.

Mendez remains quiet and attentive as Vinn brilliantly sums up in five minutes what took us half the night to discern. "It all seems so simple and obvious the way you put it now," he says. "But we've had some pretty sharp minds working on it and they didn't get anywhere close." He takes in a deep breath and lets it out slowly, closing his eyes in the process. When he opens them, he looks troubled.

"Before we go in, I guess I'll reveal one more thing since you'll see it anyway," he continues. "The murder scene tracks the last three. It's staged. I wasn't in there long enough yet to really note any details or to see if what's there matches with your two list theory. I assume it does and, if so, all hell will break loose with the department brass. No more denying the existence of a serial killer, and the fact that this is only number four out of a possible ten will cause panic, or at the very least increase the heat and pressure on subordinates like me. They'll demand answers. I probably don't need to say that this isn't the type of case we normally see, such as gangbangers with guns and jealous spouses using kitchen knives.

"Against my better judgment I'm granting you access civvies just don't get. In return you need to reaffirm that you'll give me everything, tell me every notion you have, no matter how absurd it may seem. Because absurdity appears to be the new normal with what we have here."

I wish I had pressed the "record" button on my phone as he spoke because it's a near certainty that somewhere down the road we'll need to remind him of what he just said. Both Vinn and I express our agreement. Before we have time to ask anything else, Mendez looks up at a signal from the front door. The medical examiner's ready for him.

"Like last time," he growls, our new relationship as pals and associates already forgotten, "you can look from the door but no touching. This is our scene first." With that, we follow him into the house. Vinn and I don't don gloves and make sure we touch various surfaces as we enter to explain any fingerprints I may have missed wiping away during our earlier visit.

The mail that was piled inside the front door has been removed, perhaps bagged as evidence for some rookie cop to pour over. The house looks totally different in the daylight and its details much easier to take in. Discounting the havoc that having a dozen cops searching every room and dusting for prints on virtually every surface can cause, it's clear that Stohl was a tidy, well-organized person. The small kitchen is being used as a staging area for all of the activity but to his credit Mendez makes sure that we have a spot to stand in the doorway to the bedroom. The medical examiner is still there packing up. I don't know her name but recognize her from one of the prior scenes. If age is an indication of experience, she's well versed in dead bodies. She must be in her eighties.

"I'll need to get him on the table to be sure, but initial indications are suffocation," she tells Mendez in response to his question. "Be pretty difficult to breathe with this stuck down your throat." She pulls out an evidence bag containing a yellowish ball inside, some of which has flaked off to the bottom of the bag.

"My guess is leather balm or paste," she explains. "Used to condition leather goods to remain pliable, such as that wallet in the victim's left hand." She gestures to the body. "Was balled up, compressed, and somehow made it into his mouth and down his throat about two inches, far enough to block air intake. Fibers inside his nostrils would seem to indicate that the killer wasn't taking any chances and held a pillow or something similar over his face. Again, all speculation at this point but you guys always insist."

Vinn and I move aside to let her pass then slide further inside the room while Mendez is examining the body. If he notices, he doesn't say a word. I'm not sure how long we'll be allowed here, so I let Vinn focus on the scene while I begin taking pictures, taking more time to get both broad views of the scene and up-close photos of the various elements than I had last night.

Mendez finally seems to remember our presence, sees me preoccupied with my camera, and turns to Vinn. "I know you have a good eye for detail," he tells her. "Work with me here. Start with the craftsman references."

Vinn has to pretend she's seeing all of this for the first time, so she takes a few moments to look around before responding. "As the medical examiner just mentioned, the wallet. That's not one you buy at Target. It looks to be real leather, and note the fine stitching, probably done by hand. Is there anything inside?"

Mendez carefully extracts the billfold and opens it up. It must not be the one Stohl used because there's no driver's license in the plastic window, no credit cards in the slots, and no family photos anywhere. It appears to be empty until Mendez pulls a business card out of the flaps where money is usually kept. It's the card for the Etsy seller specializing in leather goods who made the wallet. No surprise and also no help, although she's likely to be surprised with a pointless long-distance call from Chicago cops desperate for a lead.

"Of course the woodworking tools," Vinn adds. "A plane, sander, square, tape measure, chisel, hand file. I don't think you need to read anything into the fact that they're all hand tools, not power tools. They were only meant to make a point, not to be used. Then there's the balm used to choke the victim. Enough said on that.

"The killer didn't stick to one type of craft," she continues, "again probably because crafts person is such a broad term to begin with and the specialty tools once you get past the basics can be expensive. Cost may be why all of these except for the wallet are both generic and popular. Also not as easy to trace as if, say, they bought fine rawhide."

"Yeah, I'm debating whether to waste time on tracing purchases of this crap," Mendez says without enthusiasm. "Touch all bases."

"From what I can tell whoever's behind this is highly intelligent and cunning," I add. "They'll have thought about that already."

Mendez acts as if he didn't hear me. "Is that it?" he asks Vinn.

"The sample case is vintage, very well made, so it could count," she replies. "And if you want to try to track something, try that or the billfold. But no need to force a label on it because it definitely fits the salesperson category. Can you open it up?"

He does. Inside are eight small women's shoes of different styles, each neatly nestled in its own cutout. From the looks, my guess would be the case is from the 1940s or 1950s, although I'm no expert in women's fashion and Vinn is the last woman on earth to ask about something like this. In another setting at another time it would be fascinating to study but not now. Does the fact that there are shoes instead of brushes or makeup inside the case mean anything or am I overthinking?

Vinn methodically ticks off the vacuum cleaner, train ticket, and a few other items we didn't notice in our rush to get out of the house last night. Mendez takes notes, I take pictures. Mendez is about ready to kick us out when I remember an item from our prior visit.

"Detective, there's one more behind you," I tell him. "The World Book encyclopedia. If I recall my history, they were sold door-to-door at one time." In truth, I only know that from doing research on my phone on the walk back home in the early hours. As Mendez retrieves it, a hunch hits me hard. "Would you mind laying it on the clean part of the bed over here? And may I?"

He gives me an odd look and appears ready to tell me to go to hell, then shrugs his shoulders and does as I asked, which only shows how desperate he is to resolve these matters and move on with this life and career without Vinn and I in the picture.

The book is the "S" volume and is about two inches thick. I curse whoever left it for not selecting the "X" volume. I start paging through it quickly, two sets of eyes watching me carefully. It doesn't take long to strike paydirt. At about eighty pages in, stuck firmly into the crease of the binder between two pages, is a folded piece of newsprint.

"Don't touch that!" Mendez cries out as I start to reach for it. He steps between myself and the book, forcing me to move around him to see what he's doing and to get a clear view to film his actions. He pulls a tweezers out of his breast pocket, carefully plucking the paper out before resting it on the open book. We can now see that it's a clipping from a newspaper. Using the same tweezers, he unfolds one corner, then the other, then lifts the near end up and out to reveal the article.

Vinn and I both gasp as we read the byline. It's a piece written by Maggie Wong, the journalism student whose name we raised earlier as an implied threat to get Mendez to give us access in return for our agreement not to break the story to her. As a freshman, she assisted us in a prior investigation by writing an article on Chinese immigration meant to lure out a suspected killer. This is a copy of that article.

Mendez carefully refolds it and deposits it in an evidence bag. As he does so, Vinn grabs my arm hard.

"My god, Mal. Look at the entry in the book."

The book is opened to a page describing the Salvation Army. At first nothing clicks, but when it does the blood must drain from my face. I pull up my phone and clumsily work to bring up my notes on the two lists to confirm what I think I know. What I find is the very definition of horror. Mendez is looking at us with question marks in his eyes. I have trouble finding the words.

"The young woman who wrote that article is a student we know," I stammered. "A budding journalist. The page where this article was placed is about the Salvation Army, a charitable organization. The two lists, number six. The killer is a charity worker, the victim a journalist.

"Mendez, this is a threat. If we don't stop whoever this is, they're going to kill Maggie."

TWENTY TWO

"This all happened a couple of years ago, before we knew you," I explain to Mendez. "We got involved in a matter involving Chinese triads. Maggie started snooping around chasing rumors of a violent murder in the Asian community and planned to write articles that would have drawn the attention of some very dangerous individuals. The only way to prevent harm to her was to enlist her help as a journalist but under strict supervision and by surrounding her with protection. Even with those precautions, it still almost wasn't enough."

I pause and Vinn uses the opportunity to take over the narrative. "The point is, Detective," she says, "that when following what she saw as a hot lead that would add to her credibility as a journalist, Maggie didn't use the best judgment when it came to her safety. I doubt that's changed. Filling her in on the danger she's facing will have the opposite effect of what we intend. She'll want to run to the action instead of fleeing from it. She needs someone to watch over her until this is over."

"And this is your way of asking for the department's help?" Mendez responds. "I understand what you're saying and I can ask, but it's not something the department normally does. Even with a credible threat from an ex-boyfriend or husband, the standard response is to tell the woman to use the court system and get an order of protection. That policy has resulted in more than a few preventable homicides." Mendez sounds like he takes personal offense in such matters. "Here, where all we have is the suggestion of a threat from a news clipping stuck in a book, from an unknown source, inside an investigation the department would rather pretend isn't happening? Fat chance. Like I said, I'll ask, but you'd better have a backup plan in place."

I hold back on some choice words. Vinn does not, and from what I can tell made up a few new ones. Mendez takes the abuse calmly, letting her vent. We all know this isn't his fault. Once she runs out of breath, he speaks softly.

"Our best bet is to catch the bastard before he gets to number six," he says. "Unless number five has already happened and we don't know about it yet, we should have a little bit of time. As you know, in serial killings each scene provides more information and draws us closer to a solution. And he's probably made a mistake we haven't caught on to yet. What I can promise you is that I'll fill you in on everything we know. I'll send you copies of all reports and the murder book on a regular basis. I'd bring in the FBI if I thought it would do any good. But for right now, see what you can do for that girl."

That was both his attempt at comfort and his way of dismissing us from the scene. I gently take Vinn by the elbow and lead her through the house and on out to the street. Her anger is still palpable. No amount of food will work to calm her down this time.

"Call Chuck," she demands before we're ten feet away from the crime scene tape. Chuck helped pull together an unusual but highly competent team the last time Maggie needed protection. He has inroads to an unseen populace with undeniable skill sets that most of us don't even know exist. They're a valuable resource and just what we need.

"Hey, Chuck," I say, relieved that he answered. "Yeah, well, same to you. No, nothing like that this time. Do you remember Maggie? I know, how could you forget? Unfortunately she's in danger again, this time through no fault of her own. We haven't even told her about it yet, we just found out five minutes ago, but it's significant and urgent. Any chance of getting the old team together?"

"Might be tough, Mal," he responds. "You know that these people drift with the wind, change names on a regular basis, and half may have moved on or are in jail for all I know. All I can promise is to put the word out. They'll want to know at least a few details. Who are they up against, what should they be on the lookout for, what's the pay, and for how long?"

I was afraid he would ask those very questions. "In order your answers are 'We don't know,' 'It's anybody's guess,' 'we need to get back to you,' and 'indefinitely,'" I tell him.

"Well thanks for narrowing that down," he says flatly. "Mal, I care for this young woman too so I'll do my best to bait the hook, but we'll need more than that to reel them in. I'll get back to you in a couple of hours with an update."

I pass the information on to Vinn, who nods sadly but acknowledges that she expected exactly that response. Before either of us would take on a job, we needed as many details as possible for our own safety, so we can't expect others to act on less.

We walk on slowly, each of us lost in thought. Vinn finally breaks the silence. "On the one hand, we should be elated that we can identify Mill's killer and get my boss off my back. We could close the book on the investigation and walk away. Except..."

"Except now Maggie's been drawn into it," I say when Vinn goes silent. "Last night was the first night in years I slept without nightmares, and I woke up this morning happy, thinking this would be the day we bury our pasts for good. It was a false hope, wasn't it? I feel responsible for the threat against Maggie and we can't walk away yet."

"Exactly," she says. "We're stuck. And I can't decide, Mal. Do you think it's better to tell Maggie or to keep her ignorant of the threat? If we spill, she'll want details we can't give her without Mendez finding out. He'll get in trouble for the leak with his bosses who'll force him to cut off the flow of information, which makes it less likely we'll stop the killer quickly and more likely he'll go after Maggie before we catch him. And she'll put herself in the middle of it by conducting her own investigation regardless of what we tell her. But if we don't tell her and something happens which might have been prevented if she knew to take precautions, I'll never forgive myself."

"You already answered your own question," I reply. "She has to know. Besides, no matter how surreptitious the surveillance, she'll catch on to it at some point, get suspicious and nervous, and call the cops or, worse, Jenkins. If we're putting together a team, she needs to be in the huddle."

Vinn says nothing but wraps her arm in mine as we walk. Knowing her as I do, I'm sure her thoughts are the same as mine. Within the next several days or weeks, someone is going to die. It's up to us to determine who that is.

I haven't kept in touch with Maggie since we wrapped up the matter in which she played a central role, nor seen her around campus, so I'm stunned at the appearance of the woman sitting next to me in Vinn's office on Monday. Gone is the baby face of the young freshman. In its place are the features of a composed and mature woman, an air of confidence and assertiveness replacing the naïve enthusiasm of her former self. At least until Vinn filled her in on why she was called to an urgent meeting first thing on a Monday morning. Now she appears to be withdrawing within herself with a mixture of disbelief and fear, but—true to the Maggie I knew previously—tempered with more than a little excitement at the prospect of a good story.

We give her a few minutes to process the information. Eventually her eyes clear as she looks first at Vinn, then to me. She starts to speak before pausing to clear her throat, then tries again.

"What exactly are my options here? And on a scale of one to a hundred, what's the level of threat?"

Now isn't the time to sugarcoat reality. "We have to assume it's one hundred," I tell her, "due to the fact that there have already been a series of killings, the implied threat contained in the note, and how far away we seem to be from pinning this on anyone. Maggie, Vinn and I are giving this investigation everything we've got, as are the cops, but I'd be lying if I said that we're anywhere close to solving it. This threat is very, very real."

"The police aren't offering you protection," Vinn adds. "We tried to assemble a team to watch over you like the last time, but we just found out an hour ago that the best they can do is one or two at a time, and even then it'll be occasional at best. Which means we only see one viable option for you. You need to disappear until this psycho is caught. Do you have someone you can stay with for a while? Preferably as far away from Chicago as possible? Mal and I can make sure that your teachers will let you manage your classes remotely so that you don't fall behind in school."

Maggie's look of defiance frightens me, as do the words that follow. "I can't run from every nutcase that emerges," she says firmly. "Journalists receive death threats all the time, it's a sign that we're doing something right. Our job isn't just to report but to occasionally stir the pot. If I flee the city and hole up somewhere now, do you know what kind of reputation I'll get? Then what are my chances of getting a job after graduation if it becomes known that I lack a backbone? I'm the editor of the school paper, for god's sake. I need to set an example and running away isn't it."

"Maggie—" Vinn begins.

"No, Professor," Maggie interrupts. "It's my decision to make and I've made it. But that doesn't mean that I'm going to allow myself to be an easy target. I'm not stupid. Tell me what I need to know, what I need to watch out for."

"For the record, Maggie," Vinn says solemnly, "Both of us think you're making a mistake. We'll continue to try to find additional security for you but it simply won't be enough. Listen closely to what we know to date, and there's no shame in you changing your decision."

Vinn proceeds to brief her on the four murders, intentionally stressing the most gruesome details and turning to me from time to time to add my own thoughts.

I follow her strategy and even exaggerate and amplify where appropriate while still maintaining accuracy. We owe Maggie that much.

"So what you're saying," Maggie says when we're finished, "is that if your theory about the two lists is sound, and I have to admit I think you're on to something, my attacker would be a charity worker?"

"Well, yes," I respond, "but that doesn't mean they'll be in uniform, be carrying a collection box, or be otherwise identifiable when they approach you. From what we know, it's likely that the killings are done without any reference to the two list idea and then staged after the fact. You may never see them coming."

"I'll be careful," she states. "And I'll be okay, I promise. Imagine what a story this will make once it's over! I may even get national distribution."

Before Vinn and I can say another word, Maggie rises from her chair, utters a quick "thanks for the head's up," and rushes off to class. Vinn looks crestfallen.

"I can't think of anything else we could have said or done," I say, trying to mollify her, as well as convince myself. "And you have to admit that it went exactly as we thought it would."

"Damn her," Vinn mutters. "Mal, we need to catch this monster and do it soon. I don't know how or what else we can do, but we need to do something. Fast. I won't rest easy until we do."

With that, there's nothing left to say. We each have classes ourselves, and hurry to get to them on time.

TWENTY THREE

Mendez was true to his word and sent over copies of the coroner's report, his notes, and crime scene photos. While they do fill in a significant number of details about the murders of both Stohl and Mills, none of them are either helpful or in the overall picture relevant. Vinn reaches the same conclusion as she pages through the paperwork in her office between classes.

She sighs with exasperation. "At this point, Mal, I don't really care what the precise time or cause of death is, or what year the shoes in that sales case were manufactured. We're at the stage now where the two lists idea is more fact than theory, so I don't give a shit about details included to support the idea or the minutia that piles up and obscures the real focus right now. I don't even want to waste time looking for a motive. The only thing we need to do from here on is to zero in on who, not why or where or how. Find the person behind this, eliminate the threat, and start living normal lives."

"I'm with you one hundred percent," I tell her, and I mean it. "Although I'm not sure I agree that the thoroughness of the cops is a bad thing."

"You've looked through this, right?" she asks, gesturing toward the piles of paper on her desk. "Was there anything in there that referenced fingerprints, or reports of a suspicious car parked nearby, or a neighbor with security cameras pointed at the street? Anything at all that suggests the existence of a possible clue that could lead to the identity of this bastard? Or even put us in the ballpark, such as the force required to stuff that crap down the victim's throat means that the killer was likely a man?"

"Not a thing," I admit. "Ultimately, though, all of that detail you scorn can in the long term produce a profile that will put the cops on the right trail. I understand that takes time we don't have. We need a shortcut. We also need to keep in mind that the people that are doing the actual killing are only tools of whoever we're really after. Mendez aside, the police aren't looking past finding the people who are physically present at the scene doing whatever it is that makes the victims die. Given six months or a year and several more deaths, and the slow but steady methodology of the cops may pay off. Catching those people is in their book a win. To prevent any further deaths we need to find the mastermind. Identifying a strange car may lead to the killer who then provides evidence against this person, whoever it is. But my guess is that they have no direct contact with whoever's pulling their strings and won't pop out a name."

"And in the meantime Maggie dies," Vinn snarls. "So to summarize, we're once more on our own. We need to take those shortcuts you suggest, do things that maybe the cops can't and probably wouldn't sanction. Things that may even get us arrested if we're not careful. Do you agree and are you on board with this?"

"Absolutely," I say. "At least I think so. What exactly are you proposing?"

"We're not completely without a starting point. If I were to put a gun to your head and tell you to either give me a name of the serial killer or I'd pull the trigger, what would you say?"

I take a few seconds to get past the disturbing image Vinn just presented but see right away where she's heading. "Broden, of course. We're as certain as we can be that he put that puzzle that led to the latest victim in your packet. If that's true, he's either behind each of these murders or acted on behalf of who is. The cops wouldn't consider your conversation with and impression of him as enough to even pull him in for questioning. That doesn't mean we can't do some questioning of our own."

"Exactly," Vinn responds. "And don't forget that there are the other two members of the Terrible Trio that Leo's girlfriend identified. We should trust her instincts. They may or may not be involved but could have information useful to us." She pauses as she considers some unknown thought. "Not sure if we should go after them before or after Broden."

"Slow down there, Professor," I caution. "I know we're under a time constraint here, but we're getting ahead of ourselves. Since you're fond of hypotheticals, suppose Broden or either of the other two walked into your door right now. What would you ask them, or how would you handle them?"

Vinn scowls at me before leaning back in her chair to stare at the ceiling. "I know, you're right. That must be why I keep you around. Rushing ahead unprepared is worse than not doing anything at all and equally unproductive. What do you suggest? And whatever you say, it still needs to result in action of some sort very, very soon."

"Once again, we work backwards. Make a list of the information we need to get out of these people that'll either identify them as the killer or lead us in the direction of who is, then come up with a plan as to how to extract it. As we flesh this out and supplement with some online research, it'll become clear who to approach first and how."

"You and your lists," Vinn smiles. "And when have we ever come up with a plan that hasn't been blown to hell within the first five minutes? All right, unless I come up with a better idea by the end of classes today, we convene at your place tonight over some Cajun food which you're going to pick up on your way home. Now scram. I need to prepare a lab on the catalase enzyme before my 1:00."

I scram.

I rinse off the remnants of Vinn's rouge pie and my gumbo into the sink while she places four beignets on a plate and brings them into the living room for later. Apparently not too much later as there are only three left on the plate two minutes later when I join her on the couch. She already has a document open on her laptop where she's typed the names of the two lesser-known members of the Terrible Trio.

"We only did a perfunctory search of these two earlier so I thought we'd dive in a little deeper to see what we can find," she explains. "Maybe we'll stumble onto something we have in common or some unique hobby that we can fake an interest in to open up a conversation, gain their confidence."

"You make it sound like you want to have a friendly chat with them over coffee," I say. "Do you really think that's an approach that'll lead to anything that implicates

Broden in the murders? Or something that incriminates themselves? Don't forget that it's an open question as to whether either or both of them are involved somehow."

"I just don't know, Mal," Vinn responds, sounding frustrated. "We could go in there with weapons drawn and threaten to blow their brains out and that may not work any better. Let's admit it. We're floundering. These are supposedly smart people so we probably won't trick them into saying something they shouldn't or get lucky and have them slip up. And we get maybe one chance with one of them. If they're all in it together, we ask questions of one and before the door shuts behind us the other two know about it and clam up."

Vinn pauses to brush powdered sugar off her shirt. "I guess through my bitching we just eliminated one approach. I don't think we'll gain anything by talking to them at all. At least not with what we know as of now. Where does that leave us?"

"Meeting up with them and keeping silent, just staring at them until they break down and confess?" I suggest facetiously, earning a kick in the shin from Vinn. "Seriously, there are other ways to communicate besides meeting face to face. They like puzzles, right? What if we leave vague hints of some sort with the three of them, maybe obscure references to the killings that only the killer or someone with knowledge of certain details would recognize? If they're not involved or have been taken into the killer's confidence, they'll shrug them off or overlook them completely. If they're involved, though, with luck they'll get paranoid and increasingly nervous and we can draw them out that way."

"You mean make them think that we—or some anonymous person—knows something that we actually don't know? Such as the fact that we can implicate them in one or more murders that'll put them away for life?" Vinn grins. "It's devious enough that it appeals to me. It would be human nature to want to find out what we know and why we haven't turned our knowledge over to the police. The most likely assumption would be that we're looking for something in return for our silence. These people are all wealthy. They'll be convinced that we're blackmailing them for money."

"So if we give them a chance to buy our silence and they take the bait, we could be pretty sure that they're involved. That might not be the kind of proof that would support a conviction in court, but it would at least give us what we need to at that point confront them in person and put the squeeze on for additional details, even an off the record confession. With luck, they'll either rat out one or both of the other two or clear them."

Vinn sits up straight, warming to the idea. She grabs another beignet. I'm still full from dinner but take a bite off the end of one to mark it as mine. "I'm looking at this from different angles for flaws but so far it's full steam ahead," she says happily. "Of course if they think they're being blackmailed for something they didn't do and agree to meet, we may show up and find Mendez waiting for us."

"I think it's best we not inform him of our plans despite that risk," I answer. "He can't order us not to do something if he doesn't know that we're planning to do it. And we can try to make our clues subtle enough that an innocent person unfamiliar with the crime scene's staging won't recognize them for what they are. Or even notice them at all. So if we're agreed on this, what we need to do now is decide what clues to drop and how."

"Not quite yet," Vinn cautions. "We'll still need to do our due diligence on all three of them, but this time looking into their hobbies, habits, where they get their morning coffee, what car they drive, all that kind of stuff so that we can plot out the best places to leave our clues, whatever they end up being. We should be able to finish that off tonight."

"Before we start, are we going to tease all three at the same time or just one until we get a reaction one way or the other?"

"Mmm, let's talk this out," Vinn says. "We're in a rush, so my initial thought is to do all three at the same time. Stir all of the pots simultaneously. But they might feel each other out to see if we've approached the others, and if so all of them will gang up to address the issue. A united front will make it harder to crack and less likely one of them will throw an associate under the bus. Damn it, though, one at a time may be too slow. Thoughts?"

"I'm with you that approaching all three at once is too risky. One might be all we need and with luck he or she will spill on any others involved. If it's moving too slowly, we can always change tactics and go after the other two as well. If we approach all three from the outset, there's no going back."

"Agreed." Vinn sounds relieved that she gets to share the guilt if this turns out to be the wrong decision. "I say let's not do Broden first. He's so arrogant he may think he's above dealing with common blackmailers. So in researching the other two, let's also try to get a feel for their personalities to zero in on who would be the most uncomfortable and panic the easiest, be ready to deal with us the quickest, and be the fastest path to a resolution."

It feels amazing to have a plan, sketchy as it currently is. I rise to go make coffee and tea to stimulate our brains for the computer time that awaits us tonight. Reaching for my beignet on the way, I see that there's now a bite out of both ends. I tear it in half, stuff my end in my mouth, and head for the kitchen.

TWENTY FOUR

I settle in next to Vinn as she's typing Upton's name into the search bar. The same sites pop up as when we first looked into him, but this time we need to do more than a cursory peek into his life. Vinn navigates first to his profile on the website for his practice. His biography reads like it was drafted by a groupie who worships the air that he breathes.

"He wrote it himself," Vinn states with an air of certainty. "There's nothing wrong with a little puffery when trying to sell your services, but this has a 'holier than God' vibe. I wonder someday when he lies dying and looks back on his accomplishments if he'll be proud of a lifetime of tummy tucks and nose jobs for the—how does he phrase it—'elite of society.' This is helpful if we need to appeal to his ego, but let's move on."

We navigate next to Instagram, which to no one's surprise is an extension of the promotion from his website, only here of course in picture form. The good doctor has literally hundreds of posts stretching back years showing him in the company of beautiful women, most of them not his wife and including some local minor celebrities. The clear implication is that he's done work on all of them, so that he can take credit for their perfect nose or winning smile.

"Note that he promotes several charitable functions coming up," I tell Vinn. "Whether to portray himself as a philanthropist or to say that he's actually going to show up at these events, who knows. But that may be helpful if we need to know his whereabouts."

"Hmmm," Vinn ponders. "Also worth considering if that would qualify him as a charitable worker for the purposes of the two lists. We need to keep an eye on him. For now, though, let's get away from the sites he uses to show the face he wants his clients or potential clients to see," she suggests as her Facebook page fills the screen. Within seconds we're looking once more at Upton's face. "All right Doctor, what do you do when you're not cutting people up or trolling events for new patients?"

We're once more confronted with multiple pictures of Upton sharing the screen with others, only in this case the beautiful faces are those of horses. There are also several shots of he and his wife, adorned in a various floppy flowered hats, sitting under colorful umbrellas next to a white fence with out of focus horses and riders in the background beyond the fence. Same venue, several different occasions.

"He plays polo?" I ask the air. "People still play that? In Chicago?"

"Apparently so," Vinn replies, as surprised as I am. "Not the city proper but out where there are still stables. And it doesn't look like he plays at his age, but he does own a few of the horses that some players use. We might be able to find the schedule for matches or at the very least where he boards his horses if that will come in handy. I'll bet making a threat of harm to his horses would carry more weight than if we did the same to his wife."

We move through more of his social media, taking notes, but we appear to have mined most of his interests and habits within the first hour. We're ready to move on to Gretchen Connors when one more thought strikes me.

"Vinn, is there a site that lists claims against medical providers?" I ask. Vinn's eyes light up.

"Good idea," she says. It takes several minutes, but soon we're on a page of the Illinois Department of Health. "There he is. The website only goes back for five years, but he's had four claims against him during that time. Details are scarce though. Let's try something else."

Vinn types in a command, and soon we're searching court records for lawsuits against the doctor. Vinn lets out a low whistle. "Eight in the past eight years. And these are just those that made it to court, so we can assume there's more that settled before that stage." More typing as she moves from one page to the next. "Three are still pending. The other five were eventually dismissed by agreement, which probably means that they were settled. Terms confidential I'm sure. But we do have names of the plaintiffs if we need them. I'm thinking we won't. The very threat of exposing these claims and sullying his carefully curated reputation may be a powerful incentive to deal with us down the road."

"I'm not sure how we'd use that information, but it's good to have," I remark as I turn Vinn's laptop toward me and scribble down the information on the lawsuits. "Okay ready, let's see what we can find on the next one."

Gretchen Connors has no work profile or LinkedIn page. As far as we can tell her job at the insurance company is lower-level executive at best, but that doesn't stop her from placing herself among the socialites of the North Shore. Perhaps not quite the 'elite' level that Upton boasts of, but certainly the next tier. It's déjà vu when we hit her Facebook page and are deluged with photos of her with other heavily bejeweled women at events to raise money for unmarried teen mothers, or pet shelters, or to add a wing to the local library. Her pilot husband is nowhere to be found in the pictures.

"He probably volunteered for flights to Nome, Alaska rather than have to face night after night of self-congratulatory speeches and rubber chicken," Vinn notes. "Again, though, more charity work. Hard to imagine that's a coincidence, which makes me think we're on the right track with at least one of these two. Let's see what else she does besides hobnob with the moneyed crowd."

Forty-five minutes later, we haven't struck gold in the same way that we did with Upton. Connors plays bingo on Thursday nights, belongs to a bridge club that she misses as often as she goes, attends the local Presbyterian church regularly, and has owned a succession of Labrador Retrievers named Smokey. She's your average, if moderately wealthy, suburban housewife.

"It's getting late," Vinn notes as she closes her laptop. "Before we hit the sack, we should at least decide which one of them to target first."

"My initial impression is Connors," I say, "because she's a—"

"If the next word out of your mouth is 'woman,' Winters," Vinn interjects, her eyes flashing, "you're sleeping on the couch."

"Because she's a devout churchgoer and appears to have a sense of decency that Upton does not," I finish, avoiding eye contact with Vinn because that may not have been quite what I was going to say originally. "If she's involved there has to be a substantial part of her that feels guilt. If not, but she senses something is amiss with Upton and/or Broden, we may be able to appeal to her sense of right and wrong and draw her out."

"Ummph," Vinn mutters, indicating I may not yet be totally off the hook. "I agree that on the surface she doesn't appear to be the kind of person to be directing a series of murders, although you and I both know that it's the innocent-looking ones you have to watch out for. But you're right, I think Upton has such a high opinion of himself that he may be hard to break. He'll think he's invincible unless we're able to penetrate a weak spot in his defenses beyond the malpractice claims. A spot that Connors may know."

It's now after midnight and the caffeine from our tea and coffee has long ago lost its impact. "Bedtime, Vinn," I say with a yawn. "We can pick this up tomorrow."

Vinn isn't a morning person and barely made it out of bed in time to grab the blackberry with wheatgrass smoothie I prepared for her as she headed for the el and her 8:00 class. My first class today, "The Horror of Horror," isn't until 9:00 so we agree to meet up in the cafeteria for lunch. That gives me time to process what we learned about our two targets and to come up with a suggestion for how to confront Gretchen Connors.

"I've changed my mind about not talking to her and am now favoring the direct approach," I tell her as we sit in our usual spots by the window. The amount of food Vinn has before her suggests that she poured out the smoothie on her way to the train. She hates it when I try to make her eat healthy.

"You mean tell her 'hey we know you killed a couple people, how about accompanying us to the police station?'" she jests. "I don't know, Mal. We get one shot at this."

"I'm not saying we accuse her of anything or even imply that we think she's involved. I just can't think of an indirect way of getting her to address the subject of the murders, much less unwittingly implicate herself or spill on the two men. That doesn't mean we need to put all of our cards on the table, and I'm not above a little deception."

"If being sneaky is part of your plan then I'm more interested," Vinn says. "But how would we go about it? Here's my problem. If this drags on, we may still want me to attend another meeting for the purpose of checking out the other members, to see if any of them might be worth talking to. My cover's blown with Broden and with Leo's gal pal Miss Vixen, but that doesn't mean word has been spread among the others. The fewer people that know the better, at least for now. I don't think it's a good idea for me to interrogate this woman. For all we know, she'd report back to Broden and then all doors within the group will be closed."

"I wish we could use Maggie to interview her for an article in the school newspaper about the club, but under the circumstances we need to keep her as far away as possible from this mess," I muse.

"Hold on there, cowboy," Vinn says as she finishes off a fish taco. "I agree as to Maggie, but the idea of an interview itself isn't bad. Just not for a newspaper. What would entice Connors to agree to sit down for a talk with a stranger, and how could that conversation be steered to

Puzzlers Anonymous and the murders?"

We both sit silently in thought for not more than fifteen seconds before we simultaneously arrive at the same conclusion at the same time. "Charity!" we both exclaim, drawing stares from the few diners who dare to eat within three tables of the two campus outcasts.

Vinn celebrates by pushing a large spoonful of refried beans into her mouth, leaving it up to me to continue by suggesting a few details.

"I could pose as a potential donor to one of her pet charities, the conversation can be steered to her membership in the group, and I could express concern about her connection with it based on rumors about a number of the members being murdered and the possibility that a member is also the killer," I say, talking faster now as the idea begins to flesh out in my head. "The donation amount would have to be significant enough that Connors would lose any reticence about assuring me that the rumors are false and would suffer me asking pointed questions about the members, including Broden and Upton."

"We'll have to refine that connection a bit to make the fact that the donation is conditional upon your satisfaction that there aren't any killers in the puzzling group more convincing," Vinn says. "She doesn't impress me as stupid or naïve and we'll be relying on her common sense being blinded by the prospect of a big score, but that doesn't mean we can throw any flimsy connection out there.

"And," she continues hesitantly, "I have one other issue."

I look at her suspiciously. It's not like her to be shy about expressing any doubts about one of our plans. I know instinctively that this has to be about me.

"I'm sorry, Mal, but even if we clean you up you're not going to pass as the head of a charitable foundation or a wealthy patron looking for a charity to dump his money in. Remember too, I've seen your acting skills in the past and while I know you try...."

She leaves the rest unsaid, but the implication is clear and I can't say that I disagree. "I suppose you have a particular image in mind?"

"I do," she nods, relieved that I'm not upset. "We need someone who Connors will relate to, someone similar to the ladies she typically associates with, who can babble on about fashion and the latest trends, who will intrigue her, who—"

"Enough," I say. "I knew you were headed in this direction but hoped I was wrong. If we use her, I have one condition. I need to go along. Worst case scenario Broden has spread both of our names to his confederates, but chances are slim Connors knows what I look like. So I have to tag along as the financial advisor or whatever title would allow me to vet Connors and ask a few hard questions of my own."

"Fine," Vinn says, pleased with herself. "I still have my pudding to eat. Why don't you call Rebecca to see if she's got some time for us tonight."

TWENTY FIVE

"I thought about my Kate Spade, but it just doesn't shout 'money,' you know what I mean?" Rebecca's chatter about her dilemma in choosing just the right dress is entering its eighth minute. I'd cut her off except in this case her appearance really does matter, so I'm not about to do anything to seem unappreciative of her efforts. "This Versace isn't couture but could pass for it. Not so fancy that it can't be worn in the daytime but it oozes elegance, don't you think?"

"I think it's the perfect choice," I tell her, and for once I mean it. Vinn remains on the sidelines and refrains from any commentary. She knows virtually nothing about fashion and doesn't need to, as she's one of those women who enhances whatever she wears instead of the other way around.

"We need to get going," I say after looking at the time on my phone. For a simple lunch meeting this one is extensively choreographed, from Rebecca's fashion statement to arriving five minutes late, partly because that's what self-important rich people do and partly so that we don't risk Connors seeing us arrive in an Uber. The last one I took was a lime green Gremlin.

"Don't forget," Vinn finally joins in, "although you're the star of the show and will be the center of attention, you need to step aside to let Mal talk after your initial schmoozing and the woman's sales pitch for the charity of her choice. And most importantly, please don't commit to a contribution of any amount. Keep it positive but undecided."

"I know, I know," Rebecca says quickly, clearly annoyed at the reminder. "This isn't the first time I've had to put on a show, you know."

Vinn and I exchange concerned glances. It's Rebecca's history with prior investigations that has us on guard. She's not one to stay on script.

I call our Uber, thankfully another Honda Civic, which while still not appropriate for the status of the woman Rebecca is pretending to be, could be passed off as her "city car" if necessary. Our expected arrival time is seven minutes past noon, well within the fashionably late time frame.

To avoid having to travel all the way to the North Shore, when I reached out to Connors as a representative of a woman of means, I was vague as to where she lived but mentioned that she would be in the city on Saturday and would love to meet somewhere in the vicinity of Lincoln Park, the neighborhood in which many affluent Chicagoans reside. The restaurant selected by Connors, according to Yelp, appears to be a popular semi-casual but expensive spot for business lunches outside of the Loop. I'm hoping that Connors picks up the tab as a gesture meant to secure a donation.

Out of an abundance of caution, I ask our driver to drop us off two storefronts down from the restaurant, drawing the ire of my companion in her four-inch heels. I tell her to suck it up and then pause before we enter the front door.

"Rebecca, I know you're tired of hearing this, but for the next hour you're a woman of stature, accustomed to having your assistant make the intro-ductions, handle the business aspect of meals such as these, and keep the discussion on track." I notice a gleam in her eyes as I use the word "assistant." "And no, that doesn't change our dynamic in reality. I'm still the one in charge here. Understand?"

As we enter, Rebecca throws her shoulders back and her entire face seems to take on a rosy glow, her eyes focused and intent. She's in character. The ceilings are high and airy, the wooden tables surrounded by white metal chairs, wine glasses and linen napkins at the ready. It gives the impression of an indoor catered picnic. I'm immediately glad I wore a tie with the only good suit I own instead of going open collar. I would have stood out among the other diners, and not in a good way.

Our hostess tells us that we're expected and leads us to a back room, where the glass ceilings are twice as high and sunshine fills the room. Hanging plants dangle from beams crisscrossing the ceiling, threatening to drop their leaves onto the tables below for an impromptu salad. Sitting alone at a table nursing a glass of white wine sits a forlorn-looking Gretchen Connors. As soon as she notices us being brought to the table, her countenance morphs into a forced smile as she sizes us up. She rises as we approach.

"Mrs. Franklin, how charming to meet you," she squeaks, holding her hand out toward Rebecca before withdrawing it from her grasp and motioning her to sit in the chair drawn back by the hostess. Apparently it's not quite so charming to meet me, but I grab a chair anyway and quickly take the initiative before Rebecca can say a word or forget that for today her last name is Franklin and issue a correction.

"Mrs. Connors, thank you for the opportunity to meet with us today. As I mentioned on the phone, Mrs. Franklin and her foundation had a particularly good year and are looking to expand the list of beneficiaries of their annual giving. She tasked me with finding deserving groups for her largesse. In my search I noticed that your name and visage kept appearing in connection with many intriguing causes. When I brought that to her attention, she insisted on meeting you in person."

"I'm flattered, Mrs. Franklin," Connors replies without so much as a glance in my direction. "But I must say I'm surprised that we haven't crossed paths before. I'm highly cognizant of all of the local charitable organizations and donors in this part of the country. What did you say the name of your foundation is again?"

Three minutes in and we're already off the rails. I see the twitch of Rebecca's mouth that signals panic and hurry to step in.

"That's by design, Mrs. Connors. Mrs. Franklin is third generation at the helm of the foundation that bears her grandfather's name, and it's always been a source of pride for all involved that no publicity is ever a part of their giving. All donations are anonymous with no credit taken. It's much easier to be selective that way as well."

"I see," she responds, although it's clear that the woman for whom no charitable function is successful unless her name and photo make it into the society pages can't grasp the concept of not taking credit for a good deed. "Very well, Mrs. Franklin, shall we order and then discuss how I might assist you?"

I watch nervously as Rebecca peruses the menu. She's been instructed to order a salad, which is the cliché for society women who lunch and which Connors follows dutifully in requesting a kale salad. I inwardly sigh with relief when Rebecca forgoes the $25.00 cheeseburger or the breakfast burrito and goes with the Cobb salad but cringe when she asks for a side of parmesan truffle fries. Connors pretends not to notice.

"Now then," she says, her full attention on Rebecca. "How may I help?"

"As he mentioned earlier, Malcom here noticed that you appear to be involved in a number of charitable causes," Rebecca responds, so far sticking to the script. "While I like to have him do the initial screening, when it comes to making the actual decision as to how we distribute the funds the final decision is mine. And I like to do my due...my due...I like to do some research on my own." Even when we practiced she had a mental block when it came to the phrase "due diligence."

"Anyway," she continues, "I personally find emails and phone conversations less than satisfactory and prefer personal contact when it comes to parting with money. That's why I asked to meet with you. If you had to pick your own personal favorite cause of those you've been involved with for the past, say, six months, which one would it be and why?"

Connors doesn't even pause before answering. "It would have to 'Cur-tailed,' the local animal shelter," she says enthusiastically. "You see, I used to have the most adorable Cockapoo named Bootsie before I went with a bigger breed..."

I tune out as she spends the next ten minutes or so regaling us with memories of every dog she'd ever owned before transitioning into why the shelter deserved Rebecca's money and how she was sure they would honor her donation by naming a dog run after her or giving her a discount on her next pet. Rebecca does an admirable job of appearing interested while nodding and encouraging Connors to please provide more detail.

I come out of my daze when I hear Rebecca utter the trigger phrase, "Well, that sounds just perfect, Mrs. Connors." I take my cue and loudly clear my throat.

"Oh yes," Rebecca says, "there is just one more small detail. You see my foundation is extremely protective of its reputation and therefore very particular about who makes its list of recipients. You'll think this is very silly, but a tiny little matter needs to be cleared up. I'll let Malcom take it from here."

Connors looks puzzled. She'll be even more confused as I start describing the "tiny little matter" since its connection to the shelter is non-existent except through its relationship with her. We're hoping that her focus on securing Rebecca's supposedly substantial donation will blur her senses enough that she won't think too hard on this.

She looks at me the same way she would look at a filthy alley cat that showed up at her doorstep instead of having the courtesy of going directly to the shelter. "We do a deep search into individuals and groups that we work with, Mrs. Connors," I say firmly. "And I need to ask you about your affiliation with a club called 'Puzzlers Anonymous.' You belong to that organization, correct?"

She nods and I see her mind spinning trying to find the relevance. I don't give her the chance to get too far into it. "I assume you're aware that the group has had three members murdered recently and that the authorities are looking into a connection between other killings and that same group."

Connors emits a small gasp and her mouth drops open. I'll be asking Rebecca later for her opinion, but the reaction appears genuine to me. It's possible that she's shocked that the cops have made the connection, and therefore worried about being implicated, but my money is on the fact that this is the first she's heard that any members were killed at all. The cops have clearly put a lid on the victims' link through the puzzle group.

"I...I didn't... I mean..." she stammers.

"Brandon Mills, Sandra Summers, and Charlene Phelps," I tell her and her eyes open wide. "Now, what can you tell me about," I pause here as I pull out a small notepad and open it up to a blank page, "Charles Broden. I believe he heads up the group, correct? And, let's see, James Upton. He seems to hold some other position but we're not clear what exactly. Our information indicates that you're very close to both of these men."

Connors has the look of someone who just got gut-punched and doesn't know which way is up, which is exactly where we need her to be. She needs to stay in that condition for just a few minutes longer.

"I, well no, I mean of course I know them. But only from meetings. It's not like I socialize with them." She's getting defensive and slightly aggressive in her response. "If someone else in the group told you that I'm friends with those men that's simply not true. It may look that way because the three of us are, how should I say, on a different plane from the rest of them, so we sometimes stay together at the meetings. But other than that, I don't know anything about them. What I mean to say is, I've never once seen them outside of the puzzle group."

We're starting to lose her and I have to decide if it's worth continuing with that line of inquiry. I glance at Rebecca, who very subtly shakes her head. At the same time, I become aware of a persistent buzz and vibration from my pocket that won't stop. I pull my phone out and chance a quick look at the notification on the screen.

"Well, thank you Mrs. Connors, that helps clear things up," I say with a sense of urgency as I rise, pulling Rebecca up by the elbow. "We'll get back to you shortly and we appreciate your time."

"Yes, thank you dear," Rebecca coos, "it's been charming."

We leave a visibly stunned Connors and make a dash past the other diners as fast as we can go, passing the server on her way to the table with our food. I'm calling an Uber before we're even out the door.

"Malcom, what the hell—" Rebecca starts to say.

"The texts were from Vinn," I tell her. "There's been another murder."

TWENTY SIX

The crime scene is somewhere in the Market Square business district of Lake Forest, a suburb bordering Lake Michigan about twenty-five miles north of the city. Rebecca and I are silent as we ride, gazing at the homes with large, immaculate lawns set back far from the road. A million dollars might buy you a small coach house here, but if you want to be near the water you're looking at a significant multiple of that. It's a world totally foreign to both of us.

Vinn asked us to meet her at a Dunkin Donuts on the main street that traverses downtown Lake Forest, just south of our destination. We find her at a table in the back corner nursing a cup of coffee. Rebecca peels back to the counter to order her own beverage while I grab a seat across from Vinn. A few crumbs on her shirt give away that she's indulged in the fare. She sees me notice.

"I've been here awhile and have to keep ordering something to be allowed to continue sitting here while I waited for you," she explains. "If I have to face one more chunk of fried dough I'm going to throw up. Anyway, from what I understand we're about half a mile from where it happened. All I know is that it's in an office this time and between the Lake Forest cops and Mendez's crew, they have the whole area blocked off. We can't get anywhere close yet. Mendez is apoplectic. The locals took jurisdiction, which of course is right, but for the longest time wouldn't let him near the scene. I understand there have been some calls between the higher ups of each department, so for now he's allowed in as an observer. No guarantees, but he'll try to get us in along with the Chicago medical examiner once she's given the okay herself. Politics."

Rebecca slides in next to me, setting down a tray in front of her containing a bacon, egg, and cheese sandwich on a bagel, hash browns, three varieties of donuts, and a large iced coffee. Vinn's face turns green. Rebecca notices me staring at her selection.

"What? We left the restaurant before we got our meal," she says. "A girl's got to eat."

"Other than that I know very little," Vinn continues, trying her best not to look in the direction of Rebecca's food. "How did your meeting go?"

"I could have used about five more minutes to verify my conclusion," I tell her, "but unless she's a great actress she not only isn't involved, until today she knew nothing about the murders. She was clearly caught off guard when we changed direction into suspicions about members of Puzzlers Anonymous and didn't have a prepared response ready. I think Rebecca agrees with me."

Rebecca quickly swallows and sips some coffee to clear her throat. "Yes. That woman is so far stuck up her ass that she wouldn't stray outside the lines of her perfect world to sully her hands with something as gauche as a murder. I vote no."

Despite herself, Vinn can't suppress a chuckle. "The same conclusion from two different perspectives, then. I'm not sure if that's good news or not. It narrows our focus to just the two men, at least with what we know so far combined with a healthy dose of speculation and guesswork, but I was hoping that our flitty socialite would be able to offer at least some useful information about them."

"There was no time," I say. "That's where I was headed when we got your text. My guess would be there was nothing valuable to draw out of her anyway."

"Well then," Vinn concludes, "the good beauty doctor is next." She looks directly at me. "We need to think about what kind of items to leave for him to find in order to lure him out, how to use the malpractice claims to our advantage, and how to do it quickly. Our time just got cut a lot shorter."

Vinn starts to go on but the ringing of her phone cuts her off. She picks it up, but other than a few "uh huhs" and "mm mms" there's nothing from her end of the conversation to indicate who's on the other end of the line. The conversation is short.

"That was Mendez," she tells us. "The medical examiner on duty just left the city so she should be here in forty minutes or so. Part of the compromise between departments. The local guy here isn't that experienced with violent deaths and was happy to pass the buck. Mendez is going to slip us in as a part of her crew but wants to talk to us first. I assume it'll be the usual 'Don't touch' and 'Don't speak' lecture and a reminder that he'll want to debrief us immediately afterward so don't go running away. He'll meet us just at the southern end of the tapes. It's about a ten-minute walk, so we should get going."

Vinn and I rise to leave. Rebecca hesitates, giving a mournful glance at the two donuts and half a sandwich left on her tray. After a few moments and a theatrical sigh, she dumps them in the trash and joins us on our way.

We see Mendez pacing nervously inside the crime scene tape surrounding a parking lot before he notices us. From the expression on his face, either the stress of murder number five or the tension between the Chicago and Lake Forest cops has him riled and ready to burst. As it turns out, that's just the tip of the iceberg.

"This has been a shit show from minute one," he growls angrily in our direction while we're still ten feet away. "It's bad enough to be treated like crap by the local rent-a-cops here, but I've had my ears chewed off by every brass from the Superintendent on down as to why we haven't broken this thing wide open yet and how many more bodies it's going to take. That's the one and only reason—" He breaks off when he notices Rebecca trailing up behind us. "What in the hell is she doing here?"

Rebecca looks up, offended. She and Mendez have tolerated each other in the past, primarily because of her roles in bringing prior investigations to a close, but the timing of having a crossdresser in a faux couture dress, high heels, and dangling earrings at the scene of what's sure to be a gruesome dead body where Mendez is already persona non grata with the local cops isn't the best.

"She was with me when we got the news," I say calmly. "In fact we were in the middle of an interview pertaining to this case."

Mendez doesn't appear mollified. "What I started to say," he picks back up, "is that this set of highly unusual circumstances and the heavy pressure from above is the only reason I'm doing this. Don't make me regret it. When Kate gets here, she's bringing two extra sets of coveralls for you two with the idea you tag along when she goes inside and hope no one asks any questions." He looks again at Rebecca. "That doesn't include the diva here. No way in hell. She can skedaddle back home or go grab a spritzer somewhere until you're done."

Rebecca snorts, tells Vinn and I that she'll wait for our call, and turns away in a huff. Mendez waits until she's well out of ear shot.

"You have to understand," he sighs, "it's already a circus and we don't need one more clown." I look at him sharply. "You know what I mean. She doesn't belong in there no matter what she's wearing. Anyway, just like last time. Observe, take notes, and keep your traps shut. Don't do anything that would broadcast that you don't belong. You'll be under a microscope.

"Also," he scans the immediate area and lowers his voice before continuing, "don't telegraph anything, don't let them overhear you whispering, don't let them see your notes. In fact, don't take notes at all. If the local boys and girls in blue ask you anything, defer to me. As far as I'm concerned, this is my case and they're not getting any help from our side."

With that, he looks down at his phone. "She's five minutes out. Come this way."

We follow him to an isolated area between buildings just off the parking lot and wait. Fifteen minutes later Vinn and I are adorned from head to ankles in sanitary jumpsuits with booties in hand tagging along behind a no-nonsense woman of around forty, not the same examiner we met at a couple of the earlier scenes. We turn into a doorway between a trendy clothing store and a jeweler and find ourselves at the bottom of a stairway. Kate halts before going any further, turning to us.

"I don't know either of you but I trust the detective's judgment," she says. "It's not common to have a crew this large on a scene, in fact I usually work alone, but the locals have strange ideas about the big bad city, so they may not know any better. That being said, stay close and if I ask you to hand me something or to pull back a body part, just do it. Got it?"

We both murmur our assent. She then turns her attention to Mendez. "Before we head upstairs, what do we know?"

He takes a moment to gather his thoughts. "Not much yet. I was kicked out before I could take it all in so I'm going in almost cold. It's in a medical office."

Vinn and I exchange glances, which triggers a barely perceptible shaking of the head from Mendez. He knows what we know, that the next victim on the list is a surgeon and the next killer, a beautician. We each know in general terms what to expect at the scene, which are the tools of both trades, but he doesn't want us to reveal that. Not to the medical examiner nor to the local cops. Apparently they're still attempting to keep the idea of a serial killer off the radar.

"Single victim," he continues, "white male, mid to late fifties. Wasn't there long enough to guess a cause of death."

"That's why I'm here," Kate says. "And that's enough for now. Got a name?"

Mendez pulls out his notebook. "Let's see...ah, here it is. He's—he was—a plastic surgeon. Name is Dr. James Upton."

TWENTY SEVEN

The electric shock at the sound of the all too familiar name stuns Vinn and I and our faces must show it. Kate doesn't notice it as her back is to us as she starts up the stairs, but Mendez immediately senses the tension. He signals to Vinn to follow the medical examiner with a slight tilt of his head, then moves in close to me.

"What?" he asks in as low a voice as he can manage while still sounding irritated. I doubt he even knows how to whisper.

I keep my voice barely audible as well. "We've never met him but his name came up as a member of the puzzle group. From what we've learned, a close associate of the guy who probably slipped that coded puzzle into Vinn's packet. For no other reason than that, we considered him as a possible suspect. He was next on our list of people to talk to."

"Yeah, a little late for that now," Mendez grumbles. He glances up at Kate and Vinn, who are halfway up the stairs. "Dammit. We're not done with this discussion. Don't think about leaving here before we have a little chat."

We hurry to catch up, trying our best to pretend that nothing out of the ordinary just happened. The second floor consists of a long narrow hallway with doors on each side, names of various businesses stenciled on the frosted windows. A chiropractor, psychologist, and massage therapist seem to indicate that this wing is a favorite of medical providers. A small crowd of cops trying to look attentive as Mendez approaches are hanging outside a door near the end of the hall.

The four of us have to squeeze by under their curious watch.

Immediately inside the door is a small waiting room with six seats and a table full of an array of tattered magazines. A metal stand sitting on a table in the corner contains a number of colorful pamphlets with names such as "A Guide to Bust Enhancement" and "Is a Tummy Tuck Right for You?" The smell of bleach permeates the air. Kate hands out masks which we all quickly slip on. Through an open door into the next room I can make out two feet hanging off the end of a medical table.

Kate immediately takes charge, evicting two Lake Forest cops from the outer room under the pretense that her team needs room to work, but in reality it's so that they don't notice how little Vinn and I will actually contribute to the process. They put up a token resistance at first, but between her unwavering insistence, Mendez's hovering and intimidating presence, and the prospect of getting away from the overwhelming odors, they soon make for the exit.

I can tell that Mendez is chomping at the bit wanting to continue our discussion from downstairs, but he knows that this is Kate's time and to let her do her job without distraction. He also wants us to focus all of our attention on the scene, as he's doing himself. Our talk can wait. I turn my attention to the naked body lying before us.

It's immediately evident that the bleach smell is actually hydrogen peroxide, as Upton's hair has been lightened to an unnaturally light white color. Mixed in is a faint scent of nail polish from his firehouse red toenails. His face is covered in a pale green mud-like substance which Kate identifies as a facial peel. Most grotesque of all, though, are the incisions in his chest, into which have been partially inserted silicone breast enhancements. Dried blood from the cuts runs down the side of his chest and pools have formed on the floor on either side of the table. A scalpel rests on his stomach.

There's little else of note on the body, and the room itself has few enhancements. The bottle of nail polish sits on a shelf next to a hand mirror and a few implements that Kate identifies as a hair straighter and a hair curler, neither of which I've ever seen in Vinn's bathroom. There seems to have been little effort to place surgical supplies or tools in the room beyond what's on the body, but given that the corpse lies in an actual procedure room for a plastic surgeon, that may have been seen as unnecessary. On the other hand, the staging follows the pattern of each one being less pains-takingly curated than the one before.

Kate notifies us that she'll be done in another ten minutes or so and won't need any assistance, so Mendez motions us to join him in the waiting room. "Well?" he demands in a loud whisper as soon as we're clear of the door. I guess he does know how.

"Well what?" I ask. "You saw it yourself. It fits what we would expect for murder number five. Clear allusions to a beautician. The hair, toenails and polish, face peel, and so forth. The surgical references are obvious as well. The only thing I would mention is the fact that there were so few items staged and not a whole lot of effort went into it."

"I felt the same," Vinn adds. "The nail polish was sloppy. Whoever applied it didn't even try not to spill over onto his toes. The breast inserts weren't inserted more than a couple of centimeters. The whole scene could have been staged in less than five minutes, outside of the killing itself. Do we know how he died?"

"Not yet," a voice behind us says as Kate joins us. "My guess is that he was put under with gas, then either suffocated or he bled to death. You know the drill, you have to wait until I get him on the table."

"The speed worries me," Vinn continues. "It's as if whoever's behind this no longer takes the time to prep the actual killer or isn't as particular in their choice of who it is. They're in a hurry. I'm scared that they rushed this one in order to get to the next victim. The journalist. Maggie."

Kate asks Vinn to help her get the body onto a wheeled cart, leaving Mendez and I alone. I speak up before he can say anything.

"There's nothing more I can tell you about Upton than what I said earlier. He was a lead that we were just getting to. You know as much about him as we do. I'd love to be able to search this office. If he does know something about the murders, or is implicated in any way, he'd probably keep the information here instead of at his home. At least it makes sense to start here before telling his widow that you want to tear his home apart because he might have been involved in a series of murders."

"Yeah, I can't wait to run that by the District Attorney," Mendez says sourly. "But there's no way that you, me, or anyone else is going to be allowed back in here in the immediate future. The locals are locking down this whole building once they're done today. Not even the tenants will be able to get in."

He pauses as Kate and Vinn wheel out the cart with Upton covered in a sheet. Silently we follow as we push through the crowd of cops. The two locals return to their post inside the office. Oddly, Mendez tells his officers to join them in the waiting room and count to one hundred before resuming their posts in the hallway.

We're about halfway down the hallway when Mendez asks us to stop. He moves to the door of a pediatrician, bends over the doorknob for about twenty seconds, then opens the door.

"In," is all he says to Vinn and I, and that's all he needs to say before he double-times to catch up with Kate. We scurry inside, close and lock the door, and wait for the party down the hall to leave for the day.

The waiting room of the office is identical to Upton's, but instead of flyers on how to increase your bra size it's littered with picture books, puzzles, and colorful artwork of cartoon characters on the primary-colored walls. Past that, it's larger than the office down the hall. There are three exam rooms and a small break room and, of course, no dead bodies in any of them.

"It's not even 3:00 yet," Vinn notes as she looks at her phone, "We've got at least two or three hours before they leave, and even then we should probably wait until any activity outside ceases so that no one notices movement up here. If we time it right, we can go through Upton's office without having to turn on any lights that would attract attention if the cop guarding the door downstairs takes a stroll."

"Well, we do have books to pass the time," I say as I page through *The Purple Puppy Gets a Shot*. "Every time I read this one I discover something new."

"Pass," Vinn says. "I don't have enough juice left on my phone to play around. Guess I'll take a nap." She finds the one room with an exam table large enough to hold her, pulls fresh paper over it from the roll hanging off one end, and within thirty seconds is sound asleep.

I move to the kitchen, snag a juice box out of the mini-fridge, text Rebecca telling her to find her own way home, and ponder recent events. Without multiple distractions pulling my mind in various directions I'm able to clearly focus on where our investigation stands, and it's not encouraging. Yesterday we had three possible suspects. Today one has been cleared and one is dead, while the third is only on our radar because Vinn and Leo don't like him and he may have put an extra puzzle in Vinn's packet. Not exactly a lot of progress in return for the efforts we've exerted so far.

A lot depends on finding something, anything, in our search of Upton's office, but even that seems like a long shot. If he wasn't involved, we'll find nothing and won't know if that's because he's completely exonerated or just careful. If he is involved, what are the odds that there's anything to find? The one upside is that Upton certainly didn't expect to be killed, so if anything incriminating is in the office he wouldn't have known to destroy it before we come looking.

Impatient, I try to recall the exact layout and furnishings of the waiting room, reception area, and patient room for the most likely places I would hide something if I were Upton. The next thing I know Vinn is shaking me by the shoulder.

"They're on the move," she whispers. "I didn't want to take a chance that you'll snore or cry out in your sleep." I position myself at the door while Vinn moves behind the glass partition guarding the receptionist's desk and places her ear to the wall. Several sets of footsteps pass by with muted conversation. Neither one of us moves for several minutes after the hallway becomes silent.

"Pretty sure I heard keys and tape unrolling," Vinn says softly into my ear when she returns. "My guess is that they're gone. Let's give it half an hour to make sure."

The thirty minutes gives us time to perform one important task. Neither of us carries our lock picks with us unless we know we'll need them. They're not only uncomfortable to carry, being found in possession of them means jail time. We need to find a suitable replacement.

It's not as easy as it sounds. While a plastic surgeon's office contains scalpels in myriad sizes that would do the trick, no cutting procedures are performed in this pediatrician's office. Thirty-two minutes later we finally assemble our booty. One letter opener, both office and surgical scissors, tuning fork for a reflex hammer, and a couple of instruments with semi-sharp ends that we have no clue as to their use.

In the end what works is paper clips. Vinn, a virtuoso lock picker, unravels several clips before twisting them together to form an improvised version of her own favorite tool, and while it takes her longer than usual, we're still in within three minutes after she finished her creation. We carefully twist our bodies to avoid the crime scene tape blocking the door and catch our breath sitting on the floor.

We don't bother with the waiting room. It's spartan to begin with, and no one smart enough to mastermind a series of killings without getting caught would put anything incriminating where a patient could stumble upon it. Since we're not pressed for time, we work together in the same room for both the company and to share thoughts as to where to look.

We briefly debate hacking into the computer, but again storing something there would risk his receptionist or nurse asking questions about a mysterious blocked file. We search in desks, under desks and chairs, look for false drawers, riffle through books, and pour through files.

"I didn't expect to find it here where his staff spends their time," Vinn tells me when we've exhausted all possibilities, "but it's good to have made sure. If there's anything, it'll be well hidden in the other room."

The body is gone and the various props have been removed as evidence, but the odor still lingers. We saved our disposable booties from earlier and slip them on before we enter. It's more cramped than the last room and we're constantly bumping into each other. After twenty minutes, we've still found nothing. Frustration is setting in.

After five more minutes of intense searching, including going over areas the other already looked at, I'm ready to call the night a failure. "Vinn, there's no point in going on," I say angrily. "We've searched this place from floor to—"

At that moment we both look up. Sure enough, it's a drop ceiling. Without another word, Vinn helps me up onto the medical table and I push a panel up and over so that it creates a gap. I use the flashlight of my phone to scan the area. A shadow catches my attention.

"We need to move the table to get closer," I tell Vinn. It's heavy, and only after we remove all of the surgical tools and files from the drawers are we able to get it to budge. With maximum effort, we push it about fifteen inches. Hopefully enough.

It's not. There's definitely something there, taped to the ductwork. Maybe a warranty for the furnace, but I don't think so. My arm comes up about six inches short despite twisting and lunging.

"Be right back," Vinn says. She returns shortly with a small child's chair from the pediatrician's waiting room then places it on the table and holds it as I gingerly balance myself on it. It's wobbly and seems ready to topple over every time I shift my weight. With luck I can beat the laws of physics by reaching up and making a clean grab before returning back onto my perch, with neither the chair or I falling.

My initial effort to snatch the paperwork fails. I can touch it but can't get the leverage to pull it away from the ductwork. I close my eyes, give myself a mental pep talk, then push my upper body as far forward as I can. My fingers grasp the folder. I pull it away, but as I retrieve it begin to fall backward. The chair topples onto the floor and I follow it, bouncing off the table on the way.

I'm momentarily dazed and my butt hurts like hell. Vinn approaches, squats down, puts her hand forward as if to comfort me, then grabs the document out of my hands and stands up.

"I'm fine, thank you," I say from the floor.

"Priorities," she answers. I pull myself to my feet as she opens a plastic file folder and removes a single piece of printer paper from it. In small script, there are notes that fill all of the front page and half of the back. Vinn brings it closer to her face to read them.

"Not here," I tell her. She nods and places it back inside the folder. I grimace as I pull myself back onto the table to replace the ceiling tile while Vinn makes sure the office looks exactly as it did when we entered. As much as we want to see what's written on the paper, we'd rather do it from the comfort and safety of my place where we're beyond the reach of the authorities.

We walk slowly down the stairs toward the front door, but movement just outside the door stops us. I crouch down to take a look. A cop still guards the front door. We retreat to the rear exit with the same result.

"Shit," Vinn mumbles. We return to the pediatrician's office, position ourselves next to a lamp, and begin to read.

TWENTY EIGHT

Upton's small scrawl requires us to hold the paper close enough to our eyes that we end up virtually in each other's laps with heads touching. It immediately becomes evident from the different colored inks and the wide variance in legibility that this isn't a single narrative but short thoughts and questions that he compiled over time, probably jotted down whenever a thought came to him.

"It doesn't seem like he would have wanted to have to grab this sheet down from the ceiling every time he had a notation to add," I tell Vinn. "Based on all of the creases, he must have kept it in his pocket, pulling it out when he had something to add."

"I wonder if he had a premonition, then, and stored it where no one would think to look," Vinn ponders. "Or maybe he jots down thoughts on scraps and uses this as his master sheet, transferring his notes periodically. Even as it is, this doesn't exactly look like we found the Holy Grail."

She's right. The notations consist of cryptic half-thoughts which probably make sense to the person writing them but to anyone else are mostly nonsense, at least at first glance. Vinn pulls the paper closer to her face, as if proximity would reveal new insights, then hands it to me. I follow suit. For a few moments neither one of us says anything.

"There's a copy machine by the front desk," she finally says. "Can you go make several copies? We can highlight the phrases that appear to be more meaningful and take notes on the copies."

While I'm waiting for the machine to spew out collated copies, I rummage through the desk drawers to find pens and a yellow highlighter. I hand one copy to Vinn along with several pens, take one for myself, then make myself comfortable. We agree to work separately then to compare notes to see if her analytical mind and my more creative brain end up on the same wavelength.

After twenty-five minutes where the only sounds are our own breathing and an occasional curse under the breath of the neighborhood scientist, Vinn looks up at me. "Ready?" she asks.

I nod and Vinn places her page on the floor between us. My mouth drops open. Her notes are in three different colors, not counting highlighted portions, with arrows linking several of Upton's phrases, and numbers ranking each of them. The blank portion at the bottom of the second page is filled with a chart she created. I surreptitiously turn my papers over and slide them off to the side out of sight.

"The red ones are those I thought were the most revealing or useful," she explains, "while the blue are of secondary importance or only work to support a main thought, and black are either duplicate or contribute nothing of value. Each one is numbered and my chart ranks the notes within both the red and blue hues in descending order of significance."

"At first glance it looks like we're mostly on the same page," I lie. "Let's use your notes to go through this."

"There are ten red phrases in all," she continues without missing a beat. "Each of which clearly references either the murders in some way or suspicions about who's behind them. Starting at the top, not completely chronologically compared to what's on the original:

'Too many to be coincidence. Link?'
'Two members from group. Has to be inside.'
'Broden's response odd. Concerns me. Involved?'
'Confronted Broden. Takes joy speaking in puzzles, thinking I'm clueless, admitting without saying it.'
'G.C. senses nothing.'

That would be Gretchen Connors," Vinn adds.

"Yeah, I picked up on that," I reply dourly. "Go on."

"Sorry," Vinn says sheepishly, "Sometimes I forget you're not one of my students. Moving on:

'What to do, to who, is there enuf???'
'Distance self from him.'
'More than one? Then who?'"

"Wait," I stop her. "I circled that one. More than one what? Killer? And if so, how would he know that? Would've been helpful if he used footnotes."

"I think that's the most likely interpretation," Vinn says, "although it could also refer to the fact that there are multiple victims and ask who's next. But if he's referring to multiple murderers, we're in a bind because our other two suspects are ruled out. And see my arrow? Listen to these last two red notes:

'He's not alone.'
'Following orders?'"

"Yeah, I had those highlighted too. Again, 'he's not alone' could be interpreted in a couple of different ways, but when you combine it with 'following orders?' it has to lead to someone other than Broden."

"Not necessarily," Vinn says. "Maybe Upton knew of someone else that was following Broden's orders. 'He' may not be referring to Broden but to his underling. It's frustrating that Upton didn't detail whatever evidence led him to pose these questions. Or maybe he did and these are only his initial notes, so that there's more hidden somewhere else."

"Whatever the case," I tell her, "We don't have the luxury of time to look for them and if they were in his office they probably would have been stored alongside these pages. I don't think there's any doubt as to our next step, do you? We need to confront Broden. Or let Mendez have at him."

Vinn makes a face. "Do you really think this is enough for the cops to do anything? Maybe at best they'd bring him in for questioning but there's no hard evidence he's involved other than a few random, vague scribbles from a dead guy, and Broden's too smart and cagy to say anything that'll put him in jail. We need to take this head on ourselves."

"Unless Mendez gets to him first, or orders us to keep our distance from him," I say.

"Exactly. Which is why he'll never know Upton's notes exist, at least not until the time is right. Shred all of the extra copies except where we took notes. Those, along with the original, we'll fold up and put inside our shoes when we leave here. Speaking of, can you text Mendez?"

I don't respond, instead studying Vinn's expression. It's not the first time we've held something back from the cops, but before now it's mostly been our own suppositions or conclusions. This is more than that. Withholding actual evidence could land us in deep trouble or worse, prevent the cops from using their more extensive resources to catch a killer. I know what she's thinking. The wheels of official justice sometimes move too slowly and with Maggie's life at stake we can't wait for them. Going rogue may lead us to take actions that we don't want to be traced back to us. And I guess I'm okay with that. Balancing the life of a young woman who we've put in mortal danger against a few scruples is no contest.

Now's the time for Mendez to regret calling me from his own cell so that I have his after-hours number. I pull out my phone and type a text to him, hoping he's awake this late at night. "Cops at both doors, need your help to exit. Found nothing."

Vinn is looking over my shoulder. "Delete that last sentence. If he thinks our time here was a washout, he'll be in no hurry to get us out of here."

I do so and press send. Within seconds he responds with something profane, the gist of which is that we can wait until morning.

"Well that wasn't very nice," Vinn says. "I wonder what we can do to pass the time." With that she grabs my hand, pulls me to my feet, and with a twinkle in her eye leads me into the room with the adult-sized exam table.

"We don't have all day," Mendez tells us early that morning in the waiting room of the pediatrician's office. "I left a guy out front and told the local cop he could go get some coffee. So?"

"Sorry to say, not a thing," I respond, not even bothering to keep my fingers crossed behind my back. "And because we had as much time as we needed and the office is small, we did an especially thorough job. There isn't a speck of dust or a paper clip that escaped our attention."

He scrutinizes my face, using his years of experience dealing with suspects lying to his face to determine if I'm on the up and up. "It's not that I don't believe you," he finally says, no note of regret in his voice, "but I need to be sure. Spread your arms and legs." He gives me a pat down, rushing past sensitive areas but not ignoring them, then grunts in disappointment when he finds nothing. He turns to Vinn, who gives him a withering look.

"Mal at least makes me pancakes first," she snarls as she assumes the position. Mendez does a less intrusive job with her with the same end result. He's not a happy man.

"Can you get a search warrant for his home?" I ask innocently, knowing what a waste of time that would be.

"Not a chance," Mendez sighs. "Even ignoring the barrier of this guy being wealthy and a so-called pillar of the community, asking to search the home of a murder victim for no reason other than a hunch isn't going to get us anywhere. Sorry you had to spend the night here for no good reason."

He almost sounds like he means it, which only shows how off his game he is. We follow him down the stairs and after a quick look around to make sure the local guardian of the door isn't walking back with cup in hand, we exit and head out of sight before calling for an Uber. The crime scene tape from last night is gone and there's activity in a few of the local businesses.

"So we know where our focus has to shift to now," I say as we climb into the back seat of a battered MINI Cooper, being careful to avoid using a name, "but what exactly are we going to do?"

Vinn leans forward to ask the driver to turn up the music before responding and keeps her voice low. "We're out of time, so slow and methodical isn't going to work. I think we need to use the direct approach and confront him, but knowing what we know we can't risk setting up a meeting in a private setting. It has to be public, but then we're restricted as to what we can say and we can't risk pushing too far if it puts bystanders at risk."

"Agreed. We'll need to find a small place without a lot of tables, preferably outdoors. Our conversation will have to be circumspect, but he needs to know from the outset that we know what he's doing so that we can be sure that vague references aren't missed or misinterpreted. Maybe we can do some staging of our own."

Vinn looks lost in thought, a slight smile on her face. "I like it," she eventually says. "We get there early, wherever 'there' is going to be, and set the stage so that from the moment he approaches the table he knows that the meal isn't going to be a friendly social occasion."

"He's not stupid and will suspect that the moment you invite him out, regardless of the pretense," I tell her. "But he may not expect how direct we intend to be. It might be too much to expect, but if we can catch him off guard that would be ideal."

"Exactly," Vinn says, unsuccessfully stifling a yawn. "But I have no intention of extending an invitation to him—he's going to have no choice but to reach out to me to suggest a meet because he'll either be curious about what we know or will be on the defensive. But no matter what his mindset, we'll be prepared. We have no choice—we have to walk away from that meeting knowing what we need to know to put an end to this once and for all, especially discovering whether Broden's the mastermind or puppet, no matter what it takes. Even if it means that he doesn't walk away at all."

Her implication is clear, if a bit dramatic. There will be no gunfire or knife play with other people around, but we both know that either or both are inevitable. With Maggie's life at stake and our mutual pledge that this will be our final investigation no matter what, any and all action is at play. One side will live on to continue the life they had before this started, the other will not.

We each retreat into our own thoughts for the rest of the ride, fighting the temptation to sleep. As we stumble into my apartment, I immediately turn toward the bedroom with all my thoughts focused the heavenly feeling of my head sinking into the softness of my pillow. Vinn has other plans.

"Not so fast, cowboy," she teases. "Remember what I told Mendez? Pancakes first."

Other plans indeed.

TWENTY NINE

The temptation is to snuggle or sleep the day away, but we have work to do and reluctantly pull ourselves out of bed mid-afternoon. Vinn's plan to force Upton to call her instead of the other way around is simple but involves some preparation along with a couple of breaking and enterings. We'll gather some of the same items that were left at each of the crime scenes and place them where Upton can't help but spot them. The first couple he may write off as a bizarre coincidence but it won't take long before he recognizes them for what they are, a not so subtle taunting. We'll make sure of that.

We go back to my notes from each scene to find items from the stagings that are both clear references to the murder scenes and readily available to us. I read off the list for Mills' murder.

"That one's easy," I tell Vinn. "Toothbrush. We can use mine. It's about time I replaced it anyway and I have plenty of spares in a drawer in the bathroom."

"Let's try to go for two items per scene if it won't be too much trouble," Vinn adds. "Just to leave no doubt. I assume you have extra combs as well?"

"Yep." Before continuing on to the next scene, I make a quick trip and return with both a well-used toothbrush and a cheap plastic comb and place them on the coffee table. "All right, murder number two."

"We might have a couple of those things here as well," Vinn says once I've finished reading the list. "Nice that the killers were so thoughtful to use everyday objects. I know we have some fresh coffee grounds," she lifts her cup as evidence, "and I remember seeing a couple oranges or nectarines in your fruit drawer. What do you say we carefully cut one in half, scoop out the orange pulp, then fill it with the grounds?"

More often than not when Vinn says "we" in connection to a menial task, it involves only me. I don't even bother waiting for her to rise from her perch on the couch and go to the kitchen. I mess up the first try but get a nice cup made of orange peel on my second. I open the top of the coffee maker, remove the filter, and dump the still-aromatic coffee grounds into the orange. Three minutes in all, and it's added to our small pile on the table.

"It's getting a little harder as we go because the killers got less creative and left fewer items behind with the bodies," I tell her as I review my lists for the remaining murders. "And those that are used are becoming more specialized, so most of them aren't something I have in my apartment. That being said, I think we're still okay with number three."

"Not a lot of choice without spending some decent funds and waiting for Amazon to deliver," Vinn notes. "To avoid that I guess we have no choice but to go with the notebook and pen. I wish it were just a little more distinctive though."

"Why don't we make it that way," I suggest, digging through the pile of papers in our makeshift case file. Vinn immediately sees where I'm headed.

"Brilliant, Winters." she exclaims with just a little too much surprise not to make it sound insulting. "That way there'll be no doubt in his mind who's leaving all of these items in his path. I'll copy it so that it's in a woman's handwriting in case he has any doubts." I hand

Vinn one of the copies we made of the coded puzzle that Broden added to her packet from the meeting then rummage through my desk area to find a small memo book, the kind that costs less than a dollar, along with a spare pen. It doesn't take Vinn long to copy the letters. She leaves it open to the page, sticks the pen through the spiral binding, and adds it to our pile.

"All right, number four," she says and listens as I recite. "You're right, pickings are getting slim. Has to be the wallet and train ticket, right? You have an extra billfold, don't you? Most guys I know do. Bonus if it's made of leather."

I do, a nice one, but it's also got a history. It was given to me by the woman whose presence in Chicago lured me here several years ago and who I dated briefly before tragedy tore us apart. I've kept it as my one tangible reminder of her. As my relationship with Vinn deepened I often meant to give it away, but was never able to. I guess it's time to finally cut that tie with the past.

I retrieve it from the drawer of my nightstand and walk back to the living room. Vinn recognizes it for what it is and her voice softens. "I'm sorry, Mal, we can—"

"No," I interrupt, "it's time." I throw it on the pile. I then dig the wallet I'm using out of my back pocket and pull out my pass for the el. Before I hand it to Vinn I pull up an app on my phone. "Dammit," I tell her, "there's still almost $14.00 left on that thing."

"Sacrifices," she smiles as she tucks it into a flap of the wallet. "I'll buy you a new one. What's last?" she asks, but given that we were just at the murder scene yesterday it was hardly necessary.

"Nail polish," we say together.

"I have some old stuff somewhere in my apartment," she tells me. "No idea where, but we could also just buy some cheap stuff."

"You don't happen to have a beauty mask, do you?" I ask. Vinn looks at me like I just landed here from Mars. I should have known better than to ask. She can probably fit all the makeup she owns in a small hand purse. She chooses not to say anything. "Okay, great," I continue. "Let's get some dinner, decide where to plant this stuff, then get some sleep. We'll probably need to get up before the sun does tomorrow to start our day."

Before we go to bed we decide to cram the time frame for Broden's sightings of the objects into as short a period as possible. If all goes according to plan, he'll see all five sets within a few hours and culminate with the nail polish when he arrives at his job, so that the first thing he would want to do before getting down to work would be to call Vinn and set up a meeting. The downside of this plan is that it means breaking into his home, car, and office in the early hours of the morning, risking getting caught at each location. The plus side, which doesn't even come close to offsetting the downside, is that unlike his cohorts of the puzzle group, he doesn't live an hour away on the North Shore. Instead, he's in Brookfield, a west suburb a short jaunt down the Eisenhower Expressway from my place in Ukrainian Village.

While not as ritzy as homes up north, a beater car would still stand out on the streets of Brookfield, so we're more selective when it comes to choosing our Zipcar ride. We ultimately choose a minivan because no one would think that a thief would use that as a get-away car and it should blend in well within the family neighborhood in which Broden resides. The way Vinn eyes all of the seating and child-friendly features makes me uncomfortable and I add it to my mental list of topics to bring up at a later date, preferably when I'm not sober.

We don't need to watch our speed on the Ike, as anyone going less than thirty miles an hour over the limit at 3:00 a.m. will be the car that stands out. Once we're within the village limits, though, we're careful to abide by the traffic laws. As it turns out, it doesn't matter. As I'm pulling over to the curb in response to flashing lights behind me, Vinn quickly stashes her lock picks under the seat, pulls a scrap of paper out of her purse, and scribbles something on it.

"Out pretty late, folks. Something I can help you with?" The officer smiles outside my window but his right hand hovers just above the butt of his gun. As far as I can tell, he has no partner in the car checking out our plates so there's no way he can know we just picked it up from a space less than eight miles away.

"I'm sorry, officer, but we've been driving all night and I think we're a little lost," I say in my best impression of a hapless husband.

"I told you to take that last exit but did you listen to me? No," Vinn snaps. "You never listen to me. It's like you've never heard of GPS. I didn't even want to come all this way just to see your cousin but does my opinion count? And now look, you get us pulled over. This is great, just great. At least ask the nice man how to get there." As she says this Vinn throws the scrap of paper at me, which I have to grab as it begins to float toward the floor.

"I'm sorry, officer," I say meekly as I hand him the paper. "Would you be so kind as to point me in the right direction?" Vinn continues to nag me in the background and is distressingly convincing.

The cop glances past me and appears uncomfortable. He finally takes a look at the torn piece of paper. "You're not that far. La Grange is just to the south and west. Continue down this street about a mile and a half until you get to Ogden Avenue, it's a busy intersection, then turn right. The street you're looking for is a little over a mile down. You folks have a good night now."

We wait until he returns to his car and pulls around us before exhaling, then wait another few seconds until the glow of his taillights disappears from our sight. Vinn looks at me and giggles, as much out of nervousness as entertainment. We can only hope this isn't an omen for the task ahead.

Five minutes later we're slowly cruising past Broden's house, which is dark on both floors. We turn at the next intersection and park under a tree close to the alley, a virtual blind spot out of sight of most windows in the homes nearby. Our need for speed outweighs our desire for caution, so we hustle out of the car and up the alley, counting houses until we get to six, Broden's home.

So far so good. No dogs are barking, no lights coming on next door, and the back gate doesn't squeak when we open it. The garage shields us from view until we get to the yard, which we sprint across and up three steps to the back door. With Vinn's skill, we're inside in thirty seconds. I hand her the toothbrush and comb and she makes her way to the upstairs bathroom while I pull out the orange peel and remove the plastic wrap keeping the coffee grounds in place.

I'm just placing it on the granite countertop when Vinn returns. We're outside and down the stairs again in no time. Our entire time inside took less than a minute.

Surprisingly the side door to the garage is unlocked. Vinn's disappointed, but does get to work on the lock for a recent model BMW. After a few false tries, she pulls the passenger door open, positions the notebook and pen on the seat open to the page with a copy of the puzzle, and again we're in and out in a flash. Total time out of the Zipcar was probably between six and seven minutes.

Our next stop is Broden's office in Oak Brook, which coincidentally has us driving west on the same Ogden Avenue the cop told us to take not long ago. He's a financial adviser with an office strategically placed in a high-rise office building directly across from the upscale Oakbrook Center shopping mall, so that his clients can buy their mink stole and pay him to manage their millions all in one convenient trip.

We pull in the circular drive but stay on the driveway that takes us to the rear of the building rather than expose ourselves to the guard that's almost certainly snoozing at the reception desk in front. Bushes that haven't been trimmed in years line the building, but about halfway down there's a break for a metal side door that appears to be intended for utility crews and contractors. I pull over into the shadow of the building, nudging the front of the car into the bushes.

Vinn pulls the door handle down and is pleased when the door doesn't open. Another chance to show off her artistry with the picks. She misjudges the size she needs twice but on the third try gives me a wink and we're inside. Concrete steps bring us up to the fourth floor. Broden's office is halfway down the hall. We pass an office with a cleaning cart standing outside the door and faint humming from inside, which tells us we don't have much time. No second tries with the door's lock needed this time and we step into the office.

It's appointed with a false kind of luxury, with materials that mimic the real thing but to a trained eye are cheaper imitations. Replicas of famous paintings line the walls. A reception desk sits immediately inside the door from the hallway and only a few chairs await clients' posteriors. When you deal with the moneyed crowd, it's best not to keep them waiting at all.

Broden's office has an oversized desk and a real leather chair, with comfortable seating for his clients. Sickly plants sit by a window overlooking the rear parking lot and tollway just beyond. I put the wallet containing my transit pass on his chair where he can't miss it while Vinn decides to get playful and paints the handset of the phone on his desk a firehouse red with nail polish.

"As long as we're here, do you want to take a quick look around?" I whisper to Vinn as she caps the bottle of polish. Just as I finish speaking, we look up at the sound of the cleaning cart stopping outside of the door. We exchange a look of panic, then instantly as one rush to stand behind the hallway door just as it opens. The backside of a large woman carrying a trash can in one hand and a dusting mop in the other moves toward the office we just vacated. We waste no time in curling around the open door and dashing out into the hallway and to the stairway.

"Let's hope she doesn't decide to make a phone call," Vinn says with a smile as we descend the stairs. Without any further incidents we're outside, in the car, and headed for home.

THIRTY

"Sorry I missed your call," Vinn says sweetly into her phone. "I was in class all morning. What can I do for you, Mr. Broden? Is there an emergency meeting of Puzzlers Anonymous? Does the government need our help in breaking a hostile power's code?"

She holds the receiver several inches away from her ear. From my position on the other side of her desk I can't make out the words, but I can tell that Broden's voice is rising as he speaks.

"I'm sure I have no idea what you're talking about," Vinn tells him, sounding genuinely puzzled. "But if you really think it'll help, I'd be happy to meet up for coffee later today. I'm a bit tight between class time and labs, but if you don't mind coming down here I have a little time around 4:00 this afternoon. There's a little café on Taylor Street that's open until 5:00. I'll text you the address but right now I've got to get going."

She hangs up without saying goodbye and frowns at the phone in her hand for a few seconds. "He started out kind of creepily calm but wasn't very happy about the nail polish so things got a little heated, as you could hear. That's why he was forced to call from his cell. Funny that the fact that we made clear we know he's involved in a series of brutal killings didn't rile him, but a little creative artwork on his handset did."

"Did he offer to pay for our drinks in exchange for his new leather wallet and transit pass?" I ask, not expecting an answer. "So Phase One of our plan worked exactly as intended. Now what?"

"I guess I never really thought we'd be facing him this early," Vinn replies, "so I haven't given it much thought. Let's approach this backwards again since it's been working so far. Why do we think that he wants to meet? What does he want to get from us? We already showed our hand that we know he's involved in the killings, so it has to be more than that."

"If I were in his position," I respond, "I'd want to know what we're going to do about it. If we were going to turn him in to the cops, why go through this dog and pony show leaving the objects where he could find them? Why warn him? So he has to know that either we don't have enough solid evidence against him to satisfy the authorities, in which case he wonders what our plans are, or we have enough but choose not to turn it over to them, in which case he has the same question but also why the tease?"

"All right, then," Vinn says as she stares at a point on her wall behind me. "He's not going to waste time probing what we know, because if you're correct that information is irrelevant. He also won't care about our motive for getting involved. Again, not important to him. The one and only thing he wants to take away from this meeting is information on what our intentions are."

"Not quite. Not to be too morbid, but he may also want to get to know you—or us if he knows about me, which I'm sure he does—a little better in the event he decides to add us to his list of victims."

"Ugh," Vinn sighs. "Good point. So we try not to give him what he wants, keep it a mystery, while we attempt at the same time to draw him out. But draw out what exactly?"

Vinn's technique of starting from Broden's point of view has helped me bring our goals into clearer focus. "Nothing. Ideally we'd like him to say something incriminating or inadvertently point us in a direction that'll provide what we need to have Mendez and company arrest him. He's too smart for that. What I want to do is motivate him to stop where he is. Let him think that since we're on to him, his best course of action at this point is to quit killing while he still thinks he can get away with it. He needs to know that if there's one more, it's lights out for him."

"And in doing so save Maggie's or some other journalist's life," Vinn adds. "Okay, fine. We hint that we've almost got enough to corner him, that we or maybe even the cops are watching his every move, and that it would be foolhardy to even think about continuing his spree. If he believes us, he may even figure he's so much more cunning and intelligent than his pursuers that he'll stick around even after he quits killing knowing he's getting away with five deaths, or at the very least orchestrating them. But we're not going to give him that luxury, even if true." She pauses, a sadness descending over her face. "Mal, I know this means we may be faced with crossing a line that we both swore was inviolate. But I can't get Maggie's face out of my mind. We owe her."

Vinn looks up at me with a question in her eyes. She wants to know if I'm on board with taking care of business outside of legal means. I choose to pretend I didn't hear and don't respond. Right now, my goal is to stop Broden before throwing him into Mendez's care and watch from the sidelines as he gets tried, convicted, and tossed into prison for life. All of my energies are directed to making that a reality. If that doesn't happen, only then will I evaluate where I stand as to alternative justice, although her focus on Maggie reinforces the sense of urgency to do something and to do it now.

"I'd say let's lay out a plan for how to approach him today," Vinn continues after I say nothing, "but I'm sure that would be a waste of time and I've got my 11:00 class. Want to reconvene here at about 3:30?"

I nod my assent and we both head off to try to fill our students' heads with wisdom while our brains are working on a totally different problem.

We arrive at the coffee shop ten minutes early. The tables outside are full but inside it's not crowded. We don't see Broden, but then there are tables in a blind spot around a corner near the back of the shop where he may await us. Vinn comes here often because of their broad selection of coffees, not to mention the thirty-five different ways you can have them prepared. The sole mention of tea at the bottom of the long menu is "tea variety." I decide to go thirsty and set off to find a table while Vinn orders. I pass on the cushy chairs and couches as too difficult to get out of if things go sour and move to the rear to a more conventional table and chair set. No Broden back here either.

Vinn soon joins me and we wait in a nervous silence. I'm about to get up to take a peek toward the front of the shop when Broden rounds the corner with steaming cup in hand. My state of mind is such that it's the first time that I think of hot coffee as a weapon and my hand drifts down to check that the gun I have concealed hasn't moved since the last time I checked two minutes ago.

"Professor," he says as he approaches the table. "Vinn, a pleasure seeing you again. I don't believe we've met." He extends a hand and I reluctantly accept it as I introduce myself. We both know it's a charade and that he's found everything there is to find about me. He sits opposite me and to the left of Vinn.

"Enough of the pleasantries," Broden states as he adjusts himself in his chair, his voice suddenly taking on the tone of someone here on serious business. "I believe you know why I asked to meet."

"Actually, no," Vinn replies. "As I told you on the phone, I'm clueless."

"Cute choice of words," Broden says, his voice dripping with sarcasm. "Fine, if that's how you want to play it. I received your gifts this morning and if I interpret them correctly, they're meant to intimidate me due to your vast knowledge of certain events about which you actually know very little. Certainly not anything that would cause us any distress or to lead to a change of behavior. I suggest you stick to simple crossword puzzles rather than dip your amateur toes into high-level mysteries which shall forever remain enigmatic to lesser sorts such as yourselves."

"You underestimate us," I chime in. "For someone supposedly so talented at deciphering what's hidden, you're blind to the obvious fact that the walls are closing in around you."

"Oh, how I detest hubris, especially when it can't be backed up by the reality of facts," Broden says with a sick smile. "You, my poor pathetic pursuers, are the ones that are lost and you don't even know it."

"If we're such a non-threat," Vinn tells him, barely controlling what I can see is the rage building within her, "then why demand a meeting? Why drive all the way down here unless you're in a panic, looking over your shoulder frightened of the footsteps behind you?"

"Why, as a courtesy of course," Broden chuckles. "Simply to suggest—strongly—that you abandon your little quest. The inevitable by its very definition can't be stopped. It's going to happen. What you have to consider is how much more tragic your futures will be if you try to stand in the way of the chain of inexorable events. Some things can't be changed but in making the right choice now, other less fateful tasks may be avoided.

"That's what I came to say," he concludes as he stands to go. "You two have a lovely evening." With that, he turns and walks out of our sight, leaving his untouched cup of coffee behind.

"Well that didn't go according to plan," I remark bitterly. "He clearly doesn't think we're a threat to him or whatever he intends to do."

"We know exactly what he intends to do," Vinn spits. "Which means we need to double down on our efforts to convince Maggie to leave town. And he's right, we're not a threat. All we have are suppositions. I know he's involved and you know he's involved, but we can't prove it. Dammit, Mal, I was ready to choke him on his own arrogance until he stopped breathing."

"I felt the same way," I tell her. "He made me regret that we met in a public place. I'm not sure how I would have reacted if there weren't others around. But silencing him here and now might not have achieved our goal."

"I caught that too," Vinn says. "He said that our gifts wouldn't cause 'us' any distress. Either he was talking about himself in royal we-speak, which I doubt, or he slipped up and revealed that he's not alone in pulling the strings of these killings. If that's true, we really are as lost as he says we are. We figured someone else was involved but eliminated the only two people on our radar as accomplices. We're missing something here."

"Agreed," I admit sadly. "For now, let's go back to my place to regroup. You can call Maggie on the way."

THIRTY ONE

"Maggie's still not picking up," Vinn tells me as I scrounge through my fridge to see what I can throw together for dinner. "I don't like this, Mal. I'm sure she's fine, she's probably in the library with her phone on silent. Still, do you think we could head to campus after dinner to see if we can track her down? I may be overreacting, but I'll sleep better once we see her. We could also use the opportunity to bring her up to speed. If she wasn't frightened before, she'd better be scared out of her mind when I update the threat level."

"She's so stubborn I doubt it'll change her attitude," I respond, "but the sooner we tell her what we now know the better. Maybe she'll at least take additional precautions." The cupboard is nearly bare so I go to my default when I have no other food. Eggs, spinach, a couple of chicken sausages, some Parmesan cheese, potatoes, and half of a red pepper I'd roasted for a casserole a week ago. Individually unexciting, throw them together in a cast iron pan on top of the stove then transfer it to the oven and they magically transform into a tasty frittata. I get it started and turn to face Vinn, who's settled in on my couch.

"It's obvious Broden isn't going to stop. And we're no closer to knowing if he actually does have an accomplice or isn't the top dog himself and is doing this under orders from someone else. He's smart and he's devious, and it's not out of the question that referring to 'us' wasn't a slip at all but an intentional diversion to throw us off track."

"That's assuming we're on any sort of track at all," Vinn sighs sadly. "I think we need to be even more pro-active at this stage."

"Meaning?"

"Doing what we should have done before, to begin with. We took unnecessary risks when we broke into Broden's home without doing our due diligence, seeing if he lives with someone else. If we're going to go back we need to start with that. We can't risk collateral damage or witnesses."

"We're going back?" I ask. "When did we decide that?"

"Just now," Vinn answers. "I know it's a long shot to think that he's going to make this easy on us by leaving something that ties him to the murders where we can find it, but on the other hand he's so damn cocky that he may also be overconfident in his ability to get away with them. We know he underestimates us. It wouldn't surprise me if he has something incriminating set out in the open in his house with the expectation that we'll do a search but look right at it and never make the connection. It would give him a sick kind of thrill."

"I guess that's possible," I agree, "but also we're on the far side of desperate and don't have a whole lot of ideas other than breaking in and seeing what we can find."

"Yeah, there's that too," Vinn admits. "We'd better prepare to cancel some classes tomorrow. If I can verify that he keeps regular office hours, we have no choice but to go in when we know he won't be there, assuming he lives alone. Give me a little time to check."

A part of me hopes that Broden has a stay at home wife and thirteen kids in order to avoid the prospect of breaking into his house in broad daylight. I transfer dinner from the stovetop to the oven, set the timer, and nestle next to Vinn to see what she can find.

"It looks like he has office hours regularly every day from 9:00 to 4:30 and a note that says 'no appointment necessary,'" she says as she navigates Broden's website. "He's probably terrified that he won't be there if Mrs. Too Much Money stops by without an appointment after getting her hair done and he isn't there. To be safe we can call from a burner phone and make an appointment that we don't keep."

"He's been one step ahead of us this whole time," I say. "My guess is that he's expecting us to break into his home, maybe even wants us to so that he can set little traps, or as you said get his jollies knowing we won't find anything. He may stay put in his office just to give us a chance to do our thing."

"Won't he be surprised, then, when he comes home tomorrow night to find that he left a burner on under his oatmeal and the place burned down," Vinn mutters, only half in jest. "Let's move on to his personal life."

I leave her to it while I pull the frittata out of the oven, getting plates out as it rests for a few minutes. During an investigation it seems like most of our meals are eaten on the couch in front of Vinn's laptop, so she shows no surprise when I place a warm plate on her lap and hand her a fork.

"He's not exactly forthcoming with personal details on social media," she tells me between mouthfuls. "And if he has a Twitter or Instagram account I can't find it. Linkedin he uses solely for business. He posts mostly self-congratulatory announcements or monetary-related memes there. I swear, people in the financial area need to get more creative. These are putting me to sleep. The few photos from random dinners don't show a woman draped on his arm, but that's not definitive."

"Try putting his name into the court database," I suggest. Vinn types in several commands.

"Good call," she says after a few minutes of searching. "He was sued for divorce about eight years ago, and the order was entered eighteen months later. Pretty quick for Cook County, so it must've been uncontested. Do you still know how to get to the court records?"

I nod and she slides the laptop over to me. The basic timeline of court cases is accessible for free, but to look at documents from those matters requires a fee. It takes me a few tries to remember my username and password for the site since Vinn doesn't have it saved on her laptop, but after that it's easy to pull up the divorce decree in exchange for a couple of bucks.

"Wife got their second home in the city, he got Brookfield. Kids all grown at the time of the divorce. Unless he's remarried or has a girlfriend—or boyfriend—living with him, it looks like we're good."

"If that turns out to be the case we'll deal with it at the time," Vinn replies as she rises off the couch. "I'd love to sit and digest, but let's get going and find Maggie. Then tomorrow we can meet up after our 10:00 classes and head out to the suburbs. We might need some sort of costumes. Posing as exterminators would be a nice touch for the neighbors if you have coveralls. Easy to hide all sorts of weaponry under those things too."

I open the door readying to leave but immediately freeze. Blocking our way, arm raised in the process of knocking, is the imposing frame of Detective Mendez. In our many dealings with Mendez, I've seen him angry, frustrated, furious, suspicious, incensed, sore, irritated, and more, but until this moment I've never seen him nervous or nonplussed. He doesn't want to be here and his face shows it. There's only one reason I can think of for his presence and it's not good. Vinn is obviously thinking along the same lines as she joins me at the door and grips my arm hard.

"When?" she asks Mendez, her voice raspy.

"May I come in?" he replies, stepping just inside the door and closing it behind him without waiting for us to answer. "I'm so sorry to have to tell you this," he goes on, his voice breaking. "But approximately one hour ago the body of a young Asian woman was discovered just off the UIC campus in an apartment leased to one Margaret Wong. We can't—"

"When?" Vinn repeats, loudly this time. "Not when her body was found, when did it happen?"

Mendez shifts uneasily on his feet. "It's too early to be certain. Best guess based on preliminary reports? Late afternoon today, maybe even early evening. Recent. By all accounts it looks like your journalism student, but you know we need a positive ID. We don't believe she has family nearby. I'm on my way to the scene now, and I thought maybe I could give you a ride down there to take a look."

Vinn backs up to lean against the back of my couch, tears welling up in the corners of her eyes. Only when I look at her do I feel my own cheeks getting wet. We exchange glances, both of us cognizant of the timing of her death. I'm trying to remember the last time either of us has seen the other cry and am drawing a complete blank.

"Can you give us a few minutes, Detective Mendez?" I ask. "We'll meet you downstairs."

Mendez nods and turns to go, probably relieved at not being asked anything further or having to stand by awkwardly while we grieve. For a few moments neither one of us says anything, then as if by telepathy reach out to join hands.

"Dammit, Mal," Vinn says with gritted teeth, making no effort to suppress her anger. "We totally misread him again. He didn't set up our meeting this afternoon for the reasons he gave us or for the reasons we assumed. He wanted to be looking at our faces at the same time he knew that Maggie was being murdered, taking a sick pleasure in our ignorance and impotence to stop what he knew was going down while we sipped our coffee and were telling him that we knew too much for him to kill again. We fucked up and look what happened."

I pull Vinn close. "We can't look back and moan about our mistakes, Vinn. We need to concentrate on what we need to do next and how this changes things. Right now, Mendez is waiting for us. We'll discuss our next move on our way back."

"No discussion necessary," Vinn tells me, her voice still shaking. "You know what we need to do. That monster isn't going to see the sun rise."

We sit a moment longer pondering the long night ahead of us and the brutal ramifications for our lives moving forward, then head out the door to take a trip neither of us wants to take to a scene neither of us wants to see.

Mendez is waiting for us at the bottom of the stairs, an idling squad car parked in front of the house next door. He turns as we near him and we silently follow him, sliding into the rear of the car. Neither of us trusts ourselves not to say something that Mendez or the driver will overhear and which could come back to haunt us later. It's only about a three-mile drive to campus, but it's still a long, painfully quiet ride.

We stop outside a modern five-story brick corner building that stretches halfway down each street. The rounded glass entryway is a bustle of activity as a line of impatient students waits to be searched and have their identification checked by one of a number of cops who don't seem to be in any particular hurry. Mendez breezes by them, carrying us through the checkpoint in his wake.

We ride an elevator to the third floor and upon exiting have to navigate past more cops and a wheeled stretcher left outside the door by the medical examiner's crew. Before we enter the apartment, I put my arm out to hold Vinn back and stop. Mendez senses that we're no longer right behind him and turns back with an inquisitive look.

"Cover her," is all I say and he nods in understanding before proceeding inside. Thirty seconds later he motions us in.

I can tell that there are props littered around the room, including a Salvation Army-style bell, but I ignore them. None of the details of the staged scenes from the prior killings has helped us in the least so there's no sense dawdling to take them in. They'd provide nothing more than more fodder for our distress and that level is already off the charts.

Vinn and I join hands as we approach the sheet on the couch. Kate looks at us sympathetically, waits for us to give a signal, then pulls back the top of the sheet. A seething rage rushes to my head as I look upon the face of what just this morning was a living, vibrant woman with a bright future.

"That's Maggie Wong," I manage to squeak out and Vinn mumbles her assent. Mendez knows better than to ask us to stick around to evaluate the scene and arranges one of the officers in the hall to take us home.

Vinn gives her address to our escort. "No time to waste," she whispers, and we both sit back to mentally prepare for what lies ahead, not only tonight but for the rest of our lives.

THIRTY TWO

"You've never hot-wired a car?" Vinn asks incredulously back at her place. It's true. Through all of my years of covert work for an off-book government agency, getting my hands dirty in countless extreme and mostly illegal ways, stealing a car that wasn't already running isn't on my resume.

"Well you haven't either," I respond like a petulant third-grader. Given the odds that our middle of the night field trip will result in a badly injured Broden, or worse, leaving a record with Zipcar that we used its services along with the number of miles we drove is out of the question. There's no convenient public transportation out to Brookfield and neither one of us owns a car or knows someone trustworthy enough to borrow one from. That leaves only one option. Any guilt is assuaged by our rationalization that it's for a worthy cause that trumps the vehicle owner's inconvenience and the fact that we intend to bring it back. Hopefully.

Vinn opens her laptop to do a Google search before stopping herself. "Dammit," she mutters under her breath. "That would be Exhibit A at our trial."

"You're a scientist, how hard could it be?" I ask, which earns me a scowl in return. "And each of us must have seen a dozen movies where it takes a character about ten seconds to put a couple of wires together under the steering wheel and voila! Instant engine noise. We just need to concentrate to bring back one of those memories."

A nice thought in theory, but stupid in practice. After a few fruitless minutes of closed-eye concentration, we both realize the futility. Vinn admits that given an hour or two in a lab she could figure it out, but out in the field hiding from the scrutiny of a nosy public with cell phone cameras at the ready is another matter.

"There is one other possibility of someone who might know something and be willing to give us a few tips," I finally say.

"I thought of him too," Vinn admits. "Worth a try. Besides, in this neighborhood most of the cars are in the upper price ranges and will have anti-theft devices, and the street lighting is too good even in the alleys. Not so much over by you. Call up an Uber while I pack up some supplies, cowboy. Nothing suspicious about us going to your place at 11:00 at night and time's wasting."

Thirty minutes later we're exiting a dark-colored Ford Taurus, which fits exactly the kind of non-descript generic car that would be perfect for our task. On the ride over I read Vinn's eyes and could see the same idea forming in her head. A slight shake of my head and she sat back in a pout but refrained from knocking our driver out once he pulled over.

We don't even bother to stop by my apartment first but head down the darkened stairway to Leo's place. As usual, the door swings open an instant before we reach the bottom landing. I'll never know how he does that, or how he knew to have three glasses filled with an enticing amber liquid at the ready on his kitchen table.

"Not tonight, Leo," I tell him. "We need our wits about us." He eyes us curiously, then as I explain why we need his help one corner of his mouth twitches for several seconds. For Leo, that's the equivalent of uproari-ous, and in this case probably derisive, laughter. Over his shoulder I can see a photo of Megs leaning up against his toaster. He traces my discovery with his eyes, leans over to flip the picture face down, and pretends nothing just happened. Okay, Leo. We're even.

"I show," he says, rummaging in a drawer for paper and pencil. He proves himself to be a remarkably detailed artist, but despite his efforts he can tell that while Vinn and I now understand the concept, we're not ready to pass the final exam. He throws up his hands in frustration. "I show," he says again.

He gets up out of his chair, but before moving toward the door takes a match and lights his diagram on fire, dropping it into his now empty glass to finish burning to ash. His intuition, always sharp, has clearly told him that our asking for help in stealing a car means that we have plans for which no evidence should be left behind.

Leaving his unit, he leads us directly back into the shadows of the alley separating the yards of our block and those of the homes on the block to the south. We follow as he walks swiftly west, then zig zags to take us to a street several blocks away from my building. Halfway down the block a broken light leaves the street an area three houses wide in darkness. He stops next to a dark blue, older model car. I can barely see the car much less discern its make or model.

Vinn throws me a question with her eyes. Leo came here directly without a pause, and it can hardly be a coincidence that he found what appears to be the perfect car sitting in darkness. He knew it was here. Either this is his car or he's "borrowed" it himself on some prior occasion. Add that to the list of conversations for another time. Or not.

Vinn uses her picks to quickly open the driver's door then pushes a button to unlock the others and moves around to the passenger seat. I get in the middle of the back seat and lean forward. No alarm goes off and no inside lights come on. I use my flashlight to direct a beam at Leo's hands.

Leo produces a screwdriver from one of his many pockets and quickly removes the panel covering the steering column. Just as in the movies, it takes him seconds to find the correct wires, which were already stripped, twist them together, spark them with another wire, and get it started. He does it twice, then switches seats with Vinn so that she can do it herself. She's perfect the first time. Leo nods and within seconds has vanished.

I move to the passenger seat, buckle up, and without a word Vinn moves away from the curb. Trouble, here we come.

Vinn claims not to be superstitious, only cautious, but whatever the reason she takes a different exit off the expressway than the last time we visited Broden's house, which seems longer ago that just last night. The last thing we need is to be stopped again by a curious cop, which would put our plans for tonight on an indefinite hold and I don't think either one of us could tolerate even an hour more of delay.

We're pickier tonight on finding a place to park and it's harder to find the ideal space since we don't want to be on the same block as the last time. In the city, where parking spots are at a premium in many neighborhoods, a strange car blends in with the rest, but in the suburbs where everyone has a garage, the street is empty by 9:00

at night, and everyone knows the cars the neighbors drive, an unfamiliar car—or even two different cars on two consecutive nights—will draw attention. We finally settle in an area two blocks away where a commercial building on one side of the block means fewer residents looking out windows when they get out of bed for a glass of water.

"Do you think he expects us?" Vinn asks softly as we walk briskly back toward the entrance to the alley behind Broden's home.

"Yes," I answer. "Maybe not tonight, but there's no question that killing Maggie was meant to be bait. We have to enter his home tonight with the assumption that he's sitting by the back door with a shotgun or has the place boobytrapped. It's the perfect setup for him. Once inside, we're invading his home and he'll have a legal right to kill us."

"True, but it would take some explaining if he did so in some weird or unconventional way that's not reflexive, say by poisoning, which works in our favor. A gun or a heavy object we can expect, but not a viper or electric shock."

"I wouldn't put anything past him, Vinn," I caution. "He may see our deaths as a challenge, and we already know he thinks he can outwit anyone in law enforcement. He considers himself invulnerable."

I finish speaking just as we reach the entrance to the alley. Vinn pauses and holds me back from moving into it.

"You're right," she says. "Besides thinking of himself as superior to us in all ways, he's got us pegged as stupid and conventional, lumping us in with his opinion of cops in general. Which begs the question. If he really is waiting for us, and I agree with you that he may be, how do you think he expects us to gain entry to his home? What's the most logical and unimaginative entry point?"

I don't need time to think of an answer. "The back door, exactly where we're headed. It's the entry most hidden from view, the lock is easy to pick, and it's where we got in last time. So it's out. Does that mean we're going in the front way?"

"Only if we have to," Vinn says. "What do you say we have a quick and furtive look at the windows?"

We circle back to the street and soon have taken refuge in a neighbor's shrubbery, from which we can see the front and one side of Broden's home. There are no lights on anywhere on either floor, but that tells us nothing. More importantly, there are no lights and only two windows on the side of neighbor's house that faces his. I pull out my binoculars. Street and alley lamps shed just enough light for me to see.

"All of the upstairs windows, and one window on the first floor, probably a bathroom, are open a crack," I tell Vinn. "Call me cautious, but for me that falls in the 'too good to be true' category."

"Possibly," she responds. "But it's a warm night so open windows make sense, and if possible entering that way would be less risky than through one of the doors. Go to the back of the house and see if the air conditioner is running and I'll meet you under that bathroom window."

I squat behind the unit for five or six minutes and it never kicks on, nor is it warm to the touch, which tells me the open windows may not be a ruse. I return to tell Vinn and find her waiting for me with a garbage bin she pulled from the alley resting directly beneath the bathroom window.

"I took a peek," she tells me, "and don't see any obvious traps. Not saying there aren't any, so stay alert."

I hoist her up and steady her legs as she takes her time gently raising the window to its full height. Vinn should be able to get through the opening easily. For me, it'll be a tighter squeeze. I pull myself up on the lid and wait. Vinn's face appears at the window a few long minutes later.

She helps me through then puts her mouth to my ear. "Both the front and back door have a mix of broken glass and bubble wrap scattered around wherever we would have stepped. Bubble wrap is painted to blend in with the floor. The rugs that were there last night have been taken up, so the floor may squeak. Put these on," she commands as she hands me some extra thick winter socks she thought to bring with her, "and slide your feet instead of stepping."

We're so fearful of making noise that it takes us several minutes to travel to the bottom of the stairs. Once we reach it, a thought occurs to me. I tap Vinn on the shoulder and signal her to follow me back into the living room, where we huddle behind a side table, staying as still as statues.

We don't have to wait long. We sense before we see the movement as Broden appears from wherever he was hiding in the kitchen, pistol drawn, walking just as slowly as we did. He raises his arm as he nears the bottom of the staircase, expecting to find our shapes nearing the top.

Vinn feels me tense and moves with me as we jump out from the shadows. I grab the arm holding the gun while Vinn simultaneously pulls his legs out from under him, causing him to fall forward face first onto the wooden steps. I have a choice to either break his fall or to take possession of the gun as my hands slide up his flailing arms. I choose the gun. Broden hits the stairs hard, opening a bloody gash in his forehead. He's momentarily stunned, giving Vinn time to pull his arms behind his back and slip zip ties around his wrists, binding them together. Together we drag him to the living room, pushing his inert body into a chair. Vinn sits him upright while I use cables to incapacitate his legs.

It takes about fifteen minutes for Broden to pull out of his state of semiconciousness and open his eyes, then another five for those eyes to gain focus. When he does, the first thing he sees is the business end of one of Vinn's sharpest blades millimeters from his throat.

"We're going to have a little chat, Mr. Puzzle Master," she tells him. "But be forewarned. If your voice rises so much as the smallest bit above a whisper, whatever you're saying will be the last words you speak on this earth." She pauses, even flicking the knife slightly to draw blood. "Same result if either of us decides that your answers are bullshit. So now that you know the rules of the game, shall we begin?"

THIRTY THREE

Broden has two options at this stage, to cooperate or not, but if he can read the room there really isn't much of a choice at all. Nevertheless, he chooses defiance as his initial play, glaring at us both and attempting to spit at Vinn. Big mistake. In return she brings the handle of her knife down hard on the growing lump of his forehead, eliciting a yelp from Broden, which Vinn meets with a light slash across his throat. Not deep enough to cause real damage, but the theatrics of a long line of oozing blood effectively shut him up.

"Already breaking the rules, are you?" Vinn asks. "If that continues, it'll be a short night for you. You're one more noise or expectoration from a rag soaked in gasoline being stuffed into that big mouth of yours while I play mumbly peg with your fingers. I have to confess I've never been very good at that game, and it's pretty dark in here."

She looks over in my direction, which I take as a cue to begin the interrogation. I bring a chair in from the kitchen, place it close so that my knees touch his, and lean in so that our faces are inches apart. Vinn and I have play-acted tough guy scenes in the past when necessary and found amusement at our poor thespian skills later. What I'm about to do now, though, with my emotions riding high, I have too much experience with. One such session that went badly was one of the reasons I left my former job behind. I never thought I'd be in this position again and I don't like it.

"You need to listen closely," I tell him softly. "We know what you did to Maggie, so our tempers are short and as you can already see, it doesn't take much to trigger a painful reaction from Vinn here. And now that I have you up close and personal and look into your unrepentant eyes, I frankly think she's holding back too much. To save yourself, all you need to do is answer a few questions. Do you understand?"

Vinn takes his head in her hands, one grasping the top over his wound and the other under his chin directly on the cut, then forces it up and down in a nod. Broden remains silent but grits his teeth in silent agony.

"Good," I continue. "Keep that up and we're going to get along just fine. Now first up we have more of an essay question. In other words a short question containing a few subparts followed by a long and detailed answer just like you used to have in school. Got it? Tell us why you started killing, how you chose your victims, how you got other people to do the killing for you, and who else is involved. Take your time. If we feel you're deliberately leaving anything out, there will be consequences. Okay, go. We're listening."

"Screw you, you'll—" Broden begins before Vinn takes a dishrag she retrieved from the kitchen and shoves it deep into his open mouth. He begins to struggle to breathe.

"Use your nose," she tells him unsympathetically. She brandishes a second knife, longer and more menacing than the first, twirling it in front of his eyes. Flipping it up and catching it by the handle, she moves behind him, grabs a handful of Broden's hair, pulling it so tight that his eyes water, then slashes it at the base. She cuts more than his hair and another crimson line opens on the top of his head.

"No extra charge for the haircut," she taunts as she shows him her fistful of his locks before dropping them to the floor. "Now, are you ready to try again or do you need us to repeat the question?"

I pull the gag out, causing Broden to cough and his throat to spasm. I retrieve a large water bottle from my pack and begin pouring the still-freezing water into his mouth as Vinn holds his head back. He can't swallow fast enough and soon begins to thrash as he realizes he's drowning.

Vinn roughly pushes his head back upright. Excess water from his mouth pours onto his chest and down onto his lap, giving the appearance that he peed himself.

"Did we have a little accident?" Vinn mocks, then thrusts the heel of her boot hard into his crotch. Broden whimpers in pain. "Focus now, Puzzle Boy. This may be your last chance to answer our questions. A single utterance out of your mouth other than what we need to know will be all the proof we need to indicate your intent not to cooperate."

Broden's eyes are distant, his pallor a near white. We count the seconds while he regroups, then lean in to hear him speak. Instead, he begins to yell at full volume.

"Fu—." Broden never has a chance to finish what turns out to be his very last word in life. In a flash Vinn moves behind him and wraps her hands around his throat, instantly crushing his larynx as she applies the pressure. Two seconds turn into five, then five into ten. Broden's initial struggles cease, then as time passes his eyes begin to pull away from their sockets and the color of his face changes hue first to a mild red before morphing into a deeper purple. At around the forty or fifty second mark, he slumps forward then topples to the floor.

"I know what you're thinking," Vinn says to me while still gazing at the inert form lying at her feet. "I brought an arsenal of knives, why didn't I just use one and get it over fast with a quick slash?" I don't interrupt to tell her that wasn't anything close to what was on my mind but don't say anything. "I wanted his death to be slow. I wanted him to have time to realize that death was imminent and to use his last precious seconds on this planet knowing that he was dying because of what he did to Maggie. I also wanted to give you time to stop me if you had wanted to."

On this point, she's reading me better than I am myself. It never occurred to me to intervene. I didn't know it, but I wanted Broden to die and was content to be an audience to his execution. This realization brings our earlier discussions back into focus. As long as we continue to involve ourselves in these misadventures passing as investigations, the evil sides of ourselves we created as a survival technique in our past careers will never go away. The only way to reformulate our personalities to conform with who we wish we were is to make sure we're never put in this position again.

I know what comes next for Vinn because I've been there, and for all but the few people for whom taking another's life means nothing, the physiological reaction is the same. I move behind her and pull her tight in a bear hug. Almost at the same time she begins to tremble, then shake, and finally gasps for air as she uncontrollably sobs without tears. She's not sorry she killed Broden. Instead, she's sorry that it had to happen. There's a difference.

We stand in the middle of the room for maybe five or ten minutes before Vinn slides from my grasp, turns around, and pulls her arms around me. I stroke her hair, not talking because there's nothing to say. The temptation is to tell her that everything's going to be all right, but that would be a lie. Nothing will be the same ever again.

More time passes. Eventually I feel Vinn's body relax, loosen my grip, and she pushes herself away, turning around to look at the body on the floor.

"I won't say I regret what I did, Mal, because I don't," she says firmly.

"If you hadn't done it, I would have," I respond, not sure if that's true or not, but only because Vinn had the courage to do what I may not have had. I'm experiencing no remorse and if anything feel pride for her actions.

"We made a bit of a mess here, Winters," she says, returning to a more clinical view of the scene. "And I guess it's too late to second guess anyway. At this moment we need to figure out what to do from here."

"One thing we shouldn't do is stick around here any longer than we have to," I comment. "Which means no poking around. As things stand right now that probably won't yield anything we need to know anyway since I doubt Broden has the name of his killing cohort written down anywhere, if one exists at all. As far as his body is concerned, my vote is to move him to delay its discovery for as long as possible. Give us time."

"How much do you think we have, minimum?" Vinn asks.

"If he doesn't show up for work tomorrow and his secretary can't reach him by phone, her first thought won't be that he's dead. She'll wait a few days before panicking and calling in the cops to do a welfare check. Even then she'll call the suburban cops, who won't know that he's connected to a Chicago investigation so they won't do much at first. Once Mendez gets wind of the fact that he's missing, we probably have a day before he comes calling. I'd say five days at the very least. Assuming his body isn't discovered before then."

"So we should clear out in forty-eight hours," Vinn says with a sad sigh. "I'm sorry, Mal, I know this isn't the life you thought you were getting with me."

"Not your fault," I reply. "You were doing fine until I came along. But there's no time for a pity party. Where should we take him?"

"The airport," Vinn answers without hesitation. "Long-term parking. That should give us a week if the temperatures don't get too hot and he starts to smell. We'll put him in the trunk of his own car. You drive him in then walk or take the shuttle to the closest terminal. I'll circle around and pick you up at arrivals."

"Are there cameras at the entrance to the lot?" I ask.

"I don't think so," she answers. "But does it really matter?"

Vinn's right. After Maggie's murder, Vinn and I will both be at the top of Mendez's list of suspects once Broden's body is discovered or a formal search is initiated for him as a missing person. No sense sweating the fine details.

It takes no time to find his car keys, which are hanging from a coat hook attached to the wall in the kitchen. I grab Broden under the arms and drag his body to the back door, where Vinn waits to grab his feet and carry him down the stairs to the back yard. She retreats to close the door, not bothering to lock it.

Luck is on our side as no lights come on and the neighborhood dogs are all dreaming of their next meal, so the ninety seconds it takes us to get Broden inside the garage passes uneventfully. We take a few minutes to catch our breath before opening the trunk and tossing him in, but not before noticing duplicates of a few of the items left at two of the murder scenes sitting inside.

"Son of a bitch," Vinn mutters spitefully. "Serves him right." She climbs into the passenger seat as I start the car, back out of the garage, and head for the car we stole tonight. I wait as Vinn effortlessly and quickly gets the wires connected right on her first try and fires up the engine.

There are so many thoughts racing through my mind as I drive to O'Hare, Vinn keeping half a block behind me to play it safe in case I get stopped, but I'm unable to bring them into focus sufficiently to organize a game plan for the next several hours. I'm surprised when I find myself on Mannheim Road, only minutes from the long-term parking lot. I don't remember the last ten minutes of the drive.

I pull in, observe that while there are security cameras covering the lot itself, there are none that focus on drivers pulling in. I take a ticket that'll never be redeemed, move to the far corner of the lot, and park in between a large pickup truck and a white paneled van with a florist's name on the side. At this time of night the shuttle only picks up every half hour and I don't want to risk staying in one place for that long, especially once I notice the blood stains dotting the front of my shirt and pants. Keeping my head down, I slowly jog the mile or so to the international terminal, where flights land at odd hours during the night and I won't be alone waiting for a ride. I stay at the far end of the passenger pickup island where no one else is close and hover in the shadows under a broken overhead light.

Vinn pulls up a short time later. I hop in and sink into the seat as she pulls away and adrenaline begins to drain from my system. Neither of us says a word as we drive back toward the city that we'll never again call home.

THIRTY FOUR

"One suitcase? Two? Are a couple of boxes okay? It's hard to know what to pack when we don't know where we're going or how we're getting there," Vinn complains, more to herself than at me. We're standing in the living room of her condo as she takes visual inventory of the life she's so carefully curated for the last several years. "Is there any chance of getting a car?"

The sun is just starting to peek its way over the horizon and it's been too long since either of us has slept, with the prospect of a long day ahead without more than an hour or two of pillow time. We're both edgy as well as sleep-deprived but need to push through our fatigue in order to face preparing to move, a task neither of us thought we'd ever have to face again. There'll be time to work out our long-term plans later. Right now the only thing we know is that Chicago is the one place that we can't afford to be and we don't have the luxury of time to dawdle over packing decisions.

"I have an idea as to where we can head," I say, "but it's too early to make that call. As far as a car, that's not going to be an issue." I catch a spark in Vinn's eyes as I utter those words. "Not so fast, master car thief. I wasn't talking about using your newfound skills. It's easy enough to buy one for cash, no names and no questions asked. For now, I suggest traveling light. We can ask Rebecca to put all of our stuff in storage until we get settled."

"If we get settled," Vinn moans. "I'm sorry Mal. For years I refused to get too comfortable, figuring my past would catch up with me at some point and I'd have to pull up roots. I guess over time I started feeling secure.

Still not sure where all this crap came from though."

In the end, Vinn packs two large suitcases and one box of what she calls essentials, which I can see includes an impressive assortment of weaponry and her favorite coffee. As we go to leave, she pauses at the door and gazes back wistfully before closing the door with a sigh. If a tear leaves her eye I don't see it. I'm not sure I'll be able to say the same thing at my place.

We take an Uber to my apartment, where I repeat Vinn's packing endeavor, down to the same number of suitcases and a box lined with enough artillery to arm a small army, which I hide beneath my entire stash of tea. As I stare at the box, I say a silent prayer that the tea will run out before I need to touch anything resting beneath it.

We place our luggage next to the door. I scramble some eggs with whatever vegetables I find in the crisper, doing my best to use up as much food as possible. Sated, Vinn shuffles to the bedroom to take a nap while I start working the phone.

Just over an hour later, when I'm about to join Vinn for a short snooze, she stumbles out of the bedroom, her hair disheveled but her eyes wide open.

"I just got a call from an unknown number," she says, her voice unsteady. "A woman. The call woke me up so I can't recite the conversation precisely, although it was one-sided and short. The gist was that our participation is required for the next step in her quest, or plan, or something like that. And that if we don't show up, Maggie won't be the only one of our circle to suffer. She's going to text me an address."

For several long moments, Vinn and I stare at each other motionless and silent, then both of us move at the same time. "Get some coffee and tea going," she orders. "I'll look up the next set of professions on the list."

I'm barely started when I hear a small gasp from Vinn's direction. "Mal, this isn't good," she tells me. "Murder number seven. If she follows the pattern, the next victim will be a police officer. And the killer? A teacher. Mal, she wants to use us to kill a cop."

I'm stunned and say nothing. Vinn's phone then pings with the address that we're supposed to go to. Neither the coffee nor tea are quite ready yet, but I take out two mugs and pour. Vinn gulps her coffee down quickly and I do the same with my tea. We move to the boxes we just packed and begin lining ourselves with weapons wherever we can find room for them, Vinn handing me a few blades and I returning the favor by giving her two handguns. We face each other, scanning to make sure they're not in plain sight.

Any issues with sleep are no longer a factor. Our eyes are sharp, the adrenaline is flowing. If we felt any remorse for our earlier actions and the consequences they brought on, it's now buried deep inside.

"Are you ready?" Vinn asks. "Let's go to war."

The address Vinn was given is in a distressed area on Cermak Road just west of Pilsen less than two miles from our offices on the UIC campus. We don't want to risk stealing a car in broad daylight and aren't about to take public transportation when armed to the teeth, so we have little choice but to call up an Uber. Vinn finds a well-reviewed Mexican hole-in-the-wall on Yelp that serves breakfast and is only about three blocks from our destination to give as the drop-off point. We'll have to look at the menu later in the unlikely event we're ever accused of being connected to the events about to take place and are asked what we ate there.

While on our way, Vinn pulls up a picture of the building we're headed for. A stand-alone, two-story brick and cinder block building that has seen better days. On either side are fenced, weed-infested empty lots. The building's windows have security bars blocking entry and there are no side doors. Our only choices are the front or rear door, and either way we'll be expected. Stealth is not an option.

"We can't go in with guns blazing," I say as we walk west, the sun warm above us. "We don't know who's there, if anyone at all. It could be a test to see how we react. That, and we don't know if the threat to someone that we know is real."

"Doesn't mean we need to be stupid," Vinn responds. "We have to be prepared for anything and everything."

The front door is closed but unlocked. Vinn turns the knob slowly, then pushes it open quickly. I push past her, gun in hand, sweeping the room with my eyes. "Clear right," I say. Vinn answers with a "clear left."

We're in what must be a storage facility for theatrical costumes and props. Nearly every square inch of space in this front room is crammed with furniture, shelves of household items, realistic animals with glowing glass eyes, lighting, and racks of clothes from long-ago eras. The path through the room in the direction of the rear of the building is winding and barely wide enough for us to make our way through. Vinn assumes the lead, taking one step at a time before pausing to allow us to fully examine the areas around us. Dim fluorescent lighting is barely enough to illuminate what's around us and casts shadows that move as the lights flicker.

We reach a doorway with no door to the room beyond. Large, deep wooden cabinets that reach nearly to the ceiling block our view of anything but a narrow strip of the floor and the blank wall on the far side. Unlike the front room, this one is unnaturally light, nearly blinding in its brightness.

We step in cautiously and are immediately confronted with the sight of a cop in an odd uniform tied to a chair against the center of the far wall, his head drooping low but not so far as to hide a rag used as a gag stuffed into his mouth. Before we can take another step a woman's voice from another part of the room sounds.

"Keep your eyes focused on the man in the chair," she says. "Do not turn around. Walk forward slowly until I tell you to stop, then slide sideways until you're directly in front of him, both of you. Stay side by side and don't talk."

There's something familiar in the voice but I can't place it. As we continue to slowly move across the floor, looking at the man set up to be the next victim, he raises his head. I gasp as the face of Officer Jenkins stares at us, his eyes red and panicked, sweat trickling down his too-young features. I see now why his uniform didn't connect with me at first. It's the one issued to campus police, not the garb of the Chicago cops. He moans through his gag.

"Now," the voice continues, "I know what you're thinking. No way you'll kill this man. That's what they all think. I'd rather die myself than take the life of an innocent person, blah, blah, blah. But when it comes to either going through with it or watching your kid or spouse die a painful death, they always come through. Put your arms out away from your sides and slowly turn around."

We do so. Two familiar figures immediately come into view. Strapped into a chair identical to that holding Jenkins is Leo, his arms and legs bound and his mouth also gagged. The only difference from Jenkins is his attitude. His eyes show defiance, not desperation.

The woman standing above him holding a gun to his head, the owner of the voice I should have recognized, is Megan Vixen. Dressed in a cocktail dress that emphasizes her cleavage, black transparent stockings, and three-inch heels, she looks more ready to have cocktails on a Friday night than to commit three murders in the early hours of the morning. The instant I see her, and given what we learned from the past killings, I know she doesn't intend to let Vinn and I leave this place alive.

"Surprised?" she coos triumphantly. "Sexy Megs, the airhead, the bimbo, not smart enough or clever enough to keep up with the boys. I've heard that all my life. Judged, typecast, kept down because no woman this attractive could possibly have a brain and know how to use it. Relegated to second-class status even in a stupid puzzle club."

I feel Vinn tense up next to me. The irony of the situation is apparently lost on our tormentor. Vinn is the most beautiful woman I've ever met, even discounting my obvious bias, as well as the most brilliant. She can also, when necessary, be one of the most brutal. I'm counting on it. A random thought also crosses my mind.

In the early days of the investigation, a drunken Leo insisted that the killer was a woman. I doubt he's feeling any satisfaction at this stage of having been right.

Vixen continues. "You think I was born with this last name?" She chuckles. "I just thought I'd give people what they want. It fooled that idiot Broden. He thinks he's so much more intelligent than the rest of us in that moronic group of Mensa wannabes. It didn't take much effort at all to put him under my thumb. Just had to use my feminine wiles to make him think this whole idea of committing a perfect set of murders where we leave such obvious clues that the authorities are too dumb to solve was his idea. I thought about killing him but he didn't fit within the two lists, so I came up with the plan to have him use his raging insistence to prove he was so much smarter than me to take actions that put him right in the thick of each murder. Maybe someday the cops will solve them, but even then all the evidence will lead straight to Mr. Puzzle Master, not simple-minded Meggie Vixen. Even the two of you were easily pointed in the direction of the two idiots he hung out with at the meetings."

Referring to Broden in the present tense, she clearly doesn't know how he pushed Vinn and I over the edge. If she did, she might not be teasing us herself, unleashing the storm that's about to come.

"Your mistake was looking for patterns where they didn't exist," Vixen continues. "Starting within the puzzle group was the perfect shield. Solving puzzles requires making sense of the impossible, right? So you're immediately thrown off track because the only connection outside of the two lists is randomness. I started with the decision to rid the group of a couple of members that shouldn't have been allowed in to begin with. It was easy enough to find that patsy Stohl through online chats. He wanted a promotion and the rise in income that came with the new job so badly that he would do anything to get it. All it took was a little lie that I had connections I could use to make it happen and a story about a businessman who raped me to get him to rid me of the sight of that Mills person. Then that nurse fell into my lap when she reached out for help in putting her life in order in order to avoid losing time with her son. Turns out kids are a great motivator.

"After that I just found people online with the right occupations and a need pressing enough to kill. It takes a lot less than you'd think, especially once they're convinced they'll get away with it. Of the victims, I admit that after the group members only the vlogger was random. The rest all served a purpose to either silence them or in the case of that student to encourage you to go away. And of course to cause you some pain.

"Anyway," Vixen says, "enough talk. You're here for one reason and I'm sure you know what it is. Kill the cop and Leo walks free. If you don't do your job, though, your friend here will be the first to go, then the both of you, and the officer over there will have a front row seat to watch it all go down before he ultimately meets the same end. So you see, it's either three of you if you cooperate or four if you don't. And you may not believe me, but I do keep my word and let my, let's call them my 'incentives,' go. They know what I'm capable of and keep their mouths shut. It's only if they don't that bad things will happen. I'm not a monster, after all."

"Leo," I tell our friend, "I'm so sorry you got dragged into this. As far as that argument we had, I guess now is the time to drop it." I slightly stress the words "now" and "drop." Vinn's nod, meant to appear that she shares my sentiment, is her acknowledgment that she understands. We can only hope that Leo does.

"Enough chatter!" Vixen shouts as she moves directly behind Leo. "Turn around and get to it! Both of you need to do this together. And don't forget, my finger is on the trigger."

We slowly spin back to face Jenkins, who has tears streaming down his face. Vinn draws her throwing blade while I take out my pistol with the surest aim.

"We're so sorry, Jenkins, but we have no choice," Vinn says sadly but loud enough to carry behind us. "We have to do this NOW!"

With her final word, Vinn spins and throws as Leo twists his body to one side, falling several inches downward. Almost instantaneously the blade is buried in Vixen's shoulder. Her face registers shock but, still alert, she begins to move her good arm toward the gun. A split second later the bullet from my gun hits her precisely between her eyes and her body drops, the gun falling to the floor.

Vinn bends over, her hands on her knees, and begins breathing deeply. I put my hand on her shoulder.

"You were high," I say.

"Right where I aimed, you asshole," she replies with a smug smile as she rises.

We begin walking in Leo's direction but he shakes his head and uses it to gesture toward Jenkins. We turn around. Jenkins' tears continue to fall. His face is pale and his body is attempting to shake within its binds. I take one of Vinn's knives and begin to cut him free. Vinn reaches deep inside one of her pockets and pulls out a small bag of Garrett's popcorn, a mix of cheese and caramel known locally as the "Chicago Mix." She shrugs off my look of bafflement.

"Eat this," she says as she places a few fingerfuls next to Jenkins' lips. As soon as he's free and able to feed himself, she goes off in search of water while I find a fake fur coat from the front room and place it over his shoulders.

I move over to Leo, who's been more than patient staying tied up with a bloody body oozing at his feet while we attended to Jenkins. He's been busy and has loosened his bindings enough that given a few more minutes he could have freed himself.

"You might want to try a different dating service," I tell him as I untie his gag. He merely grunts as he rubs his wrists. Vinn rejoins us, removing her knife from Vixen's body and wiping it on her dress.

"Glad you were listening and picked up on Mal's code," she says to Leo. "I guess getting into that club was no accident." She pats him on the shoulder before wrapping her arm inside my elbow and pulling me to the center of the room. "So, some satisfying symmetry. What began with a puzzle ends with a puzzle." She looks in the direction of Jenkins. "Shall we?"

We walk over to Jenkins, who hasn't moved out of his chair. He's finished Vinn's popcorn and water but continues to tremble and isn't where he needs to be. Still, it's critical that he listens to what we have to say. I pull him to a standing position.

"Jenkins. London," I say to get his attention. "What you see here didn't happen. Do you understand? I'm usually not one to say 'you owe me one,' but Vinn and I can't get wrapped up in an investigation or try to justify what just went down. You'll know why eventually. We saved your life today, so you do owe us. Besides, if you still want to be a Chicago cop down the road, the way today's events went down wouldn't exactly look good on your resume."

"If you want to discover her body in a couple of days to provide a cover story as to why your DNA and fingerprints are at the scene, that's fine," Vinn continues. "Just come up with a plausible reason for why you thought to look here. And leave Leo and the two of us out. Agreed?"

Jenkins nods, still not speaking. He's on the mend and can find his own way home. By this time, Leo is heading toward the door.

"Wait up, big guy," I yell out. "Do you want a ride back? We'll gather up Rebecca from wherever she is on the way. We need to talk."

THIRTY FIVE

My block is quiet early on this Sunday morning with only an occasional jogger or dog walker passing by. The sun has yet to break the horizon but casts just enough light for Vinn and I to view the outline of the building I've called home for the last few years, and which has enough memories in its walls for a lifetime. The car I bought under an assumed name is packed and parked at the curb, ready to go. Vinn and I are not.

Rebecca is adorned in a floral, quilted, and, as she made sure to tell us, designer label house coat. She normally wouldn't be up early on the weekends so I appreciate the gesture to come out to see us off. She's avoided eye contact since she got here, even as she hands Vinn a paper bag with grease spots staining the outside.

"Snacks for the road," she says softly. Vinn and I thank her, trying to sound sincere. Rebecca has yet to gift us with one of her experimental efforts at baking that has actually been edible. Out of respect one of us, the loser of a coin flip, will be forced to take a nibble but most likely the contents of the bag will be scattered to the winds somewhere in Iowa for unfortunate birds to discover.

Leo stands off to the side, impassive as ever, the blood and grease stains on his apron impossible to wash out after so many years behind the counter at the Kuban Kabana. As he looks off to the side I follow his line of sight to a bush just a few feet to my right, where we first met as he hovered over my hungover, prone body, meat cleaver in his hand. I allow myself a grin and see the corner of Leo's mouth move upward as well. He nods at me in recognition of the memory.

Wordlessly, he hands me a well-worn cardboard box filled with bottles of liquid of every color of the rainbow, and some colors previously unknown to man. Either his supply of potent, unsourced hooch or the medicines which he was too often called upon to use in patching up Vinn or myself. In truth, I'm not sure there's a difference between the two.

"Don't forget, rent is still due on the first of the month," I manage to say to Rebecca. "You've got the account information." Since Leo paid his rent in food more often than not, we agreed that in lieu of rent he would manage the building, keeping the yard under control and arranging for my apartment to be dusted now and again. For now, the top unit will remain vacant for Vinn and I to use upon our theoretical return. All of us know that's a pretense that will never come to pass. This afternoon from the road Vinn and I will press a button that sends our bosses on campus our resignation letters. Dr. Sanders will be furious with Vinn, losing such a gem in his department, as well as for not getting the closure on his brother-in-law's death since we can't tell him about Megan without giving ourselves away. Stuart will be thrilled with my departure, at least until he discovers that I've also sent emails to all of my students telling them he'll be covering my classes.

Rebecca has been tasked with putting all of the contents of our two units into storage until we call for it as well as hiring an agent to place Vinn's condo on the market. Because we can't risk anyone tracing calls to wherever we're going, all of our communications will be by encrypted emails and through intermediaries.

Impersonal but necessary.

It's Rebecca who breaks our awkward procrastination as she moves to give Vinn a hug, then pulls me into her grasp without letting go.

"Thank you," she whispers, although for what she doesn't specify. She turns quickly away, shoulders sagging, as she hurries up the stairs to her door without looking back. Leo nods once more and walks back to his own place, leaving us standing alone. It takes us several minutes before we move ourselves. Vinn finally takes me by the hand, pulls me into a warm embrace, and kisses me deeply.

"It's time," she says.

It's growing dark when we approach the turnoff to an old logging road, making it difficult for Vinn to read an old hand-drawn map or to see the notch in a tree marking its location. I pass by it at first before Vinn corrects me, then back the car up on the shoulder. Once onto the road, we get out to drag fallen branches over to hide the entrance. If anything, the road is in even worse shape than when I first traversed it looking for seclusion the summer after the first adventure she and I shared, only to find Vinn waiting for me in the small log cabin nestled in a clearing among towering aspens.

We discovered each other that summer. As we carry our small collection of belongings inside, I think upon how much has changed in the time since, and what has remained the same. Our love has deepened, only partly through the bonding that comes with sharing multiple life-threatening situations.

Now, here in the middle of nowhere, we each hope to find what we sought in Chicago, which is a life free of violence and all reminders of the lives we thought we were leaving behind there. Our focus will be on each other and on helping the other exorcise demons of the past. Through sharing our love and passion, as well as with difficult conversations, we'll heal unseen wounds that have haunted our dreams. At least that's the plan as I see it. For all the hours it took to drive here and all of the talking we did along the way to pass the time, we both proved highly skilled in avoiding the subject of our future.

I build a small fire and for the better part of an hour we sit close together in silence, content to watch the flames dance before us. I finally wrap Vinn in my arms in an embrace warmed only partly by the heat from the fireplace, pull her close, and ask the question hovering before us in the room.

"Now what?"

"Hell if I know, cowboy," she responds quietly. "Let's just see what the world has in store for us. We could talk about what lies ahead, but as you know every plan we've ever made has been totally fucked within the first five minutes."

For five or six seconds I hold it in, then dissolve in a fit of giggles. Vinn joins in and soon we're releasing years of tension through uncontrollable laughter. As our mirth fades, we snuggle close watching the fire in silence, comfortable and warm in each other's arms. My eyes begin to grow heavy when Vinn speaks.

"Valencia Nectarina," she says. She senses my confusion. "My real name, what the initials 'V' and 'N' stand for. My parents honeymooned in Florida and I was apparently conceived in a citrus orchard. I never wanted to hear any more details."

I resist the impulse to tease but understand that this is information not easily shared, with good reason. "I think I'll stick with 'Vinn,'" I finally say.

"No, you won't," she replies. "Tomorrow we come up with new names to match our new identities. But that's then. Right now," she tells me as she rises and reaches for my hand, "I have other plans in the next room."

I let her pull me to me feet, but that's as far as we get before we both slide back down in front of the fire, shedding our clothes on the way to the floor. All thoughts of the past and the future are put on hold as we focus on the present and on each other. As we pull each other into a tight hug, as passion rises to the forefront of our minds, as the fire adds warmth to the heat we begin to generate, Vinn's eyes droop, her mouth falls open, and she begins to softly snore, her naked chest rising and falling in time next to mine. Looking for one thing, we found something else as unexpected as it is unfamiliar. Peace. I watch her sleep for a minute or more, then close my eyes and all goes dark.

ABOUT THE AUTHOR

As the voices of his characters that haunt his mind begin to dim, Thomas J. Thorson looks forward to wandering the streets of Chicago without viewing every doorstep, alley, or public gathering place as a possible venue to stage a killing. He continues to bake and create new flavors of ice cream and enjoys life in whatever form is thrown at him.

CPSIA information can be obtained
at www.ICGtesting.com
Printed in the USA
JSHW010718050223
37274JS00002B/125